EAT YOUR HEART OUT

VOLUME 1

EAT YOUR HEART OUT
Volume 1

Edited by Aaron Crocker & G K Lomax
Cover Design by Kyle Lechner
Formatted by KH Formatting

Table of Contents

Dear Reader,

I begin this letter in a space of gratitude. On behalf of the Campfire Publishing family: our team and the artists who trust us to take part in the journey of sending their stories out into the world, we are honored that you've chosen to sit around our campfire to listen to our dark tales of love gone so terribly wrong, in some cases, one might wonder, 'was it ever love at all?'

When the idea of a love-themed horror anthology first came to me, there were a couple narrative styles I knew I'd be on the lookout for while reading through submissions, I'd had this idea of a zany collection that'd really cause its reader to question the line between love, passion, and utter madness. What I found was all of that but with a depth I hadn't expected.

I'd like to add an all too quick "thank you" to G K Lomax, who's authored stories in both this anthology and "After Dark, Volume 1", for stepping up to the plate and offering to assist in edits. He has a good eye, and I'm very grateful for his help.

Within the pages of "Eat Your Heart Out, Volume 1", we have themes ranging from true love lost, ego vs. love, critics on aristocracy, delusions of grandeur, and the arranged courtship; we have love ending in slaughter, exploration of sexuality, first dances and teenage love, descents into utter madness, and so much more that I can't bear the thought of spoiling.

As I always say and will continue to not only say but mean, our campfire is a community where we strive to foster a welcome space for all with the intention of supporting a wide range of artistic voices from advanced to novice. We hope to be a writer's first acceptance letter and equally another writer's hundredth.

I hope that you, dear reader, are as entertained and terrified as we were reading through each of our selections. I hope there's pieces that prompt nostalgia, comic relief; I hope you read through stories that speak to you and lead to reflection or maybe contribute to constructive dialogue.

Our first volume of "Eat Your Heart Out" is an assortment of tales sorted to pair well with a box of mixed chocolates—there's no pattern to the layout or is there—and your favorite wine. And it is on these notes of salted caramel, whipped raspberry, or (if you're like me) the dreaded orange crème, that all of us from Campfire Publishing present to you, "Eat Your Heart Out, Volume 1".

Best Wishes,
Aaron Crocker

ERMANGARDE OF DUNWICH

R.C. MULHARE

From Arkham, you say? Old hill stories? You've come to the right place if you're looking for the strange and wondrous. But if you want the kind of things you usually put to paper, you're a long way off the usual path.

Yes, you didn't strike me as someone who likes the beaten path. The horror in '28? Hasn't enough ink been used about that? Well, that's so. I wasn't privy to much of it, not the worst. I can tell you why. Sit down, let me fetch you some coffee: what I know could take a while.

***

You've probably figured out I'm not originally from Dunwich. I came from East Chelmsford, a mill town farther down the Miskatonic River. My father disappeared when I was small, leaving Ma with Grandma and I. Grandma watched me while Ma worked a loom in one of the mills, or when I was older, when I wasn't in school. That lasted till my fifteenth summer, when Grandma took a stroke and left this world for the heavenly Jerusalem. I was old enough to start working, but Ma wouldn't hear of me breaking my hands and back in the mill. Since Grandma had taught me how to tend the flat, Ma set me up with an agency that hired out domestics.

Mister Curtis Whateley of Dunwich, one of the "undecayed" Whateleys, according to the locals, soon hired me to help his wife Zealia, who'd lost her strength after the influenza ran through Arkham in 1903. They were decent folk, members of Aylesbury's Baptist congregation, but not fire and brimstone types. Zealia treated me kindly, letting me have her collection of romantic novels and magazines to read when I wasn't working—though a farm home doesn't allow much free time during the growing season. Sunrise found me up, helping Zealia about the kitchen, while afternoons found me managing the laundry, the garden, or the chicken run. Evenings, after helping with supper or washing the dishes, I was free to read or ramble the pasture paths, though some nights found me too tired. Nights when the weather held up I went out into the dooryard, wandering past the wash-lines to the edges of the woods. But that first summer, Zealia warned me not to venture too deep into the forest, in case I fell into and cellar hole. Curtis slyly warned me about Indian spirits haunting the woods or the far less genial things that caused Sentinel Hill to rumble from time to time. Zealia hushed him for telling such outlandish tales, but Curtis chaffed, saying, "It's better she hears it from us than from Noah Whateley and his kin."

"Who are Noah and his kin?" I asked, innocently.

Zealia darted a frown at Curtis. "Not the sort of folk a young girl should ask about,"

Curtis ignored Zealia's look. "My great-uncle of some kind. We don't mingle much with his side of the family. Best not to: Noah's got crazy notions about the standing stones atop Sentinel Hill an' some've the surrounding hills. It's why you'll hear townfolk call him 'Wizard Whateley'."

Zealia she turned her attention to her magazine. "Doesn't stop you from selling him the cows you can spare."

Curtis leaned forward in his armchair. "He pays good money for 'em. It'll spend just as good as anyone else's,"

I excused myself to my small room behind the kitchen and curled up with a Robert W. Chambers novel Zealia had loaned me: a shop-girl finding love with a handsome gentleman of means reminded me of the city I'd left behind, but I soon found my reading disrupted. Through the trees, on the soft summer air, chanting drifted from the hills.

The next day, as I brought dinner to the men picking seed corn in the farther field, I heard a rumbling in the hills, like distant wheels, but there were no wagons or trucks from what I could see of the road that wound through the valleys.

One of the hired men turned his gaze towards the hills. "Old wizard's at it again,"

"What makes people call him a wizard anyway?" I asked, as I handed around the waxed paper packets of sandwiches.

Another man, a Dunwich local, emitted a laugh disguised as a cough, turning to Curtis. "Damn, yer hired girl asks crazy questions. They all this chatty in East Chelmsford?"

"Hush, Whitman, she's gettin' the lay of the land," Curtis chided. To me, he added, "You're better off not knowing the witch-things my great-uncle an' his bunch get up to on his hills. You heard about the witch-hunts in Arkham and Danvers, the accusations that flew as far as Andover and Haverhill?"

"I've heard stories about it. My Grandmother told me of an ancestor of hers who'd appeared in a farmer's wife's dreams, accusing Eliza Proctor of bewitching him with the grippe that laid him out."

"Several times great-grandfather of our'n came this way to escape the witch madness. Some say he was a witch himself, dodging the noose. One of his sons, from whose line Wizard Whateley comes, carried on the rituals, while th' other, Orland, made more've himself."

"Your ancestor?"

"You guessed it," he said.

I already had a head full of notions from the romances I'd read. I day-dreamed about the Whateley ancestor fleeing Arkham in the dead of night, books of spells and ritual tools hidden in his cart, one trusted companion or a devoted servant girl at his side. Sometimes the daydreams slowed my hands at my work; I caught it from Zealia for mixing the clean laundry with the unwashed. That didn't keep me from wandering deeper into the woods; the next time I went rambling, where I spun tales of the spirits haunting the place, doomed Native princesses and Faerie women entranced by mortal lovers.

One evening brought me to the edge of a waterhole between the hills. I stepped closer, leaning over to catch my reflection, imagining myself as a noble lady in the age of chivalry, gazing into a magic mirror to glimpse her true love.

A dark shape moved across the surface of the pond. A deep and gruff voice spoke, sounding like a grown man's. "Who 're yew?"

Cause? I looked up. A tall young man, taller than most grown men yet perhaps a year older than I, dark-haired, with a sallow complexion. His long face reminded me of a neighbor's black goat who continually raided Zealia's kitchen garden. He wore the usual loose flannel shirt, typical of men and boys around Dunwich, over brown corduroy trousers cut far looser than typically.

I stepped back. "Who are *you*?"

"Y' shouldn't be here: that pond ain't safe."

"It's on Curtis's land, I have every reason to be here; I live with his family," I snapped.

He shook his shaggy head. "Ain't that. Y'll ketch it from m' granpaw, if he catches you out here. There's spirits in that pond."

"Then hide your bootleg rotgut somewhere else," I said, thinking they'd hidden moonshine bottles in the leaf mold at the bottom. To Zealia's annoyance, Curtis allowed some of the neighbors to use his pasture pond to hide caches from the odd Prohibition agent who turned up in the hills.

"Ain't that kind of spirit, neither," the lad sighed, starting to lose patience as much as I had. "Somethin' like nymphs, but not as purty."

"You mean, the creatures in Greek mythology?" I'd perused a copy of Bullfinch's *Mythology* in the small library in my employers' home. I'd found the more romantical tales, such as Cupid and Psyche, more interesting than the hero tales. Though, I'd felt relieved when Dionysos rescued Ariadne from a lonely island.

"Somethin' like them, but they ain't slips o' girls in purty dresses."

"So who are you, if you know so much about nymphs?" I'd thought, how dare he spoil my daydreams, but he spoke with an authority that piqued my curiosity.

He hesitated, then spoke. "Wilbur, Wilbur Whateley. I know because I seen one."

"And how'd you do that?"

"Set quiet on the verge an' watch. Usually peeks out when th' sun goes down."

"All right, I will." I seated myself on my side of the pond.

He came to my side. I noted he walked with an odd gait, as if his legs had different joints from mine. "What are you doing? Get back to your side of the pond," I ordered.

"Can't. It might git ornery." He sat a yard from me. I shifted, putting more distance between us. He looked at me, his dark eyes solemn, even pained, but made no move towards me. "What's your name, anyway?"

"Ermangarde Silbey. So how long before she shows up?"

"Soon, but let's keep quite in case we skeer it," Wilbur whispered.

I took his advice. Time passed slowly; I shifted restlessly. Curtis would send Luther the hired boy looking for me. More pressingly, mosquitoes chewed my back through my dress.

Just when I'd nearly decided to leave, the water rippled. Something round and damp, draped in water weeds, broke the surface. An elfin face with large green eyes peered at me through the weeds. I started to rise for a closer look. The figure rose, its form draped in more weeds and its long dark brown hair, graceful hands lifted invitingly.

At that instant, someone grabbed my arm from behind. In that same moment, I saw the nymph for what it was—the dark flowing hair turned lank and colorless, the skin turned pasty greenish-white, the inviting eyes goggled, sliding to the top of the head like a frog's. The smiling mouth transformed into a gaping sucker lined with teeth. I scrambled backwards, falling against something soft; I looked up into Wilbur's eyes, wide and startled, as he gently pushed me from his lap and onto the leaf mold. I glanced back as the nymph dove back into the pond, a long, flat tail breaking the surface before it vanished.

"What was that?"

"Told you, t'was a nymph."

"You didn't tell me they look like that. You put me under a spell!"

He shook his head. "Ain't no spell, they look like that. Got glamour."

"That was awful!"

"Awful in th' old sense o' the word: 'awe-full'."

"I suppose from a distance, they are," I started to say.

"Wilbur? Wilbur! Get yer hooves back t'th'house! What're y'doin' 'round here this time o'day?" an old man's voice called.

A tall man wearing a worn blue robe open over gray coveralls approached, leaning on a wooden staff topped with a carving like a tangle of vines. A bronze medallion like a cluster of bubbles hung on a leather thong about his wizened neck. He eyed me, lowering his shaggy eyebrows. "Who's she?"

"This's Ermangarde, cousin, Curtis's hired girl," Wilbur said.

"Wilbur saved me from a nymph in the pond."

"Hrrrmph, best t'leave them alone and stay out the shadows, on this earth or in the sky. You keep t'your place by Curtis's hearth, and Wilbur'll keep t'his place by th'standing stones, watching for the stars to come right t'open the door for his father's kind."

I stepped back. "I've seen more than I care to. I won't keep him from his chores."

"Granpa, can I walk her to th'edge of th'wood?" Wilbur asked.

"No, you run back home," the old man growled, grabbing Wilbur's shoulder, though it sat level with his, shoving the lad behind him.

"Ermangarde? You out here?" Luther's voice called through the trees.

I looked towards the voice. "I'd better go." I hurried back, joining Luther in the woods.

"You see something in the woods? Yer face is as white as a sheet."

"Yes, I must've wandered into the wrong farm. An old man growled at me to get off his land and away from his pond."

"Tall guy? Grizzled hair? Talks like a doomsday preacher gone mad?"

"Yes, exactly."

"That was Mr. Curtis's uncle, Noah Whateley. C'mon, Zealia's worried where y'went."

I followed him back to the house, but I caught myself imagining Wilbur as some strange hybrid of the Sorcerer's Apprentice and a male Rapunzel in a tower.

I didn't see Wilbur again for months, not till autumn, close to All Hallows' Eve. While the few youngsters in Dunwich got up to the usual mischief of stealing gates and toppling outhouses the night before, Curtis didn't hold much stock in it, and I was forbidden to go out that night. I sat in the dooryard in the gloaming, watching the sun set behind the near-leafless treetops, the branches reaching for the twilit sky like skeletal hands raised in supplication.

Wilbur, now several inches taller than I remembered, approached through the trees, accompanied by his grandfather, the older man leaning more heavily on his staff than he had in the summer.

The grizzled man eyed me from under his tangled brows. "Girl, is yer master here?" Wilbur, on the other hand, cautiously kept his eyes averted towards his boots but cast surreptitious glances my way when the old man wasn't looking.

"He's inside, but I can fetch him." I suited my actions to my words. The moment I told him an elder man had come to call, Curtis looked me in the eye, saying, "Don't go outside till he's gone." But considering the old man's companion, I cautiously approached the door, listening through the keyhole. The talk between the men hardly interested me, since Wizard Whateley had come to buy some cows.

He'd come at a good time, too, since Curtis intended to cull the herd before winter. But like some latter-day Thisbe, I watched Wilbur through the keyhole. I wondered if he shared the same thoughts or if he sensed my presence, for he glanced towards the door, as if half-expecting, half-hoping to glimpse me. Unfortunately for my yearning, fortunately for my secrecy, the three headed for the cow barn. As they went, Wizard Whateley turned to Wilbur, reaching up and yanking one of the youngster's curiously leaf-shaped ears. Wilbur jolted, yelping, before replying defensively. The old man must have guessed I lingered, which sent me back to my room. I very nearly missed Zealia calling me to help with supper, which earned me a sore look when I scurried out at last.

That All Hallows' Eve night, I hardly slept. Through my garret window and the trees beyond the pasture, I saw orange torchlight glowing on Sentinel Hill. Strange chanting and even stranger sounds floated across the valley towards "the devil's hour". At length, I rose and dressed, donning my coat and letting myself out the back door. I spirited across the frosty barnyard, approaching the forest.

The trees closed in around me, bracken pulling my clothes and hair as I felt my way through the dark. At once, the forest opened up on the lower slopes of a hill, the faint starlight shining on a path. Astride the path, at the crest of the hill, rose a doorway comprised of two standing stones with a stone block for a lintel. I approached it slowly, taking shelter in the bushes outside the stones where I huddled there to watch.

Beyond the doorway a bonfire stood ready for the torch to light it. Beyond that, I spied a stone table, like an altar, amid a half circle of upright single stones and stone doorways, like a stereograph I'd seen of Stonehenge in England. Shadowy people in long cloaks, several bearing torches, flitted along the edge of the circle in a procession that wound its way towards the stone slab. One devotee played a pensive yet festive melody on a flute, while another beat a hand-drum.

The procession formed a circle, striding as one towards the stone table. They slowly marched about it, starting softly, yet growing louder at each pass, chanting strange syllables I could not understand but somehow stirred my soul.

A tall figure in a hooded cloak approached, bearing a torch. The devotees paused, turning as one to face them, their chant growing to a climax as he entered the circle of torchlight. The tall figure slid back his hood, revealing himself as Wilbur, minus his shirt and wearing what resembled thick black sheepskin leggings held up by a belt with rubbery fringe.

He approached the devotees, chanting strange words in a sonorous bass-baritone. The devotees chanted in response. With an ululating call, Wilbur tossed his torch into the unlit bonfire, which flared up towards the darkening sky in weirdly colored flames. The devotees broke the circle, dancing in abandon, circling each other and weaving between the stones. Some circled the bonfire, tossing in bundles which caused the flames to flare up in even stranger colors. The heat of the moment inspired a pair or two to fall in fierce couplings in the shadows at the edge of the circle. One woman circled Wilbur, touching his waist, the fringe at his belt flexing in response.

The sky above the circle glowed with spirals of unearthly colors whirling like galaxies. Tendrils extruded from the mass, extending towards the devotees but not touching them. The crowd cried out in mad ecstasy. The woman who pressured Wilbur tried yet again to coax him. He turned as if letting her come close, but as soon as she closed the distance between them, he held her off with one hand, shaking his head. The fringe at his hips flared into tendrils like a sea anemone. She stroked his tendrils, murmuring softly. He pushed her away firmly but not cruelly.

One of the tendrils above darkened and thickened before whipping down, seizing the ambitious female devotee by the throat. She opened her mouth in a soundless scream. Another sky-tendril thrust into her mouth. It lifted her before plunging her onto the stone table. The gathering cried out in ecstasy. The tendrils from above swarmed her, entering her ears, her nostrils, even piercing the base of her skull. She struggled against this onslaught, her muffled screams fading into papery gasps till she went limp. The tendrils pulsed as if siphoning something. The victim's body quivered, matching the rhythm of the pulsing tendrils. Her flesh shrank against her bones as if the entity had sucked her dry, till even her skin dissolved. The tendrils did not withdraw till only her bare skeleton remained, the dry bones clattering onto the stone.

The surviving devotees fell, prostrate, in awe. Wilbur gathered up the bones, wrapping them in the victim's robe before holding them and speaking as if in eulogy. He approached the bonfire and cast the bundle into it. The flames flared up, turning blue and green as they consumed what remained of the victim,

I huddled behind the bushes, frozen in terror and awe and from the chill of the ground.

The fire died down but still cast a glow that framed a shadowed figure approaching me. Fear and cold had me so frozen I did not flinch. Even the fear that Wizard Whateley had discovered me did not cross my mind.

"You been hidin' there the whole time, weren't you, Ermangarde?" Wilbur asked.

I slowly sat up, settling back on my heels. "I saw the torchlight through the forest. I had to know what happens on this hill."

"Why not jest ask me?"

"I'd heard Curtis hint at things, but I had to see for myself."

He emitted a cough of a laugh. "I dunno if yer more cracked than a bell or you're brave or what." He looked on me fondly.

"But the creature above didn't reach for me."

"You were outside the circle o'stones. The charms carved on 'em and our invocations raise a containment circle. Won't affect you unless yer inside the circle."

"So why invoke such a thing?"

"Why pray t'yer God?" He smirked, but his expression softened as he looked upward. "Because they're m'kin."

I'd read Greek myths of gods consorting with mortals, begetting heroes. He seemed more peculiar than heroic to look upon, but what would a hero even look like?

"Please tell me your godly kin haven't told you to avoid me, the way your grandfather seems to want of you and Curtis wants of me."

"Nah. My grandfather won't be the boss of me for much longer. He's been ill, 's why he ain't here t'night. And I wouldn't want you to get sacked."

"If Curtis did, I'd come to dwell with you, even if your family wouldn't have me."

He said nothing, a quiet awe showing in his eyes.

I looked away. "I should go back. Will you walk with me through the woods?"

"That far and no further." He rose and reached down to helped me to my feet.

He kept his word, as he stopped several dozen yards from the edge of the forest before bidding me farewell and returning.

I slipped into the house, flinching at every board as it creaked underfoot. If my employers suspected anything next morning, they didn't say anything at that time.

One would think those horrid sights would frighten me away from Wilbur and his circle. Instead, it awakened my curiosity and desire to understand. I had reached the age when one seriously starts questioning one's faith and beliefs. Thus, I sought to reach outside the bounds set by the Baptists. I talked Curtis into driving me to the Aylesbury town library, where I borrowed their copy of the single volume version of Frazier's *Golden Bough*, learn more about these pagan practices. Curtis took scandal at it, but Zealia argued I'd always found the fantastical intriguing. If my reading didn't interfere with my work, I'd every reason to pursue my fancies.

That following spring, I "blossomed" as the old phrase goes, going from a gangling, coltish creature, to a more lush figure. My womanly courses started that April, and my breasts swelled like buds on the branches of the trees. Zealia helped me alter some of her own out-moded dresses to fit my frame. When I ventured into town to fetch goods as needed or to pick up the mail, the older boys who passed me by took second glances at me. The coltish boys in Aylesbury started peering at me, looking my form up and down. Jeb Bishop, Mamie Bishop's nephew, started leaving things at our back door: bits of oddly colored stones, small bouquets of wildflowers, one time a fifty-cent piece. I hadn't quite set my cap on Wilbur Whateley, but close to it.

During one of those trips to the general store, I saw Wilbur there. The clerk nervously handed back his change while trying not to stare up at him. The group of old men who habitually loitered around the store's porch, murmured among themselves. One made the Sign of the Cross, another making the sign against the Evil Eye. I thought I heard one remark on my maturing appearance, which diverted the others from scrutinizing Wilbur. I passed the object of my fondness on his way out, who gave me the tiniest smile. I looked up at him, returning the smile. This set the old cronies disapproving of our silent exchange.

"Keep your eyes in your head, you goat," one snapped at Wilbur.

"I'm thinking you should do the same," I replied, coolly. Wilbur's smile turned to one of relief, albeit with concern showing in his sallow face as he departed. As I made my purchases, I overheard the cronies growling about the disrespectful present generation. I ignored them as I quit the store and headed back to the farm.

I caught it from Curtis. I explained what had happened. Zealia spoke up in my defense, chewing out Curtis for believing the words of a group of old biddies over the words of their hired girl.

Perhaps emboldened, I brought my reading material to the pond's edge. The romances gave way to anything I could find on folklore or magic. Wilbur came from time to time, bringing at times a small tome of weird lore. I, in turn, loaned him some of Zealia's romances, now my inheritance. We may have started holding hands, whispering in the gloaming.

"Do you have a sweetheart, Wil?" I asked.

"Naw, Ma won't hear of it."

"Is she preparing you for the clergy?"

"Something like it." I pressed him, but he refused to explain. "There's things I hafta show you first. Right now, m'family needs me."

As if on cue, a woman's shrill voice called through the trees, "Wilbur? You hiding out here?"

Wilbur sighed, releasing my hand. "Best be off, the both of us. Y'better return t'Curtis's place before yer missed. Ma'll burst a blood vessel if she ketches me with you."

I kissed his cheek and taking the book he'd loaned me, tucked it under my arm before scurrying back to Curtis's farm.

What did I see in him? One might think I blindly hitched my wagon to the first promising star. That in so small a town I'd few choices, given how few eligible males lived close by. In Wilbur, I found the doorway to a realm of wonder and terror and a guide who treated me with tender respect. We both in our own ways felt deeply lonely and disconnected from the world we lived in, he for his nature, I for arriving from a different part of the state. He treated me with deference, unlike some of the young men of Aylesbury. I preferred a man who carried a sense of the mysterious, unlike the lads who preferred dwelling placidly on the surface of existence, one half of a couple in a rowboat on an artificial lake, never once thinking of the terrors and wonders lurking in a natural lake between two mountains. Perhaps I fancied myself the town-born Beauty to his backwoods, eldritch Beast, or Psyche to his dark, peculiar Cupid. Fate seemed to cast a kindly eye at me for a time.

As the summer passed, I saw less of him than usual, and so I went in search of him, walking through the forest toward the farm.

At first glance, the Whateley farm looked no different from most farms in the locale— outbuildings and barns, some weathered, others more ramshackle if shored up. In one barn stood several disconsolate-looking cows, strange round marks like the marks of an octopus' tentacles surrounding bite-like injuries on their necks.

In the midst of this stood the house, a two-story gray clapboard structure like so many other Dunwich houses, except webs of boards covered the windows of the second floor. Someone had turned one window at the end of the house into a set of double doors with an earthen berm leading up to it like a ramp.

I didn't find Wilbur anywhere, no sign of him in the barn or the outbuildings. I mounted the ramp, a berm of soil with a path of cleated wooden boards leading to the second floor, the sides carpeted with grass and weeds growing up around the boards. I reached the doors, finding them latched and locked. I put my ear to them and knocked.

Nothing replied for a moment, but I smelled something odd, at once dry and earthy and yet slightly damp, around the edge of the door.

Something hit the inside of the door like someone slapping it with their arm. Something rumbled, like water in a deep pipe. I jumped back, almost stumbling down the ramp, into Wilbur's arms as he approached, leading one of their scrawny cows.

"Ermangarde, what're you doin' here?" he asked, looking down at me.

"I came looking for you." Not a lie, but not a full truth either.

"Don't go in there," he warned.

"Why not? What are you hiding in there?"

"It's not important."

"It is to me. I care about you as a friend at the least. I would like to know all that I can about you."

He sighed without parting his lips. "It's my brother."

"Why are you bringing your brother a cow?"

"Needs the milk," he replied too quickly. "Will you step aside and let me bring'er in?"

I folded my arms on my chest. "Not unless you let me see what's in there."

He unlocked the door with a key that dangled on a cord around his neck then pulled it open, leading the cow onto a platform inside.

Again, I heard that weird rushing gurgle but saw nothing in the darkness. Even the circle of light in which the cow stood did little to relieve the gloom. The cow shuffled its hooves uneasily, but he held its halter firmly.

The cow jolted; still he held her steady, grabbing the ring in her nostrils. The cow stiffened as if in fear. A sore on the side of its neck, half hidden by the hair, opened and deepened. Blood flowed slightly from it then vanished.

"It's—he's invisible?"

"My twin. Ain't like you nor me. Light o' this world doesn't work on them like it does you or I. Slides past 'um."

"Is it—he like a vampire?" I imagined a creature between man and bat, but I had a feeling that image fell short.

"No, not like in Mr. Stoker's book."

"But you can see it."

"Since we shared the same womb and the same cradle, till we outgrew it." He looked at me. "There's a way y' can see it, but that's for you to decide. A gesture called the Voorish Sign. I can teach it to y', but once y've seen 'em, you can't unsee 'em. Don't know if yer ready to cross that threshold."

"Will, I shall have no secrets with you. No pair of young people should hide things from one another."

"All right." He took my hand, gently moving my fingers, curling some back and extending others gently, turning my hand over before positioning it at a different angle. He did this three times.

The air before me roiled; a strange form grew visible and took shape. A weird mass fairly filled the interior, like a ropy heap of tendrils resembling elephant trunks covered with a greyish-greenish-purplish skin. I could barely make out a solid body.

Something moved in the mass, a shape like a half of a human face resembling Wilbur's, minus the hair and beard, turning towards us.

"Whuh… huh… Whillburr?" the mouth moved, lips twisting.

"Yes, I'm here," Wilbur said.

A tendril groped the edge of the platform, revealing suckers like an octopus's, reaching towards us. The suckers flared, showing small teeth. "Huh… whuh… who...isss?"

"This is Ermangarde. She's…she's my sweetheart," Wilbur said.

I hadn't known what to expect. I'd seen etchings of strange creatures found in the ocean depths via Bathysphere. A shudder ran down my spine and along my limbs. Wilbur pulled me close.

"Ermangarde, this is m'twin."

"It's…it's a pleasure." I kept my hands close to myself.

"To…. Tuh...taste?" the twin asked.

"No," Wilbur said, firmly. "You can't taste from her, just th'cow. Or me."

"Or…. Muh….Ma?"

"Yeah, Ma too, if she lets you."

"What're you doing there, Wilbur?" a woman's voice snapped behind us.

We both turned to see a short, middle-aged woman, her milk-white hair pulled back under a cartwheel straw hat shading her pallid face, her pinkish eyes glaring daggers at me. "Is this the young snippet yer grandfather chased off?"

"Ma, this is Ermangarde, she works for cousin Curtis an' his wife."

"Oh, the hoity-toity Whateleys, the ones who fancy themselves the local squires when they're the same stock of Horace Whateley of Arkham?"

"Ermangarde, this is m'Ma, Lavinia Whateley," Wilbur said, patiently.

"You'd better be on your way. You've seen too much and been too much of a distraction." Lavinia pulled the double doors half-shut.

The twin darted a tendril out. "Muh...Ma? Tuh...Taste?"

She swatted at the tendril, which retreated. "Get back. I've nothing for you." She eyed me from under her hat. "But her perhaps…"

I backed down the ramp. "I'd better run. Zealia will need me."

"Good. Y'need to know yer place. Will and his twin don't need you. Will in particular has a role in which you've no place," Lavinia snarled, stalking away.

Wilbur lead the cow back down the ramp, with me following him. "Sorry she caught yuh. She gets over-pr'tective."

"Did she promise you to someone?"

"No, there's no one she's marked for me. M'heart's still mine t'give."

"Is there anyone you'd give your heart to?"

"Yeah. That someone's you."

I smiled, wanting to take his hand, but I didn't dare with his mother glowering at me from below. I took my leave, hastening through the woods to give Lavinia the illusion Wilbur had sent me away. Instead, I fairly floated through the trees, returning to Curtis's house.

Wilbur had all but declared his love for me.

My mix of awe and delight must have shown on my face as I returned to the farm. Curtis, carrying an armload of wood, crossed my path in the dooryard. "Were you sneaking around Lavinia's farm?"

"I might have gone that way. I was hoping to loan Wilbur another book in exchange for the last one I'd loaned him," I admitted.

"Why do insist on spending your free time with that lot?"

"If I answer that, may I ask you a question?"

A wry smirk crossed his face. "You already asked one, but I know what you meant."

"I'm fond of Wilbur. As strange as he looks, and as peculiar as his family is, he's always treated me kindly and gently. I think he fancies me as well. But outside of the obvious reasons why do you avoid his family, besides selling your aging cows to them?"

He headed into the kitchen door, depositing his armload of wood in the box. He stood back on his heels, on the threshold, folding his arms. "That's a weighty question, but I suppose you deserve an explanation.

"The fact of the matter is, I lived with Noah and Lavinia for a time when I was young. My father died in an accident with a thresher; a year later my mother died from an influenza that went through the area. I was old enough to help around the farm but not old enough to run it myself, and so I was sent to live with my father's next of kin, namely, Noah and his family. I'd been raised a Christian, but I'd begun to ask questions about the faith. Noah took this as a sign I wanted to turn it aside, and so, out of curiosity, I joined his coven. For a while, I took part in their circles on Sentinel Hill, till the time Wizard Whateley tried to finagle me into serving as a channel for that weird god of his. I wanted no further part of it. I'd seen what emerged from the sky and

I wanted no part of how it handled its devotees. By that time, I was old enough to take possession of this farm and move away from his lot.

"I might also have had a place in my heart for Lavinia, despite our blood ties. I tried convincing her to come with me, but she'd gotten in too deep. Even if she had left that world, I doubt she would've lasted before she slid back into that life, and her last state would've been worse than her first."

"So you have firsthand knowledge of their practices?"

"Yes, and if you knew what went on and probably still goes on, you'd die of fear if it didn't break your mind first."

"Do I want to know a mild version?" I feigned innocence, pretending to have little idea of what entities her lover dealt with.

Curtis looked me in the eyes as if to drill the information into my mind. "They sacrifice people to their gods. That included Lavinia's mother Abigail."

I stepped back. "What do you mean?"

He described the same manner of things I'd seen that Halloween on Sentinel Hill. I listened, quivering and glancing away, my recollections bolstering my image as a shocked innocent.

Curtis fell silent, eyeing me with pain and annoyed concern. "Now that you know my reasons, do I have your word?"

"That I won't go back there to visit Wilbur? But you do business with him."

"I sell him our fading cows and find others for him to keep him from feeding humans to that thing or whatever he has shut up there."

"I still have a book on loan to Wilbur. After he returns it, I'll do what I can to convince him to stay away."

"See that you do." Curtis turned his back on me.

I stalled for a time returning the book I had from Wilbur. One late afternoon in August, when the sun's angle starts to lower and the nights feel autumnal, I'd gone out to the kitchen garden; a rumble came from Sentinel Hill. A great flock of whippoorwills burst from the woods, shrieking and wheeling about before darting away.

Luther, coming from the pasture with one of the cows, stopped and stared up at the screaming birds. "What's Wizard Whateley up to now?"

The next morning, Wilbur arrived at the kitchen door, clad in an ill-fitting black frock coat straining over his broad shoulders, his solemn face quietly sorrowful. Curtis, seeing him approach, went to the door, holding up one hand to hold me off. Even in the kitchen, I could hear Wilbur's rumbling voice.

"My grandfather, yer great-uncle, passed away last night. Would y' want to come pay yer respects?"

"I'd rather not, but tell your mother she has my condolences," Curtis replied.

Curtis shut the door a shade harder than necessary. I kept my attention riveted on washing the breakfast dishes. "I'm sure you heard all that."

"I heard you talking with Wilbur."

"It's a family matter, though I suppose you'll be relieved to hear Noah Whateley's dead."

"I see." I'd tell a half-truth, if I didn't admit my heart skipped with relief. Never again would that old madman manhandle Wilbur or growl at me because of our fondness for each other.

The late summer passed into autumn. Then one day, early in October, I found the book I'd loaned Wilbur, laying on the top step of the back porch, wrapped in brown paper, a note written on the inside:

"I miss seeing you. I hope youve enjoyed the book Ive lent you.. Come back to me when you have a moment.

"W."

I hesitated till the end of October to return the book. I tried to be as stealthy as he had. But as I passed the herb garden at the edge of their barnyard, Lavinia rose up behind the raspberry canes surrounding it, her pinkish-violet eyes glaring under her sunhat. "What brings you aroun' he'ah?" she asked in a tone of "as if I didn't know".

"I was going for a walk, enjoying the day as the laundry airs," I said, as innocent, I hoped as the babe newborn.

She crossed her arms on her chest. "You c'n walk yerself back to Cuh'tis's place Wilbur's got his duties."

"I was about to ask where he is."

"Well, y' can't see 'um. You've seen 'um too much, too often. Y've turnt his head." She stumped toward me, glaring at me as if she could paralyze me with a look. I stood there like a bird frightened by a snake, not sure whether to fly or stay still.

"How have I turned his head?" I asked, deciding it better to stand my ground.

"He has work to do, but you ain't a part of it."

"If he wants help, I'd be honored to help him. Have you ever asked him what he wants?"

"He's told me what he wants," she said, but somehow, I didn't believe her. I started towards the house. She whipped one hand out like a snake striking, grabbing my wrist. I all but fell onto my face. She jerked me back. I tried shaking her off, but she gripped my arm harder. Finding my free arm, she grabbed me by my other wrist.

"Let me go! If you don't want me, why are you grabbing me?" I shook my arms hard, trying to remove her, but she dug her work-hardened fingers into me.

As luck would have it, Wilbur approached, leading one of their spindly-looking cows, which pulled on her rope as if she knew what awaited her. Wilbur stopped to stare at us.

"Maw, let her alone. Let her go!" he ordered.

"This why you weren't to be seen at May Day for the Great Rite?" Lavinia snapped. I knew enough from reading Frazer to know what she meant. I knew it meant more to his magick than it did any romantical pairing, but my heartstrings jangled before my heart sank into my belly.

"'s got nothin' to do with that," Wilbur snapped, his eyes pained as if he felt as I did.

The cow tossed her head, throwing Wilbur off, and ran for freedom. Wilbur pelted after her. I tried yet again to break free of Lavinia's grip. Seeing the cow veering towards her, Lavinia darted toward the house, dragging me towards the ramp leading to the second-floor doors, now barred with a thick beam as well as locked.

A series of thuds resounded behind the doors, as if the twin wanted to escape, or it heard the commotion outside and objected to the noise. Lavinia released me enough to wrestle the beam up, The latch loosened. The door flew open and a tendril whipped out, flailing toward us.

"Maw, no! Let her go. I'm begging you!" Wilbur shouted from the ground. Lavinia shoved me towards the tendril. I stumbled, falling on my face. The tendril whipped over my prone form, reaching for Lavinia.

The tendril suctioned itself onto her neck. Another whipped out, attaching to her forehead. She barked at it, as if ordering the twin to release her. Instead, a third tendril plunged into her open mouth. She tried grappling with her offspring, but the tendrils pulsed like the tendrils of the sky beast.

I screamed. I wanted to rush the thing and haul her free, but she hadn't tried to break free. Instead, her pink eyes took on a look of resignation. Her flesh shrank against her bones.

Wilbur rushed to his mother, wrenching her free. The tendrils flared. Roaring, Wilbur kicked them. The tendrils stiffened as if stunned. Wilbur shoved one door shut. Breaking from my trance, I slammed the other closed. Wilbur barred the doors, locking them.

At that moment, a flock of whippoorwills broke from the trees, wheeling and calling. Wilbur dropped to his knees beside his mother, feeling under her jaw. His twin thumped at the door.

"She's gone," Wilbur said, in a small, nerveless voice.

"Is there anything I can do for you?"

He didn't look up. "You can leave me with her. I need a moment." I left as ordered, as if under a spell, returning to Curtis's farm.

I let myself in by the kitchen door. Zealia had started chopping carrots for a soup. "Ermangarde, you look as though you've seen a ghost."

"No—I saw Lavinia Whateley fall to her death." I couldn't have told her the bald truth.

Zealia wiped her hands on her apron. "I was afraid she'd come to a bad end. Can you take over the soup?" I did as asked, preparing the ingredients like a sleepwalker.

I dimly heard Zealia and Curtis speaking quietly, then a door open and close. Zealia returned, checking the bread baking in the oven.

The yard door opened. Curtis entered, his face bearing an ambiguous frown. "You were there when Lavinia was injured?"

"I was there when it happened."

"What brought you to their farm?"

"I was returning a book I realized I still had."

"You're not going back, not any time soon."

Late on the night after Halloween, I dressed in my one black dress, not knowing what else to wear to the kind of funeral his coven might hold and let myself out, crossing the yard and heading for the woods, the firelight my guide.

Atop Sentinel Hill, beside the stone altar, the remains of a pyre smoldered. Wilbur sat beside it, watching the smoking coals and what lay amongst them. A few coven members, some wearing fine suits and gowns under their black ceremonial robes, lingered nearby. They eyed me, suspicious as I approached Wilbur.

"She's a friend, lives across the woods," Wilbur said.

I sat beside him. "They got 'er," he said, without looking up.

"I'm sorry." I didn't feel it.

"Don't be. She's gone back where we all come from, to th' elements that make up everything." Some might consider his philosophy cold, but his approach had as much value as another would while beating their breast and tearing their hair in abject woe. I put my hand upon his upper arm, feeling how cool he seemed compared to other folk. He looked down at my hand, so tiny and slender against his thick, muscled limb. He slid his arm gently from under my touch. At first, I dreaded that he might rebuff me. Instead, he put his arm about my shoulder, offering me comfort, as if apologizing for the way his mother, the deceased, had treated me. I nestled against him, no mind to the musk of his clothes and skin.

After a long moment, he spoke, "Was wonderin', I'd have t' show yew the gestures t' make an' teach y'the wurds, but would you wish t' be the Priestess at the next Sabbat we holds?"

My heart jerked a beat or two. "I would, but what would Curtis say? They don't know that I've come here."

His dark eyes grew grave. "Hrrm. The'ah's that."

"She had grand plans for me, things she'd promised 'fore m' twin an' me was born."

"You can tell me about them, if you wish."

He looked at me. "You knew I ain't human, not entirely. Me and m'twin stand between this world and the realm of Yog-Sothoth, our Father, Who is the Gate and the Key. Grandpa intended us to be the first of a line, bridging the gap between Earth and the Beyond; in return, our Father showed him a cache of pirate gold hidden in a cliff cave above the Miskatonic River. Too much industry here, too many factories dumping poison into the water, too many automobiles and chimneys and locomotives blowing smoke into the air. The rate we're going, humans won't leave a blade of grass or a single tree standing. So… Ma gave herself to Yog-Sothoth, promising to bear His offspring if they'd become the means of cleansin' th'Earth. Only blood of His blood can open the way when the time comes right, when the stars an' planets form the right configuration."

I leaned closer, into his line of sight. "But did you and your twin choose this?"

"Only life we've known."

"Have you thought of going to Boston or Arkham? Seeing more of the world?"

"You seen how people look at me. You got the only eyes that don't stare."

"Because I love you and you've shown me so many wonders. Do I factor into this grand plan?"

"Ma thought you distracted me. She wasn't wrong, but not for the reasons she thought. I ast you to be my High Priestess. Would you rather keep this between us alone?"

"Oh, yes, I would rather."

He drew me onto his lap, pulling me close to nestle my head into the side of his neck, where I breathed in his warm, goatish scent. Work in the barnyard had worn down my citified preciousness towards odors.

He lifted my face to his. I leaned in, narrowing the gap; he closed the distance, laying his lips against mine.

Something slipped from under his shirt, twining about my waist. Without breaking the kiss, I glanced down. A sinuous tendril, like those of his twin only smaller, held me against his chest.

I broke the kiss. "If you must reveal your charms, perhaps I should return the favor." We'd played at love that summer, but now our play grew serious. Despite the November chill and the late hour, our puppy love matured into the love of man and woman, even if the man claimed parentage from another world.

I shan't elaborate on the physiological particulars. Too many scribblers have tried quizzing me on the organic processes involved. But allow a woman some privacy?

Suffice it to say, we lay entwined till the fire burned down and the sky darkened to its deepest indigo-black. I dozed off in Wilbur's embrace, awakening to wonder if I'd had an All Hallows' Eve dream, to find myself laying on the porch of Curtis's house, my clothes neatly buttoned up and carefully arranged. Except for a blissful soreness, I thought I'd dreamt this.

I let myself in, tiptoeing through the kitchen, intending to head to my room.

"A bit late to go out pranking. Aren't you old for hanging tick-tacks on the neighbors' windows," Zealia said sleepily from a chair. I froze in my tracks. "Have you been out with Lavinia's brat, though he's grown a bit tall and broad to call him that."

"I've been out with my sweetheart," I said, telling the truth in part.

"Are you too shy to admit it?"

I turned to look at her, unable to tell her.

"I gather I said the truth you can't speak. Let's not tell this to Curtis. He won't take it well. Go on, head off to bed before he finds out."

I went to my room, collapsing on the bed and falling immediately to sleep.

As fate or luck or the ones beyond would have it, I missed my monthly courses. I tried hiding it, but Zealia took notice, as did Curtis. I would not say who had begotten this child, and so he took it that someone had forced my situation. Rather than subject me to scrutiny, he was willing to claim the child as his, though Zealia wouldn't hear of it. Arkham folk tended to be more delicate about scandal and propriety, things Dunwich folk shrugged at, but he reminded her this wasn't Arkham.

"No one thought twice about Lavinia's brat and who got her with him, whose name *she* didn't take," I overheard him say one night.

"She's not Lavinia. She's not Dunwich folk, neither," Zealia argued.

"She's more akin to this place than you are," Curtis replied, sagely.

They considered sending me back to my mother, but I was too old for that, nor did I want to go. Still, as my condition grew noticeable, they sent me to a discreet home near Keene, New Hampshire, run by members of a nursing order of Catholic Sisters. I expected them to judge my condition, but the Sisters treated me more kindly than anyone in East Chelmsford or even Dunwich could have. They treated the three or four other women in straits similar to mine as if we were their own daughters. They even allowed me to send letters to Wilbur. Yet I never received a reply from him.

One morning, late in the summer and late in my pregnancy, one of the Sisters came to my room, telling me I had a visitor before letting Curtis enter – my condition had kept me off my feet for a month – though she kept the door open and remained in the hallway, keeping watch discreetly.

I noticed a hint of gray on Curtis's temples which I hadn't seen before. His face looked more lined than I remembered, as if a fright had aged him.

"Wilbur's gone," he told me.

"I know this."

"How?

"He never answered my letters, and the most recent were returned to me, marked 'Deceased'. How did it happen?"

"He tried breaking into the Miskatonic University library. The watchdogs chewed his sorry hide." He glanced at my belly, under the bedcovers. "Is it his?"

I looked him in the eye. "Yes."

He shook his head, as if to escape my gaze. "Why'd you let yourself get tangled up with the like of him?"

"We were both lonely people who didn't always feel at home." I had to change the subject, lest my heart overflowed. "What about the thing in the house?"

"Busted out, a week, maybe ten days ago. It flattened the Bishop house, killed several herds, till Professor Armitage from Miskatonic University and a few of us sent it packin' wherever it come from."

"It was looking for Wilbur."

He looked at me as if I'd sprouted fins for hands and feet, then shook his head, fumbling a farewell, along with a promise to bring me and the child home when the time came.

That night I went into labor: the shock of the news must have made the child restless within me. The child of Wilbur's wanted to see the world that couldn't nor wouldn't contain his sire or his uncle. I couldn't help thinking Armitage had done a kindness to Wilbur's twin, sending them back where their father awaited. I only wished that Wilbur might've gone as well, or that he might have lived to see his sons

Yes, I gave birth to twins, though the Sisters laid only one in my arms. The other they wouldn't speak of, telling me it had passed. Due to deformities, they wouldn't let me see it. But the fear and confusion in their eyes told me more. The Sister Infirmarian gave the one child and I a thorough examination, declaring us fit to return home. The Sister Portress offered to drive us to Dunwich, but I told her I could take a bus to the closest train station and find my way. But first I had to find the twin.

I roamed the woods separating the convent grounds from the surrounding farms, softly reciting the chants Wilbur had taught me, making the Voorish Sign, stopping only to tend to my son.

As day faded into night, I found an opossum carcass drained of its blood, a round sucker mark on its neck, like something Wilbur's twin had left on its donors. Not far away, I found my son's twin, cowering in a thicket. I knelt, speaking soothingly, and telling them we would return home to Dunwich.

After a long trip via trains, buses and hitching a ride on a pick-up truck loaded with sweet-corn, we arrived in Dunwich. I found the town changed; whole stands of trees had flattened; several houses and farms lay in ruin. A few farms stood abandoned, while others looked as though the occupants had planned to remove themselves for greener pastures. I approached Curtis's house carrying young Will in a basket, the smaller twin tucked away in my satchel of clothing. Curtis came out to the front porch to meet me and lead me into the front parlor. Zealia, wrapped in a shawl, sat ensconced in her rocking chair. She smiled to me wanly, asking me to bring young Will closer. She smiled on him, tutting at how much he resembled his father. I asked if I might have my old room back. Without hesitation, they admitted they'd given it to a new young woman they'd hired to tend the house, but I could spend the night if I chose. Curtis told me that the lawyer handling Wilbur's estate had approached them as the next of kin, informing him of the disposition of Wilbur's property. I agreed to spend the night.

Next morning, Curtis brought me to the law office of Wardsworth and Matherton in Aylesbury, where, once I confirmed my identity, Mr. Matherton informed me that Wilbur had left me the farm and the contents of a safe deposit box at the town's one bank.

I went first to the bank, where the manager initially snubbed me before taking it upon himself to guide me to the box, one of the largest.

Inside lay a cache of golden coins. The Whateleys, had they so chosen, could have moved to Arkham, had they opted to blend in with "polite society". But what are social graces to those who dance with entities from beyond?

I converted one gold coin to ready cash, returning with Curtis to his house, where I collected my effects and my sons. Taking my leave, I walked through the wood to what remained of the farm. An outbuilding which Wilbur had refit as a dwelling had somehow survived his twin's frightened rampage. I entered, bringing my sons with me.

Among Wilbur's effects, I found his Book of Shadows. Between the pages, I found several loose sheets written in a tenderer hand. These I am more willing to share:

> *"Dear Ermangarde,*
>
> *"Zealia told me of your confinement, but neither she nor Curtis would tell me where they had sent you to rest. I'd come to their dooryard. Curtis accosted me, telling me to go away. I asked why I hadn't seen you in over a month. He told me of yor indisposition and that you had returned to yor people. Yet he would not tell me where you had gone. And so I write this in the hope that somehow, you will find your way back to me."*

At a later date, a month before I gave birth, he'd added, *"I hope that somehow, by some means, I can better explain wat I had been born to achieve. Per my family's calling, I have been seeking the means to open a door into the realm of my father, Yog-Sothoth, the Guardian of the Gate Who Is the Gate. I am seeking a grimoire containing the proper words and rites to unlock this gate. The copy we possess lacks the full text, but the rare text library at Miskatonic University in Arkham has a complete version. I shall go up to Arkham to acquire that text, however possible, by copying it, borrowing it, or if necessary, stealing it from under the noses of those would-be intellectuals, all research and no application. I will open a door and escort my twin through it to dwell with our father and his kind. And I remain here to search for you. I suspect why you have been sent away, and if my suspicion proves true, I will take responsibility for our offspring as their father and your lover."*

The letters ended there, along with the entries in his Book of Shadows. I have contacted Professor Armitage's successor, who seems exponentially more cooperative in sharing information.

I made a life here for my sons. In due time, perhaps we will find a way to the world of their father's people. I've gathered a few of Wilbur's surviving circle, though we'll never likely have the reach their grandfather once had. The growing skepticism of this age and its over-reliance on science has stifled folks' interest in the wondrous, though I've heard of an odd physicist in Berkeley, California, a scion of old New England stock, has some understanding of parallel realms and the mathemagic that might allow one to cross between them with ease. I might've contacted him, though I doubt a rational man of science would consider the words of a backwoods New England widow. Yes, I'm known as "Widow Whateley", though Wilbur and I had never wed in the eyes of the Commonwealth of Massachusetts.

***

Why do I keep these practices? Wilbur would have wanted it this way. I keep the hope that some night, when the stars come right, the veil will part, and he'll be there waiting for me. That night, we'll step across, young Will, his brother, and I, and the four of us won't be parted again.

It's almost sundown. Tonight's the equinox. Young Will's been setting up on Sentinel Hill as we speak. You're welcome to join us: you can put that and what you witness into your book.

EACH MAN KILLS THE THING HE LOVES

G K LOMAX

Yet each man kills the thing he loves,
By each let this be heard,
Some do it with a bitter look,
Some with a flattering word,
The coward does it with a kiss,
The brave man with a sword.
Oscar Wilde: The Ballad of Reading Gaol

I've never been able to tolerate cruelty.

I'm not talking about being against cruelty to one's fellow man – that ought to go without saying, even if, all too often, it doesn't. No, I'm talking about cruelty to animals. When I see someone whip a horse or kick a dog I – well, I have to say that I suffer. I seem actually to feel the blows. Presumably only in my imagination, but that doesn't make the experience any less unpleasant. I once tried to describe these feelings to Father Louis. He nodded and said that I clearly had a sympathetic nature. Then, because he's an educated man and likes to show off his learning, he explained that he was using the word sympathetic in both senses. I think I understood what he meant. Eventually. Then he recounted some anecdotes about St Francis of Assisi, and pointed out that although the Bible describes our Saviour as breaking bread, it doesn't mention him eating meat.

I don't go that far. I've never had the heart (or the stomach) to slaughter any animal myself, but I accept that it must be done. When it's my animal, I insist that it's done as swiftly and as painlessly as possible, and whilst they're living I make sure their lives are as comfortable as possible. Enough food, clean straw regularly, room to roam within reason. My neighbours say that this makes me a bad farmer, but I get by.

All this is by way of a preamble to explain that when I found the wolf caught in the trap, there was little doubt what I'd do.

It was the last week in January, in the bitterest winter I'd ever experienced. We're used to deep snow and harsh frosts in the Vosges, but this was exceptional. Old Alphonse said it was the worst winter he could remember, and he was born in 1811, so his memory goes back a long way. Certainly it was the only winter I'd ever known that forced the wolves down from their usual haunts.

There are still wolves in the Vosges. Mostly they've learnt to avoid man and stay in the forested areas of the peaks. Some men (not me, you'll not be surprised to hear) like to hunt them occasionally, although kills are rare. Still, they're up there, and there they would've stayed if hunger hadn't driven them down to our farms.

The first incident was on Christmas Eve. We'd dutifully filed into the church for the Midnight Mass when Jean Genappe heard his dogs barking furiously. His farm was more than two kilometres away, but sound carries a long way in still night air. Jean knows a bark of alarm when he hears one and left the church at a run. Several other men followed him, but they were too late. Wolves had got into Jean's sheep pen, where they'd killed four of his flock and one of his dogs.

That wasn't the only attack, nor the village's only loss. It wasn't long before men started rooting around in barns to find long-disused traps. There were predictable arguments about where best to site them, so as best to protect the village. I say village because that's how we think of ourselves, but we're really a collection of small farms spread over ten or twelve square kilometres. That meant that a few traps had to cover a lot of ground, with everyone wanting his own farm better fortified, so to speak, than those of his neighbours. Eventually, however, some sort of compromise was reached, and a line of traps was set along the edge of the forest to the north, which is where we thought the wolves were coming from.

The traps were vicious things. Baited with fresh meat, they'd spring shut with hideous force. The sharp teeth would bite deep into its victim's leg, and if the bone wasn't snapped into the bargain it would be a surprise. Maybe it was necessary, but the very thought of its cruelty made me feel sick. I said nothing, however.

∗∗∗

It was just after dawn when I found the wolf. As every man in the village did, I regularly went up to the forest to gather firewood. I remember that it was a bright, windless morning (wind is the winter killer, not snow) and I was feeling quite cheerful as I dragged my sled behind me.

Cheerful, that is, until I heard the sound of whimpering.

I followed the sound, until I came across the wolf – the biggest I'd ever seen – with its left forepaw cruelly caught. The wolf growled at me, so I approached carefully: it's difficult to explain to animals that you mean them no harm, and I was in no mood to be savaged whilst playing Good Samaritan. The wolf's leg didn't seem to be broken, which was something. Looking closer, I saw it was and old and rusty trap, so perhaps its springs had lost much of their force. That did mean, however, that the wolf might be able to chase me after I freed it. No man has been killed by a wolf for hundreds of years, as far as I know. Not in France, anyway, but that didn't mean it could never happen again.

I approached cautiously. For reasons I don't really understand, I spoke soothingly to it, and held my open hands wide in a non-threatening gesture. Not that I expected the wolf to understand – and yet somehow it seemed to me that it did. It stopped growling at any rate, and looked me in the eye. I held its gaze. Its eyes were big and yellow, with narrow black slits. It didn't blink. After a few moments, I felt – and I can't explain why – that we'd achieved some sort of understanding.

I crouched down and took hold of the trap with both hands. It seemed stuck at first, then I jerked the jaws open far enough for the wolf to remove its leg. It moved haltingly at first – it seemed that it was trying to see if it could put any weight on the leg. It seemed that it could; a little anyway. It scampered a few yards into the trees.

I let the trap shut so that it was rendered harmless, then turned back to my sled. I'd only gone a few paces when there was movement behind me. I turned just as the wolf leaped up at me. Taken by surprise, I sat down heavily in the snow. The wolf put its paws on my chest. I smelt its breath. For a moment I was terrified. Was my throat about to be ripped out?

Then the wolf licked my face. I was so surprised I laughed out loud. The wolf put its head on one side, seemingly puzzled by the sound. Then it turned and scampered off into the trees.

I felt like St Francis.

* * *

I thought no more about the business for a day or so. There was some muttering in the village about a trap that had sprung without trapping anything, but old Alphonse (who enjoyed being the oldest man in the village and the fount of folk wisdom) said that such things weren't unknown. "I once knew a trap to be sprung by a falling pine cone," he said. Men nodded wisely, and no-one questioned.

Then the hare showed up.

I found it on my doorstep one morning. Dead and bloody. Killed by something with teeth and large jaws. Such as a wolf.

My mind raced. Were animals capable of showing gratitude or even of understanding the concept? I thought that they were. Dogs certainly are, and they're not very different from wolves. The more I thought about it, the more certain I became that the hare had been left by my wolf (my wolf?). It couldn't have been too hard for the wolf to work out which house was mine: if a dog can follow a scent, so can a wolf.

I thought again about St Francis – then with a flash that made me so dizzy I had to sit down, I remembered a story I'd heard in my childhood. There was once a wolf that terrorised the town of – I couldn't remember. St Francis went alone into the forest and spoke to the wolf. The wolf listened and followed St Francis obediently back to the town. The wolf, St Francis explained, had only acted out of hunger. If the townsfolk would feed the wolf, it would leave them and their livestock alone.

I was unsure what to do about the hare. For one who's squeamish about killing an animal, I'm surprisingly unemotional when it comes to skinning, cleaning and cooking one that's already dead. I think this is because I'm actually sympathetic towards the spark of life in an animal. Once that's gone, it's gone. The flesh is nothing by comparison.

Still, the hare gave me pause. Eventually, I thrust it into the snow that had piled up against the west wall of my house. One good thing about winter is that it's easy to preserve meat.

***

The next day was Sunday. More than that, it was the Feast of Candlemas. We always celebrate Candlemas diligently in our village. Quite apart from its relevance to the life of our Saviour, we consider that this is the day on which we can say that the worst of the winter is behind us, and that we can look forward to the renewal of the world. Not that we don't get snow in March or hard frosts as late as Easter sometimes, but there you are. On this particular year it happened that Candlemas – the second of February – fell on a Sunday, so there was an especial feeling in the air as we crowded into our small church. As usual, a profusion of candles was burning, filling the church with light, and making every surface sparkle. I edged my way towards the bye-altar, dropped a couple of sous into the box and lit one myself. I didn't ask for anything specific. I never do. I have few wants. Health, peace, and a farm that produces just enough. God already knows that I want these things: he doesn't need reminding.

Then I threaded my way to the back of the church. There isn't room for everyone to sit, and I hate to push myself forward.

Father Louis was on good form. He likes a packed house. He made reference to the harshness of the winter, but reminded us that stoicism and perseverance in times of trial were solid Christian virtues. We nodded. The Vosges breed tough people. He moved on to the bounties we could expect in the spring, comparing them to the far greater bounties we could expect in the hereafter, but I'm afraid I'd stopped giving him my full attention. Standing at the back of the church meant that I had a good view of most of the congregation. I was running my eye over them idly with no fixed purpose when a young woman in the rearmost pew turned and looked at me. Our eyes met for a moment, and she smiled at me.

Confused and embarrassed I shifted my gaze back to Father Louis and tried to concentrate on his words as he reached the climax of his sermon. Tried without success.

I'm a single man, and a solitary one – or as solitary as it's possible to be in a village where everyone minds everyone else's business. There was a time when I was younger when I showed an interest in the girls, but I was always shy and awkward around them, and none of them showed much interest in me. I wasn't much of a catch, anyway. My farm was one of the smallest, and as for my personal qualities, I was no beau. I was large-framed; strong but slow. Slow of foot, and not much faster when it came to wits. It was no great marvel when the girls of the village looked elsewhere for mates.

I wasn't too disappointed, to be honest, though my mother was. She kept dropping hints about grandchildren, so I persevered to please her. Without success, or much enthusiasm to be honest. My mother's been in her grave these last five years, and I've accepted (with little reluctance, I have to admit) that I'm one of life's bachelors. Last September I turned thirty. I think part of me was relieved to be able to say that I was no longer young.

And yet. A woman's smile carries its own magic, and I don't suppose any man is completely immune, no matter what his age.

I knew who she was, of course. Everyone knows everyone, remember. Her name was Claudette. She had no other name; she was a foundling, her parentage unknown. She'd been taken in by M Deladier, and works for him in some fashion. M Deladier's the richest man in the village. That's probably not saying much; I'm sure there are many people, even in Epinal, who would regard him as little more than a peasant, but up here a man who owns fifty hectares and who's been known to have had furniture delivered from Nancy is accounted wealthy.

Claudette isn't seen much in the village. She works for M Deladier as a cook or a maid (there are rumours, mostly put forward by men with too much wine in them, that she serves M Deladier in other, less virtuous, ways as well). She's not quite plain, though few would call her pretty. Hard work takes its toll on women-folk in these parts. She rarely ventures out. Other than in church, I'd probably laid eyes on her less than a dozen times, and I'd certainly never spoken to her, nor she to me.

Yet she'd smiled at me. Or had she? As I thought about it, doubts entered my mind. The church had been crowded; perhaps her smile had been meant for someone standing close to me. Further, she'd had to turn round and look over her shoulder before smiling. Unless she had eyes in the back of her head, how had she known where I – or anyone else – was standing?

These thoughts occupied my mind for the rest of the service, to the extent that I was taken by surprise when it ended. I stepped out into the bright daylight and started home. After a few paces I stopped. It's traditional in our village for the Candlemas service to be followed by a celebration lunch, with music, dancing and other jollities. I hadn't attended one for some years, as large gatherings make me uncomfortable, but things were suddenly different.

The Candlemas lunch is held in M Deladier's barn. Actually, most of the village's celebrations are held there – those that aren't held in the open air, that is – as it's the largest one in the village. It's got to the stage were the Preparation of the Barn is a ceremony in itself. The men all go to empty the barn the day before an event is to be held and move everything into the barns of M Deladier's neighbours; and the women go to sweep out the place. It still smells of silage, of course, but we're used to that.

Claudette works for M Deladier. The village will gather in M Deladier's barn. Therefore…

It's customary for everyone to make a contribution of food or drink at such gatherings. I felt mortified that I had nothing suitable at home – or did I? Before he died, my grandfather had bought a case of brandy, and had issued instructions that the family should drink one bottle at his funeral, and that each member of the family should be similarly honoured when their time came. There was supposed to be some special distinction for whoever got the last bottle, but I can't remember what it was. Grandfather, Grandmother, my father, my mother, two uncles, one aunt, my only cousin, my brother … there were three bottles left. Reflecting that if I died single, there'd be two bottles left unused, so to speak, I grabbed one, washed the dust off it and hurried to the dance.

M Deladier was surprised to see me and even more surprised when I gave him the bottle. It's rare for anything stronger than wine to be served at such events, but it was a good brand and well-aged, so he accepted it with thanks. He probably thought I was being socially awkward – and, to be honest, he wouldn't have been far wrong.

The barn was crowded and, for all that there was still snow outside, hot. The air was heavy with the sound of twenty conversations happening at once. There was no sign of Claudette. I stood there, feeling foolish and uncertain. Part of me wanted to turn and flee. Someone pressed a glass of wine into my hand, and I sipped it slowly.

Minutes passed – three, four, I'm not sure. Then I saw her. She entered from a door at the far end, carrying a tray of pastries which she put it on a table with the rest of the food. I felt a moment of outrage on her behalf: even at a village celebration she was treated as a servant.

The pastries were the final touch, it seemed, for M Deladier called out for everyone to help themselves. People crowded round the table, and I followed. I didn't feel particularly hungry, but Claudette was standing behind the table, and I wanted to be close to her. I took bread, cheese and a leg of chicken. I was about to turn away when Claudette caught my eye. She smiled. I wanted to say something to her; I knew I *ought* to say something to her; but I could form no words. She didn't say anything either, but there was much in her smile, in her eyes.

Kindness, sympathy, understanding – or was I just imagining these things?

She glanced down at the tray of pastries. Hesitantly, I took one. I bit into it. It's bad manners – and bad for the digestion – to start one's meal with dessert, but I was incapable of thinking clearly. The pastry tasted of honey and almonds. It was heavenly – though that probably *was* my imagination.

I finished the pastry and left the other items untouched on my plate. Claudette served others, though I felt (imagination again?) that her attention was on me. Then the music started.

Our village is well-blessed with musicians. Jules Benoit plays the violin like an angel. If he'd been born in Paris, he'd play at the Opera. Here, he plays it wherever he happens to be. He even plays to his sheep when he drives them to pasture. He says it improves their mood and therefore their wool. Victor Perrin is a passable clarinettist, and M Deladier's daughters play piano and flute. Our little ensemble is rounded off by Raymond Tissot on a drum which, he swears, belonged to his grandfather, a drummer-boy at the Battle of Austerlitz.

People started to dance. A rustic frolic by Parisian standards I don't doubt, but we like our traditions. I watched for a while. It had been some years since I'd danced our dances, but I knew the steps. I'd been taught them as a boy. I felt the pull of the rhythm. I felt a longing; I felt a fear.

After some moments of anguish, the longing proved the greater. I turned to Claudette, who was watching me with an expression I couldn't read. I opened my mouth, but no words would come. All I could manage was to hold out my hand to her and make a sort of half bow.

Mercifully, it was enough. She took my hand and we joined the throng.

It was an energetic dance, with much circling and stamping. At the end of each measure, the man has to spin his partner round. As I did so, I was mortified to see Claudette wince with pain. Stammering apologies, I led her back to the refreshment table.

"It's nothing," Claudette said. "Or at least, it's nothing you need to apologise for. I hurt my arm earlier, that's all."

I looked down and saw that she had a bandage which wasn't quite covered by the sleeve of her dress. "Do you want to sit down?" I asked her.

"No," she said, "I want to dance."

With that she led me back onto the floor. I made sure to spin her by one arm only after that, and she experienced no more discomfort; or if she did, she didn't let it show.

I don't know how many dances we danced together. Five, six, seven … all I'm sure of is that I experienced a level of happiness that I'd forgotten existed. I felt younger than I had for many years.

Time went by in a blur, and. I was surprised to suddenly notice that our little band was packing up and people were saying their good-byes. I was uncertain what to do next, and was quite relieved when M Deladier came up to me. He had two glasses in his hand, one of which he gave to me.

"You've not had any brandy," he said, reprovingly, "and since it was you who brought it, I must insist that you join me in a toast. *Santé!*"

He clinked his glass against mine and tossed off the contents in one go. I felt obliged to do the same. I'm not much accustomed to strong drink, and the fiery liquid scorched its way down my throat and set my guts ablaze. I had to force myself not to cough. M Deladier smiled at me, thanked me again for bringing such an excellent vintage, then withdrew.

I turned back to Claudette (to whom M Deladier hadn't offered any brandy, I suddenly realised). She looked at me, expectantly. It was clearly up to me to do or say something, but I was at a loss.

Eventually, Claudette turned away. "I must help with clearing up," she said.

"Wait!"

I was shocked to hear myself utter that word. Claudette turned back to me.

"I …" I began, then felt my face redden. Panic was about to overwhelm me utterly, but at last – and maybe only because the brandy had given me courage – I said, "would you like to have supper with me? Tomorrow?"

Suddenly it was her turn to look bashful. "Yes, I would like that very much," she said, not looking me in the face. "Now I really must go and help out."

***

Living alone has turned me into a passable cook. Well, I've not made myself sick, at any rate. This, however was the first time I'd faced the trial of cooking for anyone outside my own family. For a long time I couldn't decide what to prepare; but then I remembered the hare the wolf had left. I reckoned it would make a passable stew with the addition of some onions, carrots, red wine and herbs.

I retrieved the hare from the snow, skinned it and gutted it. I was cutting the flesh into small chunks when a thought flashed into my head. There was more than enough meat for two… The more I thought about it, the more it seemed fitting. I wrapped one leg together with the entrails in a piece of sacking and set out for the forest. I left my offering near the place where I'd encountered the wolf. I was distressed to see that the trap had been re-set. This posed me a dilemma. The smell of the entrails would no doubt attract a wolf (I liked to think would be the same wolf) and it would lay heavy on my conscience if I was instrumental in my wolf (or any wolf) being caught. There seemed only one thing to do. I took a fallen branch and sprung the trap, rendering it harmless. Then I hurried back home.

I don't have much use for clocks or watches. Winter or summer I get up with the sun. I eat when I'm hungry and go to bed when I'm tired. This meant that when I'd invited Claudette for supper, I hadn't thought to specify what time that meant. Being February, it obviously meant after dark, but that still left me in an agony of doubt. I found myself flitting between the stove and the window, alternately fussing over the stew (I had to fight the urge to add more salt every time I tasted it) and watching for Claudette's approach.

There's a clock in M Deladier's house. A big one, almost as tall as a man. He acquired it three years ago, and made such a fuss about its arrival (and the huge, though unspecified price he'd paid for it) that half the village turned out to witness it being ceremoniously carried into his house. I suppose the clock means that everything happens at set times. Breakfast at seven, lunch at one … I wondered if the Deladier family was eating their dinner whilst I was waiting. M

Deladier would undoubtedly call the evening meal dinner rather than supper as I'd done when inviting Claudette. I wondered if that marked me as irredeemably rustic. I wondered whether Claudette was obliged to serve the Deladiers while they ate their dinner, meaning she'd only be able to get away afterwards. I wondered if she'd be forbidden to leave the house at all. I wondered if she'd changed her mind about accepting my invitation. I wondered if I was making a fool of myself.

I wondered – and worried – about many things. Then, just when I'd given up hope, Claudette's approach was signalled by my dog, Bruno. To be sure, he signals the arrival of any visitor, but it did seem that he barked particularly vigorously on this occasion. My mind was on other things so I dismissed the thought. Nor did I think much of the fact that when Claudette entered my cottage, Bruno shot out into the night.

***

I probably made a fool of myself over the next few minutes. My tongue suddenly seemed too big for my mouth and I made a hash of even the simplest of sentences. I took Claudette's coat, sat her in the best chair – the one that doesn't wobble when you sit on it. She was wearing a plain brown dress that had been mended many times. The sleeves were long, and I couldn't see if she still had the bandage on her arm.

I served supper. Stew, bread, wine. Claudette breathed in the scent of the stew when I set her plate in front of her. There was an expression on her face that I couldn't read. I assumed she was assessing my abilities as a cook. I was in an agony of suspense. Then, at long last, she tasted it. She smiled at me and said it was good. I smiled back, hoping she wasn't just being polite.

"How long have you lived with the Deladiers?" I asked, I knew I had to make conversation, and this was the only thing I could think of.

"Since I was a child. I was a foundling, as you know."

"Do you know who … I mean, before he took you in …" I felt myself blushing and wasn't able to complete the question.

Claudette either didn't notice this, or was kind enough to pretend that she hadn't, "No," she said, "I was very young. I can't remember a single thing about my very early childhood."

"Do you wonder about it?"

"Sometimes, but not often. What good would it serve?"

"You're probably right," I said, though I thought she was definitely wrong. How can anyone live their life if they don't know who they are? "Does M Deladier treat you well?" I asked.

"I suppose so. He needn't have taken me in, for a start."

No, I thought he needn't. But the thought occurred to me that by doing so, he'd gained an extra servant; one who felt herself beholden to him; and perhaps one he didn't even need to pay. One of the reasons that M Deladier was able to be extravagant with money in some ways was by being frugal in others. I didn't think that Claudette was a slave, exactly, but she might be effectively a serf.

"Does he work you hard?"

"Everyone in the village works hard. Including you. Life can be hard in the mountains."

"I suppose it can, but I wouldn't want to live anywhere else. What I meant, though, was whether M Deladier makes you work particularly hard. Compared to his other servants, I mean."

Claudette put her head on one side whilst she considered the question. "No," she said at last. "No, I don't think so. I have my duties. Cleaning, washing clothes, helping Berthe in the kitchen, weeding the vegetable garden. Things that have to be done in any house."

"And helping with the farm?"

"Oh no. M Deladier's most particular about that. My duties lie in the house and its garden, not the farm. M Deladier has told me quite firmly that I'm not to go near any of the animals. I have to stay indoors as much as possible." She shrugged. "The kitchen garden's walled, so it counts as indoors, M Deladier says."

Well, that explained why I'd seen so little of her over the – how many years was it? I tried to guess her age. I've never been good at that sort of thing, but in Claudette's case I was particularly uncertain. She was no longer a girl, that was plain, but whilst the rest of her face suggested that she was two- or three-and-twenty, her eyes told another story. They looked – older. Not old, as such; they weren't the eyes of a matriarch; but there was something about them. Wisdom, perhaps? I gazed into those eyes for a spell. As well as wise, they were beautiful. I'd taken them to be brown at first, but now I saw that there were flecks of gold to be seen. The effect was mesmerising, almost bewitching. I felt that I could drown in them.

I don't remember much of the rest of the evening. I know that we talked easily, almost as if we'd known each other all of our lives. I felt like a green lad, but in a good way – as though I was falling in love for the first time. Maybe that's what I was doing.

I produced some cheese for dessert, and boiled some passable coffee. As we sipped it, I felt a feeling of panic rise within me. How was such an evening supposed to end? I didn't know – but I was sure that if I handled things badly it would spoil everything. Mercifully, Claudette came to my rescue (wittingly or unwittingly, I couldn't tell). "Thank-you for a pleasant evening," she said, "but I must get back to M Deladier's house. He makes sure all the doors are locked before he goes to bed."

"Will you … would you like to come again?" I asked, helping her on with her coat.

"Very much, but it might be some time before I'm able to. Good-bye" With that she opened the door and stepped out into the night.

I watched her until she was swallowed up by the darkness. I wondered why she hadn't brought a lantern – and how foolish I'd been not to offer to lend her one. I stayed peering into the night for a long time. After a while, Bruno reappeared and slunk in. I closed the door and went to bed.

***

The next day dawned as days will, and I rose to the work of the farm. I fed the pigs, collected eggs from the chickens, checked on my sheep. I even made a start on digging out the drainage ditch between my land and that of the widow Clement. It was a hard and dirty job which I'd been putting off for weeks, but on this particular morning my soul was lighter than it had been since I couldn't remember when. I actually sang to myself as I laboured. The image of Claudette was before me as I did so, and I imagined what it would be like for her to join me in duet. Was this what love felt like? I wasn't sure; but even if it wasn't, it was a feeling worth cherishing.

Which is why I was annoyed as well as disconcerted when M Deladier interrupted me.

I straightened up and removed my cap. The village doesn't have a mayor, nor any official officials, so to speak. We've never felt the need. There's a gendarmerie down in the valley, but they rarely trouble us and we try never to trouble them. Nevertheless, M Deladier commands a degree of respect. I waited to see what he wanted.

He seemed affable at first. He wished me a good morning and thanked me again for the most excellent brandy I'd brought to the Candlemas lunch. I waited for him to get to the point. M Deladier has never been to sort to pay social calls for no reason.

"Claudette visited you yesterday evening," he said.

"Yes," I said. His expression had changed. It wasn't quite stern, but the bonhomie had vanished.

"May I ask what your intentions are regarding her?"

That was a difficult question to answer, mostly because I didn't know myself. It was the sort of question asked by a father when a young man's interest in his daughter has become serious.

I settled for honesty. "I don't know, Monsieur." A long pause. "I confess to a lack of experience in such matters." A longer pause, which M Deladier showed no inclination to break. "I hope I've not given offence?"

"No, no," M Deladier reassured me, in a way that was far from reassuring. "I know you're a decent sort who would never over-step the bounds. Nevertheless, I feel obliged to have this conversation with you. As a friend."

One thing I was certain of was that M Deladier was not my friend. Oh, he wasn't a bad man by any stretch of the imagination. He was honest in his dealings, and always outwardly polite; but he was jealous of his status as the village's leading citizen.

"Claudette, is a foundling as you know," M Deladier said. "I took her in when she was child."

"That was very generous of you, Monsieur," I said. There was a sudden flash in M Deladier's eyes that suggested that I'd said something out of turn.

"I took her in, as I said," M Deladier repeated, "which means that, although she's no kin of mine, I feel a level of responsibility towards her."

I'm no great reader of men, but it was plain that M Deladier wasn't being entirely open with me.

"As such," M Deladier went on, "I've come to ask you not to, well, not to seek to get to know her any better. It's not that I think you're an unsavoury character," he hastened to assure me. "Far from it, in fact, which is why I've come here to warn you … yes, to warn you. I must tell you frankly that any … relationship … with Claudette can only end badly. I wouldn't want you to get hurt."

This made little sense to me. My mind was filled with a dozen questions, all vying for attention at once. "Do you know who her parents were, Monsieur?" I asked.

Why I asked that particular question rather than any of the others that occurred to me, I don't know; but M Deladier's reaction to it suggested that it was one he'd been hoping I wouldn't ask.

"Yes," he said slowly, "I'm afraid I do. "And now I've taken up enough of your time. I wish you good day." He turned and walked away without waiting for any comment from me.

I leant on my spade and pondered what had just happened. I think the most puzzling aspect was that M Deladier was making much of my supposed 'relationship' with Claudette – almost as though he thought I was on the verge of popping the question. To be sure, courtships in our part of the world were generally quite short, but to think of tying the knot after few dances and a supper would've been considered fast work.

Then there was the fact that he'd seemed to warn me. Not warn me off, like a jealous father to an unsuitable suitor for his daughter's hand, but to warn me about – well, that was the mystery.

I pondered the matter. After a while, a possible explanation suggested itself. It was possible, I supposed, that Claudette was M Deladier's illegitimate daughter, got by some mistress. I was pretty sure he'd never had a mistress in the village – such a thing would've been impossible to keep secret – but he might've had one in Epinal, where he went on business from time to time.

If that mistress had died or run off, that would've left M Deladier in a quandary. It might've led to him taking Claudette in out of responsibility rather than generosity, which is why he'd reacted as he had when I'd praised him for it. I don't think he was concerned for my reputation should I marry someone of no family, but it was possible that her true parentage might become known as a result. I could well believe that that was something which would trouble him.

I didn't know at the time how right my hunch was – and how wrong.

***

I reacted to M Deladier's visit the way I do to most things that puzzle or upset me. I put it out of my mind and carried on with life as usual. I finished digging out the ditch, and if the work wasn't as enjoyable as it had been when I started it, the effort it required did at least prevent me from thinking too much. Then I got my barn (which could fit inside M Deladier's four or five times) ready to act as my lambing shed. I had seven ewes in lamb, and though I didn't reckon any of them would be ready to drop for two or three weeks, I thought it would be as well to be prepared if wolves were on the prowl. I also, after some thought, got my long-unused shotgun out from its cupboard and cleaned it. Whatever my feelings about cruelty to animals, if a wolf threatened one of my lambs, then not even St Francis would be able to stop me from shooting it.

The weather remained cold but clear. Even to me, who was long accustomed to the sight, the country looked stunningly beautiful under its brilliant white covering. I pity people who live in lands where it never snows.

I decided to take advantage of the still weather and dragged my sled up to the forest to gather more wood. It was about an hour's walk, and my heart was light. I came to the place where I'd freed the wolf. There was no sign of any trap, but that was no surprise; a wise hunter never sets his traps in the same place twice running. I looked around for the new location. I told myself it was so that I didn't accidentally step in a trap myself – they're indiscriminate, after all. There were none to be seen, however. I poked my stick at a few likely places in case one was hidden under the snow but found none. I loaded my sled and started back downhill.

As I neared home, I heard Bruno barking. I rarely took him with me when I went up the mountain. As with most of the village, I thought that protecting livestock was a dog's prime duty. Bruno certainly took his responsibilities seriously, and was making quite a noise – though I couldn't see what has alarmed him.

Leaving my sled, I covered the last kilometre or so at a sort of half run, which is the best that anyone can manage in winter. Bruno ran to meet me and was clearly relieved that I'd returned. I checked the sheep fold. All my animals were present and correct, though it was plain that something had disturbed them. I walked among them for a bit, hoping that my presence would calm them. It did, up to a point.

I checked the barn, the hen coop, the pig-sty. Nothing amiss. I looked around for tracks or other signs that wolves had been near. Nothing. I shrugged. I petted Bruno and told him he was a good dog, I opened the door of my cottage.

Claudette was waiting for me inside.

"I'm sorry," she said.

"For what?" I asked, totally at a loss.

"I – I should've waited outside, only…"

"Of course you shouldn't." Which was true. Nobody locks their doors in our village (well, nobody except M Deladier, and even he only does so at night). It's considered polite to knock, or at least call out, but no-one would expect a visitor to wait outside in winter. Then again, perhaps Claudette hadn't done much visiting and wasn't aware of the norms. I hastened to assure her that she'd done nothing wrong and was indeed most welcome.

"I think I upset your dog," Claudette said.

"Oh, don't mind Bruno. He's…" I looked around. I'd expected Bruno to follow me into the house as he usually does. Instead, he was nowhere to be seen. "Oh well, if he hasn't got the sense to come in out of the cold," I said, "that's his problem."

"He doesn't like me," Claudette said. "He growled and showed his teeth and everything. I think he would've bitten me if I hadn't hidden indoors."

"He just doesn't know you yet," I said. Which was true, I supposed, but Bruno's behaviour struck me as out of character, to say the least. In retrospect, I should've given the matter more thought, but other things seemed more important.

"Won't M Deladier be angry with you for …" I wanted to say "for coming here," but instead I lamely said, "for leaving his house without permission?"

"M Deladier's gone to Epinal. He won't be back until tomorrow. As for the rest of the household, Berthe has promised to say she sent me on some errand if I'm missed. She's good to me, Berthe is." The implication was that nobody else was, but neither of us said so.

"I brought some of those pasties you liked," Claudette said. She opened a small bundle and showed them to me. We shared them with some coffee. They tasted even better than they had in M Deladier's barn.

"Did you make them yourself?" I asked.

"Yes."

"You're a very good cook."

"It's Berthe's recipe," Claudette said. "She taught it to me. I'm glad you like them." Then she suddenly became serious. "I know M Deladier came to see you," she said.

"Yes."

"What did he say?"

I considered how to answer. I didn't want to say anything that might offend Claudette, but I didn't want to lie to her, either. "He told me that I shouldn't see you any more."

"Did he say why?"

"Not directly. It seemed to me …" An interesting choice of words I realised, as I uttered them. They gave me scope to 'interpret' what M Deladier had said, without telling any actual lies. "It seemed to me that he was concerned that I shouldn't …" I stopped. M Deladier had pretty much implied that I was considering marrying Claudette, but I couldn't say that to her.

"Is he unkind to you?" I asked.

Claudette considered. "No, not unkind as such. He doesn't beat me, or anything like that. But I don't want to talk about him. That's not what I came for."

"What did you …?" I realised the foolishness of the question before I'd finished asking it.

It's not true to say that I'd never kissed a girl before then. I'd had the usual youthful experiences, including taking a girl up to a hay-loft. Three times. The third and last time, however, had been when I was one-and-twenty. Now, standing in front of Claudette these experiences seemed impossibly remote and quite useless as a guide. I felt as though I was sixteen again. I wanted to say something but couldn't think what.

Mercifully, Claudette took the initiative. She came and stood close to me. I noticed for the first time how tall she was – no more than ten centimetres shorter than I, one of the tallest men in the village. She said nothing but planted a soft kiss on my cheek.

Then things happened quite quickly.

***

Later, lying exhausted in bed, I contemplated how suddenly a man's life can change. As a lover, Claudette was vigorous, generous and enthusiastic. Quite noisy as well. Those experiences in the hay-loft, I now realised, were nothing.

I also realised that I'd finally fallen in love.

"That was lovely," Claudette murmured.

"It was," I replied. Then, and probably only because I felt I had to say something, I asked, "Why me?"

"Of course you," Claudette said, making it clear that she thought it was a stupid question. When I still seemed uncertain, she added, "Because you're kind."

"I try to be," I said. "But when was I kind to you?"

"At the Candlemas lunch. You asked me to dance."

"Surely others have asked you to do so?"

"Never. The boys all avoid me, even if they don't know why. I can't really blame them, I suppose."

Well if she couldn't, I could.

"Of course, I already knew you were kind," she added.

Looking back, I should've noted the oddness of that remark; but who's at their most rational when they're in love?

"Claudette," I began. "I …" My guts felt like water. The next few moments could turn out to be the best of my life – or the worst. "Claudette, I don't care what M Deladier says. I'm going to ask him for your hand in marriage. If you'll have me, that is."

"Of course I'll have you," she said, snuggling up close to me, "but don't ask M Deladier; *tell* him."

‖ ‖ ‖

For the next few days I was walking on air. For some reason, M Deladier was delayed in Epinal by business (or possibly a new mistress) so I didn't have the chance to ask or tell him anything. However, this did mean that it was fairly easy for Claudette to visit me of an evening. Not that she did so unobserved. Very little happens in the village without everyone finding out about it soon enough. No-one said anything, at least not to my face. This was another thing I should've thought odd but didn't. I mean, if a man is about to get married, it's natural for his friends (or his neighbours at least – I'm not sure that I have any actual friends) to offer their congratulations. I received none. Instead, I got some strange looks – not least from the widow Clement, who looked at me sadly, and shook her head.

If I ascribed any reason at all for this odd behaviour, it was that people thought that M Deladier would be angered. There was nothing he could actually do to me to vent his anger, I thought, but disharmony is never a good thing in a small community.

Still, Claudette and I were engaged, even if we'd made no public announcement. I did think about this and decided that it would be best to ask Father Louis to do so on Sunday. Not even M Deladier would dare to make a scene in church.

It also occurred to me that I ought to give Claudette something to mark our betrothal. A ring possibly, or… Or something that had belonged to my mother. Yes, I'd almost forgotten that she'd owned a necklace. A fine silver chain, from which was suspended a piece of amber in the shape of a tear-drop. It had originally belonged, she'd told me, to her great-grandmother, which made it well over a hundred years old. It had been passed down the generations; each mother giving it to her eldest son, to present to his bride. I still remembered the embarrassment I'd felt when my mother explained the tradition to me. Each of us knew at the time that the chances of me finding a bride were slim. Now, however… I retrieved the necklace from the box where I keep my few valuables. I thought I felt my mother looking down from heaven and smiling at me.

Claudette was delighted with my gift. I don't think she'd received many gifts before. There were tears in her eyes as I fastened it for her. Then she tucked it inside her blouse. I was a trifle disappointed at this, but she told me it was a necessary precaution. "I'll wear it openly when we're married," she said.

***

The next day it snowed hard and kept snowing. Twenty centimetres at least – and that was just where it lay level. Some of the drifts were taller than a man. Twice I had to dig my way out of my cottage. There was no chance of going to church – or anywhere else. It was one of those spells where all one can do is to survive and wait. Fortunately, we're used to doing that in the Vosges.

After the snow came the wolves. Each night we heard them howling. Each night a little nearer.

The first attack came on Jules Benoit's place. Four sheep with their throats torn out. That's what makes a farmer hate wolves. If they killed only what they needed to survive, that would be one thing. We wouldn't like it, but we would at least understand. Wolves, however, kill more than they need. They do it for fun, for wicked pleasure.

The next night there were two separate attacks; the night after that, three. No matter how many traps we set, no matter how alert our dogs were, no matter how many men sat up all night cradling a shotgun, sheep were lost. The livelihood of the village was being lost. Something had to be done.

I wasn't surprised to hear a knock on my door one evening. Indeed, I'd been expecting it. There were perhaps twenty men with shotguns and rifles, each wearing many layers against the cold. Nothing was said. I just nodded. I hadn't suffered any attacks myself, but there are times when a village has to act as one. I put on both of my coats, picked up my shotgun and my show-shoes and joined the party. I decided to leave Bruno behind. If it came to a fight between him and a wolf, I couldn't see him winning.

It took nearly two hours to trudge up to the tree-line. No-one said much. We took turns in hauling three laden sleds. Half-way up I donned my snow-shoes. They made walking a little easier but not much.

The moon rose, full and bright. Those who live in towns might be surprised that our party set off at night, but that's when wolves are at their most active. Besides, most of us had been standing watch at night and sleeping during the day.

We reached the trees. One of the sledges was up-ended and the carcass of a sheep was tipped onto the snow. Bait. Someone produced a knife and eviscerated it, spreading its entrails so that the smell of it would carry a good distance. M Deladier (I hadn't realised he was with us until he spoke. He must've arrived back in the village just before the snow) assumed command. He told off four or five men to wait a discreet distance away, in the hope that a wolf would show up. The rest of us he divided into two parties. He sent one to the right with the second sled, the other he led to the left with the third. I was included in his party, probably by chance as we were so muffled and bundled up that our own mothers wouldn't recognise us. He then ordered all lanterns to be extinguished, other than his own – a dark lantern with a shutter that could be raised or lowered as convenient. He kept it lowered so that no light escaped.

We set off, I and another man hauling the sled. We walked what seemed a long way. If the moon hadn't been so bright we'd've blundered about helplessly. As it was, we made slow and painful progress.

At least, M Deladier called a halt. "Here," he said. There was no reason as far as I could see for choosing that particular spot, but M Deladier was used to taking charge, and I suppose we were used to letting him do so. The sheep was hacked at, bloody chunks were scattered, we settled down to wait. I chose a spot about twenty metres away and lay prone. As I did so the wind, which had been almost non-existent before, began to blow steadily from the north. I burrowed into the snow. Wind, as I've mentioned before, is winter's killer, and the north wind is the worst. A man half-buried in snow, however, is sheltered from the worst the wind can do.

We waited. M Deladier was a few paces to my right. I still thought this was mere chance, and that he wouldn't realise it was me unless I spoke aloud, which I resolved not to do. I'd no idea, of course, how much village gossip he'd picked up since his return, and whether or not he knew about me and Claudette, but I decided not to take any chances.

We waited, we waited, we waited. I've no idea for how long.

I did my best to stay silent and motionless, but M Deladier was forever fidgeting and sighing with impatience. I wanted to tell him not to be such an idiot, but I didn't dare.

Mercifully, the wind died down. Quite suddenly. The silence which resulted was portentous and eerie. M Deladier kept raising his head to look about him. I didn't know whether he'd scare off any wolf in the vicinity or invite them to attack him. I wasn't sure which would be worse.

Then a sound. A snuffling, close by. It put me in mind of a dog trying to decide if a rabbit-hole was worth investigating. It also put me in mind of a wolf sizing me up. I brought my shotgun up to my shoulder.

More snuffling, and the faint but distinct sound of something large moving through the trees. The moon's light didn't penetrate the dense shadow beneath their branches. It occurred to me suddenly that we were bathed in moonlight, but that our adversaries – if adversaries they were – had the advantage of being invisible to us.

More sounds. I was convinced now that a pack of wolves were before us – but they didn't seem to be behaving like wolves. A wolf – or a pack of wolves – either attacks or flees. These seemed to be – what? Toying with us? Testing our nerves?

If the latter, they succeeded. The one whose nerve broke was M Deladier. The crack of his expensive rifle split the night and echoed off the mountainside. I don't suppose he hit anything. He was a poor shot at the best of times. Firing at something he couldn't even see was unlikely to have improved his marksmanship. The report did shatter the tension, though. All at once dark shapes were running full tilt towards us, barking their challenge. Guns fired. Someone screamed.

M Deladier got off another ineffective shot, then a wolf was upon him. I raised my shotgun – but feared to fire for fear of hitting man instead of beast. Instead, I got to my feet and staggered towards him, possibly with the intention of clubbing the wolf with the stock of my shotgun. I never got the chance, though. Just before I reached the two struggling figures something crashed into my back and sent me sprawling.

I lost hold of my gun. I tried to rise, but a wolf was on top of me. It closed its jaws on my shoulder. I had time to be thankful for the two coats that I was wearing, meaning that no teeth penetrated my flesh, then the wolf began to shake me vigorously. I tried to crawl away and beat at it at the same time. Ineffectually; but somehow in the struggle I found myself flipped over so that I was lying on my back. In an instant the wolf's paws were on my chest. It gave a vicious growl, and I realised that it was about to sink its teeth into my throat.

At that point a second and larger wolf crashed into the first, knocking it off of me. There was some confused snarling, and the smaller wolf was soon running back into the forest. I meanwhile, was frantically feeling about for my shotgun. In so doing, I knocked over M Deladier's dark lantern. The shutter flew up and a beam of light stabbed the darkness.

Before me I saw, unmistakably, the wolf I'd rescued from the trap. My mind instantly recalled a story from my childhood: Androcles and the Lion. I smiled to myself.

Then I saw something else and fainted.

***

When I woke up, I was in my own bed. It took me a while to gather my senses. There was someone sitting on a chair by the bed. Claudette.

"Oh good, you're awake," she said. "How do you feel?"

I didn't answer. Instead I raised myself up into a sitting position and looked at her coldly. "I know," I said.

"What do you know?" Claudette asked.

"I know that a wolf I freed from a trap saved my life last night. I also know that the wolf had a necklace round its neck. Silver, with an amber pendant. The one you're wearing now. Difficult to see against a furred neck unless a light shines directly on it but unmistakeable if it does. I also realise that I missed a lot of clues these last few days. Clues which make sense now."

"The bandaged arm, the fact that M Deladier won't let me near his animals, the fact that your dog was suspicious of me?"

"Those. Plus the fact that you said you knew I was kind before I asked you to dance."

"Yes, that was a slip."

"Plus the fact that you knew I was behind you in church. You smelled me, didn't you?"

"I did."

"So you're …"

"A werewolf, yes."

"There was a full moon last night, wasn't there?"

"Yes. The fireside tales you've heard about werewolves aren't entirely true, but a full moon does exert a strong pull on my wolf side."

"And the wolves of the forest? Are they…"

"No. Just ordinary wolves. They're afraid of me, actually. The attacks on the village were truly carried out due to hunger. I just helped them to be a little more organised, that's all."

"All?"

"All God's creatures have to eat."

"Do you think you count as one of God's creatures?"

"He made the world and everything that's in it, so yes."

"I see. And would you have told me before or after our wedding?"

Claudette had the grace to look ashamed. "I don't know. Truly. I was in an agony of indecision. There was one thing I was certain of, though. I was certain that I loved you. I still do."

"Why?"

"Because you're kind. Other than Berthe, you're the only one in the village who was ever kind to me."

"Because everyone else knows you're a werewolf?"

"No. Most people don't like me without knowing why they don't like me. Like your dog doesn't like me without understanding why."

"So no-one else knows?"

"M Deladier."

"He knows, yet he still took you in?"

"Yes. He's my father."

"Your father? Is he a werewolf, too?"

"No, but my mother was. He met her in human form. I presume he took her as a mistress, unknowing. He found out soon after my birth. He killed her."

"I thought werewolves were hard to kill. Silver bullets and such."

"A myth, sadly."

"I see. I'm surprised you didn't kill him when you found out."

"I couldn't. He's my father. I can't say I love him or respect him, but I can't lift my hand – or my paw – against him. He made it down from the mountain, by the way. He's in bed now, with bandages and a bottle, feeling sorry for himself."

"How did I get back here?"

"I carried you. He, I might add, ran for his life, leaving everyone else behind him."

"That doesn't surprise me. Were any of the others …"

"Injured? Yes. Killed? No."

"That's something. Your doing?"

"Yes."

I heaved a great sigh. "Well, that's me caught up. The question remains: what now?"

"That's up to you."

"Yes, I was afraid it might be." I lay back and stared at the ceiling for a long time. "Tell me," I said at last, "if we do get married, will our children be werewolves?"

"The boys, no. The girls, yes. It passes down the female line, or it does in my family."

I was silent for a long time. Then, "How do you know that? Your mother can't have told you, as she was killed just after your birth."

Claudette didn't answer.

"There are others, aren't there?"

"Some."

"Berthe?"

"No."

Had there been a slight hesitation before that denial? I wasn't sure but decided not to press the point. Instead I thought about marrying a monster. Yes, I used that term. In my head, anyway. Claudette might think she was one of God's creatures, but I didn't – couldn't – share her opinion.

I also thought about *not* marrying a monster. They say hell hath no fury like a woman scorned. What would a werewolf scorned be like?

I got out of bed and opened a chest. My father served with the French army in the war against the Prussians. It was an inglorious business, he told us, but he did come back with a Prussian cavalry sword. This I retrieved from the chest.

I unsheathed it.

Claudette said nothing, did nothing.

"I'm sorry, my love," I said.

Claudette nodded, then stood up slowly, presenting me with an easy target. "I said it was up to you," she said. "I thought it over whilst waiting for you to wake up. I said I love you, and I do. More than anything I want to be your wife; but if that can't be, I want nothing at all."

I wondered whether I should say something at this point. Make a speech, bid Claudette farewell. My soul was too empty to do so, however. I just thrust. The idea that werewolves are hard to kill is indeed just a myth.

Afterwards I went into the kitchen to boil some coffee. As I did so, my eye fell on the almanac on the wall. I noted the date. The fourteenth of February. St Valentine's Day. The day for lovers.

THE THINGS WE DO FOR LOVE

BP CHRISTY

Twenty-five years is time enough to name every crack in the walls.

Ellen is that narrow one that spider-webs up the eastern side. Tucker is that wide one stemming from a chip over in the corner. But my favorite is Mia. She's the deepest, and on sunny days a pinhole of sunlight shines through her.

We went to college together, Mia and I. She was absolutely radiant the first time we met. God, my palms were sweating like crazy. I remember she wore a baby-blue button-up shirt that was just big enough to peek at what was underneath if I leaned forward in my chair far enough. I was so close to her that I could smell her hair; it smelled like some kind of fruit.

I remember the way she fit into a pair of jeans made teachers uncomfortable. It was funny how they'd refuse to look directly at her, even if she asked a question. It was also the reason guys showed up to class early. It definitely got my attention. I'd fight my way in to get the perfect seat in the back where I could watch her without making it too obvious, you know, to be aloof. She liked it when I watched.

And she had real fire, too. One time I accidentally ran into her on purpose in the hall, and she told me to watch where the fuck I was going, but the way we locked eyes said something completely different. Love at first sight sounds corny, but I assure you it exists.

The girls in high school never responded to me like that.

It was fate that we met.

The only thing standing in the way was her "boyfriend," Marcus. I don't know why she put up with that guy, the way he treated her.

Papaya. Her hair smelled like papaya.

I'd do it all over again exactly the same way for her any day of the week.

Don't judge; we're in love.

November 8, 1999

A tray of drinks crashes to the dance floor as I drag a waitress down with me.

Aside from the music, the club is totally silent. All eyes are on me and the waitress who's frantically trying to pick up her scattered tips. It isn't until someone laughs that anyone says a word.

There's no way of knowing what Mia's saying to Marcus, but there's lots of hand-waving and yelling from her, and he's flexing and pointing at me. Is she defending me? Who is going to defend her?

Whiskey's soaking into my underwear, but I'm not about to get up until Marcus gets thrown out. He looks almost as angry as the waitress sweeping up broken glass with her apron. I offer to help, and she flips me the bird and stomps off.

There's more laughing.

The fat-lip Marcus just gave me feels like a night crawler in my mouth.

Bouncers finally escort him to the door. My molars rattle around and there's a shard of glass in my palm, but seeing her walk out with him really hurts.

It feels like gravity's tacked a few hundred pounds on my shoulders, so it must not be easy for Tommy, my best friend, to haul me to the exit. Time pauses as we walk home, only playing when Tommy gives me a hard time. I stumble over an uneven part of the sidewalk.

"I can't believe you just sat there and did freaking nothing!" Tommy laughs and blows a cloud of frozen breath into his hands.

My apartment keys rub into where broken glass cut my palm, yet I squeeze harder on them every time he speaks.

"But I gotta admit you took it like a champ," he says, dancing around like a prize fighter jabbing at the air.

I tuck my chin to my chest and avoid eye contact.

"Oh buck up, Champ, you knew she was with that guy," he says. "So it shouldn't be too shocking that you got tapped on the chin for bumpin' and grindin' on her." He starts dancing with a mailbox, exaggerating the way danced with Mia. "Still, I gotta give you credit for doing *something* after drooling over her all year."

I stare at him from the corners of my eyes.

He stops laughing and coughs. "Sorry. It was kind of cold how she didn't even look back, though. Nope, she just bitched about how he embarrassed her."

I liked it better when I thought she was defending me. The night crawler pops like a zit between my teeth. I swallow a mouthful of blood.

The night replays in my head while I half-heartedly listen to Tommy drone on and on; reliving the image of me freezing up when Marcus came through the crowd, pushing people out of his way. It isn't how I want to remember an evening that was otherwise magical. I can still smell the cheap whiskey that got spilled in the rush – in fact, I'm starting to chafe from it.

"I can't even imagine how embarrassing it must be to get punked out in front of your dream chick like that," says Tommy.

We've covered this, but he's like a dog with a bone.

"Ah hell, dude, let it go. Fish; sea; however that old saying goes. Let's get a beer. My treat."

Nodding in agreement, I kick a rock out of my way.

"Come on, say it," says Tommy, spinning me around to look him in the face.

This is me, letting it go, I tell him, circling my face with my fingers.

"You see! Tommy, with a supporting cast of alcoholic beverages, will now make your humiliation at the hands of that bad man fade away into a luscious haze of self-abuse," he says and pushes me through a pub door. Usually pubs won't serve minors, but in a college town people tend to look the other way.

Of course I don't let it go. Who could? While Tommy's at the jukebox, I mentally replay the event again while picking the wrapper off my bottle. The crowd, the lights, the girl, the getting punched in the face is all so painfully clear that it needs a *creative reimagining*.

In the new version, Mia stays behind to see if I'm okay.

She's so thoughtful. A smile stretches awkwardly across my swollen face.

"That's more like it," Tommy says and clinks our bottles together.

November 10, 1999

The classroom clock ticks louder with every passing second and my knee bounces at eighty-miles-per-hour. There's a stench of body odor lingering in the air, and I hope to God it isn't me, not while sitting so close to Mia. The number two pencil in my fist is now riddled with little half-moons from my fingernails.

She's wearing a lacy red camisole with a gray crushed-velvet hoodie. Her hair is up, but a couple of curly strands have escaped and dangle free. Once in a while she'll reach back to rub where they tickle her neck. Her nails are painted pink and shimmer iridescently when the light hits them just right.

That night at the club still haunts me. That punch caused a pretty big rift in our relationship. Tonguing at the scar inside my lip, I dig splinters and yellow paint from under my fingernails.

In the newest version, Marcus swings and misses. My fist drives into his chin with a crack, which is a nice thought, but you can't change the past.

There should be a rematch.

Maybe it'll happen in another club, or maybe in the parking lot. Regardless of where, it'll be cool to see Marcus' head snap back as he topples to the ground in a heap.

Maybe he'll cry.

He'll probably cry.

Mia looks back at me and my pulse quickens. I wink as we make eye contact. She furls her brows and turns around, frowning. She must have smelled me.

A splinter stings under my fingernail, and highlights my fingertip in red.

November 22, 1999

Sweat seeps through my t-shirt as I bob and weave, thrusting jab after jab in front of the bathroom mirror. Metallica's "Seek and Destroy" is blaring.

Tommy's only complained a few times so far about the noise level or about having to take a piss, which isn't bad. He usually interrupts me a lot more when I'm training.

In the latest version of the rematch, there are chanting spectators and stern dialogue between us – two combatants squaring off on the field of battle for the love of Mia. He gets in some lucky shots, but the fight ends with a thunderous right-cross that blasts him against the side of a car, which he slides down, unconscious.

Mia throws her arms around me, and we walk off into the sunset. It'll be glorious. A fairytale beginning to our public relationship.

Panting and dripping sweat on the sink, I catch my reflection in the mirror and spit on it.

DECEMBER 13, 1999

"He doesn't deserve her," I tell Tommy as the point guard steals the basketball out of the visiting team's hands. The crowd cheers and jumps to their feet. The smell of stale beer and processed meat pours in from every direction of the arena.

"Wuf?" he says through a mouthful of half-chewed hotdog.

"That neanderthal Marcus doesn't deserve a woman like Mia," I explain. The words reverberate through the almost-empty plastic cup of warm beer-foam.

He swigs his beer to help choke down the hotdog, and says, "Oh, good, for a second I thought you found out about me and your mom."

I ask him why he can't be serious for once.

"Really, I don't know what you see in her," he says – and whistles at the players. "Seriously, dude, I don't think you're her type."

"You don't see how she looks at me," I shoot back and throw down my empty cup.

"Whoa! I'm just saying that she's more into the *bad boy* thing is all."

"Like sneaking up and sucker-punching me in the middle of a dance is such a '*bad boy*' thing," I say with finger quotes.

Tommy now has the same look on his face that Mia had in class. "Are you talking about when you got punched last month?" The slob wipes ketchup off his chin. "Whatever. But, if you insist on doing something stupid, I suggest you not go toe-to-toe with his big ass. You'll probably have to shank him or something when he's not looking."

We laugh at the absurdity of stabbing someone, but it does offer a colorful new spin on my gladiatorial scenario. It wouldn't be a mortal wound; it'd just be enough to make him think twice about trying to punk me out in front of Mia again. It would send a clear message that he's to back off for good.

The ball flies through the air and swishes through the net as the game clock buzzes.

January 3, 2000

It's a new year. A new millennium. A time for fresh starts.

"Looking for anything in particular?" says the pawn shop owner from behind the glass counter. I've been crouched down, admiring the knife selection so long that my knees hurt. His breath is rank from drinking burnt coffee and cigarettes, and his gut is testing the limits of his stained polo shirt.

I tell him that I'm looking for a knife that will make a statement. Scratching the stubble on his chins, he tells me that it all depends on the statement I want to make. He begins to showcase the various knives and the message each would send.

"If you're looking to be all fancy, you can't go wrong with a butterfly knife. Of course, you'll need a lot of practice time with it before you even begin to look remotely cool," he says, and takes one out of the case.

"It's too small," I tell him, and ask if he has anything bigger, more masculine. My hands leave fogged, sweaty handprints on the display case. He quickly puts the butterfly knife away, probably because I'll get the blade dirty.

He looks me up and down and taps fingers on the glass. Every one of his fingers has a gold ring that clinks with each tap. "Son," he says, "what exactly do you plan on doing with a knife anyway?"

I tell him that I've been threatened by a much bigger guy and just need something to scare him off, which was close enough to the truth. Mia is in harm's way, and Marcus has threatened, even assaulted me before.

The employee hesitates and looks into my eyes. "I'll take your word for it." He reaches back under the counter. "I have just what you are looking for."

JANUARY 16, 2000

From around a snow-capped hedge, I see Mia on a bench, basking in the first full sun of the new year. She's wearing a pair of light-blue jeans and a tie-dye shirt with the State Fair logo peeking out from her coat. She's reading a book and swinging her feet around.

Pressing my thumb into my palm, I massage it while watching her feet sway back and forth. If I concentrate hard enough, I read that my soulmate will feel it.

The rumbling of a shoddy exhaust system breaks the serenity. My thumb stops massaging her feet as Marcus's rusted Camaro flies dangerously around the corner and screeches to a stop. The piece of junk vomits exhaust and smoke from burning oil, making a poisonous black fog at his feet as he steps out of the car. He's not even trying to hide his true face anymore. He *is* the Devil.

He whistles and yells that they're running late for a movie while she tries to pick up her things.

She yells back that it's his fault that they're late in the first place.

Good for her, but how long can she keep it up? She doesn't deserve that. Marcus is easily over six-feet-tall and about 220 pounds of angry muscle. She won't stand a chance when he attacks.

I chew on the thick scar inside my mouth.

After making sure campus security isn't watching, I slip my hand into my pocket and caress the cold metal handle of my new Carson Design M16-14 Special Forces Combo Edge Tactical Knife, slightly opening the subdued black, four-inch retractable blade then letting it snap closed.

She deserves a hero.

FEBRUARY 11, 2000

Tommy's avoiding eye contact with me as he carries out the last box of his belongings.

We haven't said a word to each other since he'd decided to move out after his jealousy drove a wedge between us. The choice was between him and Mia, and love trumps friendship. I suck down a beer and flip through a magazine roughly, tearing the pages a little. Seeing a bikini that Mia would look stunning in, I tell Tommy to check it out, just to break the tension.

He stops in the doorway. "You need serious help. There is no *you and Mia*," he says.

Before I can say anything back, he's gone.

My beer bottle explodes against the door in a shower of brown glass.

FEBRUARY 14, 2000

Sleet falls hard enough to make my hair mat to my forehead, but not quite hard enough to soak through my coat yet. The whiskey I've been sipping is keeping me warm. I've been standing under a leafless tree in the middle of a parking lot island reciting the dialog of what's to come for a while.

Marcus is late picking her up. Villains are always late.

Mia's stretching out on a bench under an awning with a book in hand. If I know Mia, it's Dickinson she's reading.

She's as enchanting now as the night Marcus punched me from behind at the club. That had been the first time she said she needed me to deliver her from him. I still can't believe how I blushed when we kissed.

The knife rests heavily in my pocket.

Whispering into the wind, I tell her that I'm here, and even though we are too far apart for her ears to hear me, I know that her heart can.

The familiar roar of Marcus's car echoes off the brick campus buildings. His stereo is loud enough that I can hear the lyrics of whatever death metal song he's listening to.

There's cold rainwater trickling down my burning cheeks. Stepping off the muddy island, I splash through the puddles and make a beeline straight for Marcus, who is yelling for Mia to move her ass from the warmth of his car. His arm is hanging out of the open window, a cigarette burns between his fingers, that tap to the beat of the music.

My stomach tightens. I flip the knife open.

The sting of the cigarette being extinguished against my free hand barely registers as I pin his arm to the car door and thrust my knife blindly through the open window.

I open my eyes.

The blade lodges in his neck. He's gurgling and thrashing around. The car's horn honks as he struggles. The harder he fights against it, the deeper the knife slices in. I can feel his heartbeat vibrating through the blade. He stares up at me blankly with his mouth gaping open as he paws weakly at my arm. He kind of looks like a fish out of water that's gasping for air. The gash in his neck looks like ragged gills.

My stomach tightens again, and I throw up down the side of the car.

Mia's screaming. Why? She knows this is the only way to be free from his tyranny. We've talked about it a thousand times. This is how much her happiness means to me.

Why is she running?

I yank the knife out and run after her, pleading for her to stop. I scream over and over that I love her until my throat is hoarse.

PRESENT DAY

Twenty-five years I've been in this cell.

It doesn't matter that she testified against me, as long as she's free. But they got it wrong. How can they say it was murder when it was in defense of another?

Twenty-five wasted years; years that would otherwise have been spent with Mia.

We'd have three kids: two girls and a boy. Our son is the youngest. His sisters give him such a hard time, and we just laugh and laugh whenever we show the video from when they were little, and the girls dressed him up in their mom's clothes. He hates it when we do that.

I saved her.

That's what you do for the people you love.

CUCKOOS

TIM JEFFREYS

Calvin eased his foot off the accelerator then pulled over at the edge of the road.

Earlier, when he'd stopped at the petrol station to buy daffodils, he'd expected Beks to say something on his return to the car. But she hadn't. Perhaps she thought the flowers were for his mother since that was where he'd told her they were going today. Nor had she questioned why he'd taken the moorland road out of the village instead of heading towards Gledholt. Not daring to look at her, he'd kept driving along that road. Fifteen minutes. Twenty. She remained silent. Now though, as he wrenched on the handbrake, she turned to him, narrowing her eyes. "Why have we stopped here, Cal? Babe? What're we doing?"

"I'll just be a minute."

Grabbing the flowers from the dash, he climbed out of the car, slammed the driver's side door behind him then walked out onto the moor. He could sense Beks watching him through the side-window, but he didn't look back. Once out on the moor, he was surprised by how featureless the landscape was. A flat expanse of thick and sodden brownish-green grass rolled out for miles in every direction.

Is this the place?

He remembered the ancient weather-eroded boundary stone which stood close to the road. That night, three months earlier, he'd mistaken it for a gravestone. It might even have been why he chose this spot.

There are other graves here.

But maybe there were similar boundary stones dotted about the moor. He couldn't be sure it was the same one he'd seen that night.

He'd thought there'd be something else, some other landmark to orientate himself by. Something he'd recognise. He hadn't marked the spot where he'd buried the body. Of course he hadn't. He'd never thought he'd be returning to it. Also, to his mind, an obviously-placed marker, even just a rock, would alert someone to the fact that there was a body buried beneath.

You keep my secret, and I'll keep yours.

Not that, at the time, he'd been capable of thinking about anything other than making the ground where he'd dug appear as unspoiled as possible. His mind a stew of grief, confusion, desolation, and fear, it was a miracle he'd been able to think clearly about anything. Maybe the truth was that he hadn't wanted to create a grave. If there was a grave, then there was a person in that grave. And if there was a person in that grave, who was it? And who was the person currently sitting in the passenger seat of his car, watching him through the side-window? A person couldn't be in two places at once. A person couldn't be both dead and alive.

The sky was overcast. A gusty wind, carrying scatterings of icy rain, traversed the moor. It flattened his coat and jeans against his body. He yanked up the hood of his coat then tucked his hands under his armpits. He continued walking away from the road, pushing against the wind, scanning the ground for signs of disturbed soil. He found none no matter which direction he walked in. Either he'd covered his tracks too well that night, or this wasn't the place.

You keep my secret...

Halting, he looked first one way and then the other. He scanned the low hills in the distance. He couldn't see the village. He could see no signs of civilisation, in fact, other than the one road snaking over the moor. It was an awful, bleak place to be buried. Lonely. Desolate. She deserved better.

Taking the daffodils from the plastic wrapping, he laid them on the ground in front of him. It wasn't the exact spot, he knew that, but she was here somewhere. Somewhere on this moor. Somewhere under this earth.

Turning to head back to the car, he flinched at a voice.

"What're you doing?"

Beks stood a few feet away, leaning with her weight on one leg, hands in the pockets of her jacket, looking at him, her eyes dark with disapproval.

"I told you I wouldn't be long," he said. "You should've waited in the car. It's cold out here."

"I wanted to see what you were doing," she said. "What *are* you doing?"

"Nothing," he said. Then – knowing he shouldn't, he added, "Paying my respects."

"Respects?" She glanced around, then back at him. "To who?"

To the woman whose body we wrapped in a sheet, put in the boot of my car, then buried somewhere around here, or some other place just like it, he could've said. *To the woman whose house we took over. To the woman whose clothes you wear.*

But he could say none of this. Saying it would make it real.

He shrugged, and threw up his hands.

"Don't be a fool," she said, throwing him a frigid look. She crouched to snatch the daffodils from the ground. "If someone sees these flowers, they might start thinking there's a grave somewhere around here. Is that what you want?"

"Do you know where it is?" he said, looking into her eyes. "Do you remember?"

"Cal," she said, moving closer so that her face was inches from his. They'd slept in the same bed, side by side, for the past three months, had sex countless times, snuggled on the sofa to watch TV, sat down together at the dining table to eat, and talked about what the future might hold for them. Now her proximity sent a bolt of terror through him. He tried not to let it show. He looked into her eyes, told himself, *It's Beks. It's just Beks.* He only had to see her eyes to know. He'd never met anyone with eyes as green as hers. He'd always thought they were like jewels, like emeralds. He used to love gazing into them. Now - though he wanted to run from her, run as fast as he could - those eyes held him rooted to the spot.

It isn't Beks. Beks is dead.

He'd lied to himself for the past three months. How? Perhaps it was guilt or grief, or was it fear? Dread? He'd let himself believe. But that morning in bed, when she'd rolled over and slid a hand across his chest, he'd felt a shudder go through him. The memory came back. In truth, it'd never gone away. He'd just been pushing it from his mind all this time. The memory of how he'd buried Beks' body in a shallow grave out on the moor. And he was afraid now. Afraid of what this thing, this doppelgänger, this *whatever-the-hell-it-was* would do if it found out the fog in his mind had cleared. And now that it had cleared, how long could he go on pretending?

"I worry about you sometimes," Beks, or the thing that looked like Beks, continued. She ran a hand along his arm, sending a shiver of repulsion through him. "You get some strange ideas in your head. Weird fantasies. What's the matter? Aren't you happy?"

"I...I am happy," Calvin said, looking away, avoiding her eyes now.

"We love each other. Right?"

"Yes."

It took all his willpower not to flinch in disgust when she touched his hand.

"No one can take that away from us."

"Let's..." He swallowed. "Let's go back to the car."

He thought she must have noticed his unease, but she smiled, turned, and began walking back towards the road. He watched her for a moment. Then, flitting his eyes downwards, he saw a flat jagged stone in the grass. Looking towards the road, he checked for other cars. There were none. No one to see. As he started walking, he crouched to pluck the stone from the ground. Gaining on Beks, heart pounding, his ears filled with the rushing of his own blood; he examined the back of her head, thinking about the best way to deliver the blow. He could slam the stone into the side of her cranium from behind. At the very least, it would stun her. It would give him time to deliver a few more blows. He didn't know what it would take to kill a thing like that.

He drew a deep breath.

Close to her back, he was adjusting the weight of the stone in his hand when, as if sensing his intentions, she halted and craned her head around. He dropped the stone, covering the dull thud of it hitting the ground by saying, "All right?"

She didn't answer, but ran her narrowed gaze up and down his body. Then she smiled.

It's just Beks.

"Come on," he said, picking up his pace again, passing her, keeping his eyes focused on the car. "It's freezing."

***

Banjo, the black Labrador belonging to Calvin's mother, began barking and howling the moment Beks stepped inside the front door. Calvin's mother yelled at the dog to stop, but he wouldn't.

"Put him outside," she finally told Calvin, pressing the back of one hand to her forehead.

Calvin led the dog by the collar to the back door and let him out into the long junk-strewn rear garden. Even then, the dog stood behind the door, barking furiously. Calvin had never known Banjo to get into a frenzy over anyone. He normally wagged his tail at visitors.

Returning along the hall, he looked in on the living room. Beks was there, perched on the sofa and smiling at something she saw on the TV, seemingly unfazed by Banjo's behaviour. Not wanting to be alone with her, Calvin crossed into the kitchen to help his mother prepare the tea.

"How's life in the drug-dealer's house?" she said. "Don't you ever worry he'll come home?"

"He won't be back," Calvin said, pouring water from the kettle into three mugs.

His mother turned to stare at him. "How can you be sure? Nasty piece of work, he was. Can't imagine he'll be too happy if he comes home one day and finds you shacked-up with his missus."

"I just know, okay?"

She gave him a searching look. He waited for her to ask if he knew something about Royce Peglar's disappearance, but to his relief she didn't. He didn't want to have to lie to her.

By way of diversion, he said, "What the hell's got into Banjo? Never seen him get worked up before."

His mother huffed, glancing towards the kitchen door. "The dog's a good judge of character, that's all."

Calvin looked up from stirring the tea. "What's that supposed to mean?"

She was silent a moment, then said, "I don't know what you're doing with that little missy in there, Calvin. She was always trouble. I remember how she used to be up there in your room with you all the time after she got back from school. God knows what went on. You always had the door shut. What was she then? Fourteen? Fifteen? Had you twisted around her little finger." She paused to light a cigarette and take a drag on it. "Her mam and dad couldn't have cared less where she was. Not surprising she went off and married that thug, Royce Peglar, considering the madhouse she grew up in. The street's been a lot quieter since her dad died. You know that."

Calvin waved at the smoke his mother exhaled. "Isn't it time you quit the cancer sticks, Mum?"

She chuckled. "Hark at him, lecturing me."

"Me and Beks were meant to be," he said. He took a deep breath to stop the tears welling behind his eyes.

His mother huffed again. She stood half-turned away from him, leaning against the edge of the counter, taking drags on her cigarette and exhaling with a long sigh. "It's your funeral."

She pointed towards the room across the hall, from which could be heard the noise of the television. "Shall we go in? Shouldn't leave her all by herself." She paused to suck on her cigarette. "She'll be loading her handbag up with all my best silver."

"Beks isn't a thief, Mum," Calvin said, shaking his head. "And you don't have any silver, best or otherwise."

"Better go in anyway. Keep an eye on her."

"I wanted to ask you something first."

Perhaps picking up on the edge in his voice, her eyes widened. "Yes?"

"Do you remember when you used to take me to visit Granddad at the nursing home when I was a kid? You'd leave me there with him, remember, and he'd tell me stories about these monsters that lived on the moor."

"Did he? I don't remember that."

"He said they wanted my heart. I thought he meant to eat it. I was afraid of the moors for years."

She laughed. "His mind was gone, Calvin. He didn't know what he was talking about. He probably didn't even know who he was talking to. That's why I couldn't stay there with you. He had no idea who I was, and I couldn't stand it. Some days he'd call me by his mammie's name, Jean. He thought I was his mother. It tore me up."

"Then he never told *you* any stories like that?"

Calvin could still hear Banjo barking outside the back door. The damn dog just wouldn't let up. "Maybe when you were little?"

"Your granddad wasn't one for bedtime stories, son," his mother said. "He was usually drunk by the time he got home from work. Us kids put all our energies into staying out of his way."

"So you never heard stories about monsters that live on the moor? From anyone?"

She frowned, and shook her head. "Old people are full of talk." Then, before he could press her further, she took one of the mugs of tea and left the kitchen.

Picking up the two remaining mugs, Calvin carried them into the living room and placed one on the coffee table in front of Beks.

Glancing up, Beks smiled at him before returning her attention to the TV. He looked to see what she was watching. It was a cartoon. *Teen Titans GO!* One Calvin had liked to watch sometimes because it made him laugh. It was about a gang of superheroes. One of them, the green one – Calvin couldn't remember his name – could change into any animal he wanted. That was his superpower.

"I like this," Beks said.

When she glanced up again to meet his eyes, he looked away.

He could hear his mother talking to Banjo through the back door, using a soothing voice, telling him to quieten down. Entering the room a minute or so later, she said to Calvin:

"We had a dog when I was little. A Jack Russell. Bess."

"Bess?"

"I just remembered."

"Remembered what?"

She thumbed in the direction of the back door. "Bess used to go nuts like this whenever your Great Aunt Agnes came to the house. Agnes was a hill walker. Always out tramping about the moors."

Calvin didn't chance a look at Beks, but he sensed she too was listening to his mother. "Oh?"

"Yes. And she married a fella she met on one of her walks. Guy. He always wanted us kids to call him Uncle Guy, but we wouldn't. We didn't like him. There was just something off about him. It was him that Bess used to go crazy at. Like I said…" She shot a meaningful glance at Beks. "Dogs are good at getting the mark of people."

Concerned, Calvin looked at Beks and saw that she was staring at his mother. Not in an offended or even a murderous way, as he'd imagined, but in a quiet contemplative way which was somehow worse. She inspected the other woman as if she wanted to learn something about her, or understand her simply by looking. Shifting her head to one side, she met Calvin's eyes. And smiled.

***

When they were back in the car, Calvin found that it wouldn't start.

"Come on," he breathed, as he twisted the key in the ignition. "Come on."

Watching him intently, Beks said, "You love her?"

He stopped working the ignition, sat back in his seat, and turned to her. "What?"

"Your mother. You love her?"

"Of course. She's my mother, isn't she? Even if she is half-senile." He tried the key in the ignition again, and the engine came to life. "Oh, thank Christ."

Before he pulled the car away from the kurb, Beks craned her head to stare at his mother's house.

"She doesn't like me."

"Huh?"

"She doesn't like me. She hates me."

"She doesn't…" *She doesn't know you*, he'd meant to say but his words faltered. When he tried again, he put too much emphasis on the final word and his attempt at reassurance curdled. "She doesn't know *you*."

***

That night, when Beks came to bed, Calvin put his back to her and feigned sleep. She wasn't fooled. After she fell in beside him, one of her hands went searching under the duvet.

"Oh," she said, laughing under her breath, "someone's awake."

Before he could do anything to prevent it, she had turned him onto his back and straddled him.

Throughout, he kept his eyes squeezed shut. Then when it was over, he brushed her off him with one arm and lay flushed and nauseated, with sweat trickling along his jaw-line and pooling in the hollow of his chest. "Need some air," he said, getting up and crossing to the window. He pushed it open a few inches and took a deep gulp of the cold air that rushed in.

He couldn't help wondering what that thing looked like when it wasn't impersonating someone.

He sat on the edge of the bed, staring out of the window at the blue-black night until he judged, from the sound of her breathing, that Beks was asleep.

Have to stop referring to it as Beks. It's not Beks.

It's...

Scared that he was losing his grip on reality, he lay awake replaying his memory of the day Beks, the real Beks, died. He recalled how he'd rushed to her house, this house, after she called him and told him Royce was home. That couldn't be, because he'd taken care of Royce himself, out on the moor, and dumped his body in the reservoir. As he'd stormed up the driveway, Beks had come hurrying out to meet him. Royce had been watching from an upstairs window. How this was possible he didn't know at the time, although he did now. He and Beks had argued. He hadn't meant to push her. He was angry. He'd wanted to get away from her. It wasn't his fault she'd fallen. She'd been wearing those ridiculous block heels. It wasn't his fault, either, that she'd been standing so close to that stone fountain.

He remembered the blood. So much blood, pooling under her head.

It was the next part of the memory he didn't trust. The part where another Beks had come out of the house and told him they had to get rid of the body. Because if they didn't, this new Beks said, he'd go to prison. The whole thing, she told him, had been caught on Royce Peglar's security cameras.

Everything can be exactly how you want it to be. I'll keep your secret if you keep mine.

Rolling his head to the side, he tried to make out the face on the pillow next to his. In the near dark, shadows in the hollows of Beks' face turned it into a death mask.

It could be whoever it wanted to be. That was clear. It did what it did to survive. First it had become Royce. That was why he'd been there in the window of his house that day Calvin had stormed up the drive. Then it had become Beks. If pushed, who would it become next? He recalled how he'd seen it studying his mother earlier that day, running its eyes along her frame as if it were trying to learn her. Yes, that was it, that's what it had been doing, learning her. Was that what they did? Learned you, studied you, in order to become you? Feeling cold, he drew the duvet tighter around himself.

He lay wide-awake, knowing he wouldn't sleep. As the clock on the bedside table ticked away the minutes and the hours, those words of his mother's kept returning to his mind: *Old people are full of talk.* He'd thought at the time that she'd meant this as a way of dismissing the stories his granddad told. The more he thought about it, the more he wondered if what she'd meant was that it was the old people who were always talking about monsters on the moor. It was the old people of the village who knew about such things.

The old people.

***

He imagined he saw suspicion in Beks' eyes the next morning when he told her he was going into Dobcroft to see about some work, but she didn't protest or insist on going with him. She shouldn't have been suspicious. They'd talked about how one of them was eventually going to have to get a job. The house was paid for, but there would be bills, and they still had to live. They didn't(,) of course(,) discuss the fact that they lived in a house neither of them had any right to be in, cuckoos who'd usurped the rightful birds from their nest: something that was becoming more apparent to Calvin with each passing day. Royce was fish-food and here was Calvin sleeping in his bed, drinking his Loch Lomond Single Malt, and wearing his silk dressing gown; whilst Beks lay in a shallow grave on the moor, while something that looked just like her sat at her dressing table, rifling through her make-up box, and spraying itself with her Gris Dior.

He left her watching cartoons. It was *Teen Titans GO!* again. He heard her chuckling as he stepped out of the front door.

In Dobcroft, leaving his Citroen in the carpark behind the All-in-One, he walked the streets, wondering where he could find some old people to talk to. The sky was grey and a fine misty rain fell, on and off. Outside the Barclays, a man who looked to be in his seventies, dressed in a ratty coat, had stationed himself next to the cash machine. He had a few coins in one hand which he looked at in a ponderous way, as if wondering if they were enough and where he might get more if they weren't. Then he'd glance up the street in the direction of The Royal Oak pub.

Recognising the ploy, Calvin fished some change out of his pocket and approached him.

"Not got enough for a pint?" he said.

The old man looked at him, showing a bashful smile. "No, lad."

"Let me help you out." Calvin slipped the man a few pound coins.

"God bless you, son."

"Glad to help an old war hero. Have you always lived around here?"

"All my life. Born and raised in Dobcroft."

"Do you know anything about shape-shifters?"

The old man's expression hardened. "Sorry?"

"Shape-shifters. Things that can impersonate us. Look like us. Things that live out on the moor."

The old man shook his head, already beginning to slide away towards The Royal Oak. "I don't know what you mean by that."

Hearing someone call his name called, Calvin turned around. The old man took off for the pub. Approaching from the opposite end of the street was Freddie Kear. He was dressed in a white tracksuit, probably a knock-of from Huddersfield market, and a baseball cap which he wore with the peak turned to one side. He looked like he belonged on a *Top of the Pops* re-run from 1990.

"Hey, Calvin," he said, "heard you was living the high life now?"

Calvin hardened his expression. "What's that?"

"Ain't you been living in the big man's house ever since he done his disappearing act?"

"Maybe. What's it got to do with you?"

Freddie sniggered and made hand gestures as if he thought he was some American rapper. "You know that's a dangerous position, man. Heard you been putting it to his missus on the sly too."

Calvin pressed his lips together, before he nodded and said, "Ah yes. That reminds me."

Drawing one arm back, he gave Freddie a swift punch in the nose, hard enough to knock the cap off his head and send him sprawling against the wall of the bank.

"What the fuck, Cal?" Freddie said, clutching both hands to his face. "What did ya do that for?"

"Royce told me it was you who squealed to him about my car stinking of Beks' perfume. And there's me trying to do you a favour.

How's your mother, by the way? Back home, is she? Out of the hospital?"

Freddie glared, pointing at him with one wavering hand. "Royce said he had a plan for you."

"Yeah, well. His plan went sideways."

Lashing out, he punched Freddie again in the side of the head, knocking him to the ground this time. Leaving him sprawled on the pavement(,) he headed after the old man in the direction of The Royal Oak.

***

Apart from Hattie behind the bar, the pub was full of old men, some with dogs laid out by their feet. The man Calvin had spoken to outside had installed himself alone in a nook behind the door, where he sat nursing a pint of bitter. Calvin ordered a pint for himself then carried it to the man's table.

"Mind if I join you?"

Raising his watery eyes, the old man gave no sign of recognition. He said nothing, so Calvin pulled a stool out from under the table. The old man sipped his ale and fixed his solemn gaze on the far end of the bar.

"I asked you about shape-shifters. Outside, remember? Things on the moor that can look like other people."

Meeting Calvin's gaze, the old man narrowed his eyes. "Did you say shape-shifters?"

"My granddad used to talk about them. He used to tell me stories about them when I was a kid. He said there were things living on the moor that could change their shape. Like the guy in that cartoon. You ever seen *Teen Titans GO!?* But they're not people. They're monsters. Like trolls or something.""

"Trolls?" The old man's eye brightened. "I've seen trolls."

"Have you? Where?"

"Norway. Far north. Years back. Nineteen seventy-five or seventy-six. Before you were born, lad."

"What were you doing in Norway?"

"Serving with the Commando Royal Marine Commandos" the old man said.

Calvin looked the old man up and down. "Really?"

"Yes. We were the only ski-trained troops in the forces back then. Nowadays, all the commando units are ski-trained." The old man prodded his own chest with one finger. "I learned to ski in a small town called Berjka, just outside the Arctic Circle." He leaned closer to Calvin as if to impart a secret. "Would you believe not one man on that course could get to the bottom of a very gentle slope of about six feet long without falling over."

"That true?" Calvin said. He went on tentatively. "And you saw trolls there?"

"Yes," the old man said. "Trolls, or Trollsen as the locals called them." A smirk touched the corners of his mouth. "We saw them in shops, cafes and such like. They were dolls, models. They varied from about two to six feet tall."

"You old bastard," Calvin said, drawing back. "I thought you were talking about actual real live trolls."

The old man furrowed his brow. "Are you out of your mind, lad? Things like that aren't real."

"Was a time," said a voice from behind Calvin, "everyone around here knew someone who'd had a shifter in their house."

Twisting around on the stool, Calvin found himself facing a whippet-thin man with long white hair. Calvin had never seen him in the village before. He had an ageing rocker look. Bushy grey sideburns ran down either side of his face.

"Sorry?"

The man nodded. "Your granddad was a smart fella. He was trying to warn you. People don't talk about those things anymore. That doesn't mean they're not still out there."

"You mean they're real?"

The man craned his head forward, peering into Calvin's eyes. "If you don't know that already, why are you in here asking about them?"

"Did you ever know someone?" Calvin said. "Someone who had one in their house, I mean?"

"For all you know," the man said, straightening up. "I might be one of those things myself."

"Seriously though," Calvin said.

"Serious? I am being serious. That's the thing with those shifters, you never know where they are." He threw out one arm. "Everyone in this pub could be one."

Calvin let his eyes roam the pub, taking in the old men sitting alone or in twos or threes, the dogs lounging under the tables, the harried-looking woman behind the bar.

He faced the old rocker again. "If those things exist, they could be everywhere, couldn't they? All over the world."

"Those things are clever," the old rocker went on as if Calvin hadn't spoken. "Once they're found out, they move on and become someone else. Everything's a cover up. Do you think we really went to the moon? Huh?"

"What?"

"Neil Armstrong. The moon landings. Do you think he really went to the moon in a bit of aluminium wrapped in tinfoil? 'Course he didn't. It was all faked."

Calvin shook his head. "What's that got to do with…what we were talking about?"

"Everything! What I'm telling you is that you can't trust anything in this world. Nothing's what you think it is."

The man's voice had risen, drawing attention from other tables. From the gloom at the far end of the pub, a voice called out, "Pete's starting early on his conspiracy theories."

A few men laughed.

One man at a nearby table addressed Calvin. "Has he told you the one about the lizard people yet, lad?"

Without answering, Calvin swivelled around on his stool, putting his back to the long-haired man who was beginning an argument with the man who'd mentioned lizard people. He took a swig from his pint. The old man sitting opposite stared at him fixedly. Then he spoke, almost in a whisper. Something about the moor.

Calvin leaned towards him. "What did you say?"

"They can't leave the moor. They're tied to it. They won't go far from it."

"The moor?"

Calvin waited for him to say more but the old man's eyes dulled again, and he slumped back into silence. Calvin took a long swig from his pint, then rose and left the pub.

***

When he arrived back at the house – he still couldn't think of it as *his* house, it wasn't *his* house – there was no sign of Beks. When he looked in the garage, he saw that her Fiat was there. He'd not seen her drive it in all the month's he'd lived with her. Wherever she'd gone, she'd gone on foot. Unless someone had stopped at the house to pick her up. But who would've done that?

Some garden tools Royce Peglar kept at the rear of the garage had been knocked over. *Had Beks been in here?* he wondered. *Looking for something? If so, what?*

Have to stop thinking of it as Beks.

After setting the tools upright, he returned to the house.

For the rest of the day, he watched TV without really seeing it, and listened for the sound of her key in the door.

He thought about what the old rocker in the pub had said. *Those things are clever. Once they're found out, they move on and become someone else.*

Could that be what had happened? Because he'd processed that the thing wasn't Beks, had it left to become someone else? Moved on? Was he free of it now?

He waited.

When it went dark outside and Beks still hadn't returned, he felt a sudden and acute sense of levity. For no reason, he laughed out loud. Closing the curtains, he poured himself a whiskey.

It's gone, he thought. *It's gone, and it's not coming back.*

***

"Beks is gone," he told his mother.

He'd spent three days alone at Royce Peglar's house, dreading the sound of a key in the lock. By the end of those three days, he was convinced that the thing that had been impersonating Beks was not coming back.

"What're you going to do?" she said, keeping her eyes fixed on the TV. When he'd arrived at the house, he'd found her sitting in the living room, chain-smoking and watching TV with the curtains drawn. The room had a stale smell, and was hung with smoke. "Stay up there at that house?"

"I don't see how I can. Without Beks, I've got no right to be there."

Looking up, she smiled for the first time since he'd arrived. "So, you're coming home?"

"I don't know yet."

Only now did he notice what she was watching on the TV. Cartoons. Though she watched TV around the clock some days – soap operas, talk shows, and true crime documentaries – he'd never known her to watch cartoons.

"Since when did you like this stuff?" he said.

"I'm waiting for the one I like."

Something about the way she said this unsettled him.

"Which one is that?"

She frowned. "I don't know the name."

"How long have you been sitting there? It stinks in here. Wouldn't you like to go outside? The sun's out."

"No."

"Open a window at least."

When she didn't respond, Calvin crossed to the window himself and pushed it open a few inches. As he did, he noticed a chew toy of Banjo's on the sill, and realised he hadn't seen the dog since he arrived.

"Where's Banjo?" he said, turning again to his mother.

"Don't know. He got out."

"Got out? You never let him out by himself. Where is he?"

"I told you. He got out."

When he stood between her and the TV, she waved at him. "Move," she said. "It's starting."

Looking at the TV, he saw the opening credits for *Teen Titans GO!*

He stared at his mother, catching the waver in his voice when he said, "Since when did you like this?"

"I've always liked it," she said. "Shift."

Thinking, hoping, that Banjo was in the garden, he went to the back door. The key was in the lock, as always. He opened the door and stepped out.

"Banjo? Banjo? Here, boy!"

He walked the length of the garden. Rusted lawn chairs were propped against the fence. Car parts and liquor bottles littered the overgrown grass. A flowerpot was filled with cigarette butts. In a spot towards the rear it looked as if someone had been digging. There was an area of flattened dirt about a metre long and half a metre wide. Glancing around, he saw a spade lying, discarded, in the long grass. He couldn't remember his mother ever owning a spade.

He returned to the house, his heart beating so fast he could scarcely draw breath.

"Have you been digging?" he said as he entered the living room.

His mother half sat up in her chair. "Huh?"

"In the backyard. It looks like someone's been digging."

"What would I be digging out there for?"

"Where's Banjo? Why're you watching kid's TV? Mum? Where's the dog? What is this? What's going on?"

He clutched at her arm.

She darted her eyes at him, her face full of fury. "What the hell's got into you, Calvin?"

***

Your mother. You love her?

Of course. Of course. He should've known. Should've seen it coming.

He sat in his car, rested his head against his arms which were folded across the steering wheel, and sobbed. When the sobs tapered off, he sat up straight, wiped the tears from his face, gritted his teeth and looked through the windscreen at his mother's house. Right now, that thing was in there. Most likely, it was laughing to itself. Thinking it had fooled him. But he was smarter than it was Did it think they could go on like this, the two of them? Continue this charade? This game of who's who? Did it think it could go on toying with him, becoming one person after another as the bodies piled up?

No. Because he wouldn't allow it. It was time for it to end.

***

He watched the house until long after dark. What was that thing doing in there? He pictured it in his mind, sitting in his mother's armchair, smoking his mother's cigarettes, smiling to itself, waiting for him to return.

So, you're coming home?

It had gone eleven o'clock when the downstairs lights went out. A short time after, the light flickered on, briefly, behind the drawn curtains of his mother's bedroom window.

He watched a group of teenagers loitering under a streetlamp further along the street, passing a bottle of cider between them. He felt sorry for them. He'd been one of them once, stuck in a village that had nothing to offer. Nothing to do except stay out late and roam the streets, drinking cheap cider from the All-In-One, and looking to see what trouble he could get into. He and his friends had liked to vandalise cars. That had been their thing. One day they'd made a mistake and smashed the headlights and knocked off the wing-mirrors on an old camper van belonging to Brian Torrington, a retired semi-professional boxer. He'd come out of the house and given each of them a smack in the head. He then said he'd go to the police unless they all went for a try-out at the boxing club he ran twice-weekly at the village hall. They'd all said they would. Calvin had been the only one who turned up. Brian Torrington, it turned out, had saved him, given him something to channel his anger and frustration into. Something better than drinking cheap cider and vandalising cars. Until he didn't want to do it anymore.

When at last the teenagers left, he climbed out of the car. He shivered at the cold. The street was silent, most of the houses, including that of his mother, in darkness.

The gate hinges creaked as he entered his mother's front garden. Pausing, he looked at the upstairs window. When, after a moment or two, no light came on, he continued to the front door. As quietly as he could, he used his key to let himself in, closing the door softly behind him. For a few seconds, he stood in the darkened hallway, trying to steady his breathing. He pictured that thing lying awake in bed, listening. Padding to the living room, he felt for the light-switch and flicked it long enough to see the pack of cigarettes and lighter forgotten on the arm of the chair his mother – no, not his mother, the thing that looked like her – had been sitting in earlier. Flicking the light off, he searched the dark with his hands for the cigarettes and lighter. Slipping a cigarette from the pack, he lit it and, after a moment's hesitation, dropped it onto the seat of the armchair.

Have to make it look like an accident.

He stood in the dark until flames leapt up the seatback. Then he inched backwards out of the room. In the doorway, he paused, shocked at how suddenly the armchair went up in flames. Black smoke began to fill the room, burning his throat, though he resisted the urge to cough. Rushing to the front door, he stepped out, sucking at the fresh air. Again, he closed the door as gently as he could. Then he was away down the path to where his car waited. He glanced back once before climbing in behind the driving wheel, and saw flames climbing the living room curtains. He looked up at his mother's bedroom window. No lights were on.

Burn.

As he drove away, something crossed through the headlights of his car. A fox he thought at first. But no, it was a black dog. It halted for a moment in the middle of the road to stare at him, light reflecting in its eyes. Then it was gone, vanishing between two parked cars. Stopping the car, he stared after it.

His lips moved. "Banjo?"

***

He steered his car up the driveway to Royce Peglar's house, hardly knowing where he was. Approaching the house, he was startled to see lights in the downstairs windows. How could that be? Had he forgotten to turn them off? But it had been daylight when he left the house. Why would he have turned on any lights?

Was she…?

Abandoning his car at the top of the drive, he popped the driver's door and half-fell out. Clambering to his feet, he ran to the front door. His hands were shaking so badly, it seemed to take him an age to fit the key into the lock.

Once the door was open, he bustled in, heading straight for the lounge. What he found there made him catch his breath. His legs weakening under him, he had to grip onto the doorframe.

Beks didn't look up. She occupied an armchair, dressed in only a pink bathrobe and with a towel wrapped around her head. She had one long leg crossed over the other, and was idly filing her nails.

How could she - it – how could *it* have escaped the house-fire? How could it have got here so quickly? Before him. That was impossible.

A thought far worse came then. Had it even been at the house? Had he just burned his mother in her own bed?

He wanted to yell at her. *Who are you? Tell me who you are!* But he couldn't make a sound.

When at last she raised her eyes to him, she smiled and said softly, "Cal."

"You're…you're back," he spluttered.

Without raising her voice, she casually said, "I had to go away for a few days. I had some stuff to do." She returned to filing her nails. There was a short silence before she went on, "I told you right at the start, Cal. Everything can be how you want it to be. We can have a nice life together, you and me. Here in this house. It's ours now. It belongs to us."

In his mind's eye, he saw flames climbing the stairs of his mother's house. He turned back towards the front door then halted. No point going back. Too late. Too late now.

His hands slid down the doorframe, and he collapsed to his knees with a small exclamation as if he'd been punched in the stomach. Thinking he might puke, he leaned forward, propping himself on his hands.

Looking up again, Beks showed him a quizzical smile as if she hadn't noticed his distress. She sighed. "It's really very simple," she said. "All I want you to do, Cal, is tell me that you love me."

Raising his eyes, he stared at her.

Her expression showed curiosity. Pity. She cocked her head. A smile played again at the corner's of her lips. "Well, Cal? Do you?"

Anger flooded his mind. With a roar, he pushed himself to his feet, and flew forward. He unloaded a volley of punches to her face as he fell on her. The armchair overturned and they crashed to a heap on the floor. As they wrestled and thrashed around, Calvin was suddenly aware that she – it – possessed a strength it'd not yet revealed to him. He tried to get his hands around its throat, but its arms were like iron girders, holding him off. Though its head snapped back when he punched it in the face, he felt no give in its body. Seizing fistfuls of his shirt, it rolled him over itself and onto his back. Then it was up and straddling his chest, pinning its arms with its knees, its hands fastening around his throat. Its face floated about him, shadowed. It gritted its teeth. Its eyes were livid.

"Your mother talked too much, Cal," it said. "Always did, even when she was little." It grinned, nodding its head. "That's right, I remember her. A grubby little windbag. Didn't want to sit on Uncle Guy's knee, didn't want to call him 'uncle'. I told your Aunt Agnes at the time: that one's trouble. She should've been strangled at birth."

The only response he could make was a squawking sound. Its hands were fixed so tightly around his throat that he couldn't get a breath.

"Why do you fight me, Cal," it said. "Why do you question me? Isn't it so much easier to pretend? I can be anyone I want to be. Any*thing* I want to be. I'm doing this for you, Cal. Isn't it what you always wanted? You and Beks together forever? Meant to be?"

Just when he thought he'd black out, it loosed its grip on his throat. Raising his head from the floor, he sucked in a long breath, before sinking to the floor again.

It peered into his eyes, its hands held tantalizingly just above his throat.

"Isn't it?"

His nodded rigorously. "Yes. Yes." His voice was a rasp.

"Then say it," it said.

"I love you," he managed. "I love you. I love you…"

Blood

An Excerpt From The Elizabeth Chronicles 1.5

Mark Mackey

Dear Diary-March 17th

With the upcoming school ballroom style dance tomorrow night, I think it's high time to start looking for a date Almost losing my life and head a little over two weeks ago to Shelby and a sharp axe, it's a good thing she's going to be locked up permanently in a psychiatric facility. She sure needs it. So I'm feeling pretty tired so I'm going to put an end to my writing for the night.

***

The silvery light from the full moon lit Brynn Culvers' way as she traveled home. She'd spent the majority of the afternoon studying at the Mason Public Library. In her mind, it was one of the best and most favored places throughout the small Nevada town. Luckily tonight, for the first time in nearly a week, the temperature was only in the sixties. It made her trip home bearable.

Brynn's being an only child to her parents Clayton and Stevie suited her quite well in that that she didn't have to split their attention with a brother or sister.

"Oh come on don't you think that's a bit selfish?" her best friend April Lawters had once asked her.

"No, uh-uh, no brother or sister competing against me for my parents' affections is absolutely perfect, April."

"If you say so, Brynn."

***

Continuing along, Brynn was caught off guard. Passing by Julie's Diner, she almost crashed into someone making a sudden exit.

"Hey just what the heck is the matter with you?" Brynn cried out.

And then she saw his face.

The sight of it almost instantly filled her with immediate desire. He was absolutely gorgeous.

"Hey I'm sorry, I should have watched where I was going," he said in a velvety smooth voice.

Hearing him speak was like bells ringing in her ears. Not coming as one bit of a surprise to Brynn, felt desire grow within her.

"No it's all right, I should have watched where I was walking as well. So I've never seen you around here before."

"My family just moved here last night."

"Welcome to Mason."

"Thanks. Hey you should let me make up for my almost crashing into you by treating you to Coke, coffee, ice cream, maybe?"

"Shouldn't you tell me your name first?" Brynn asked.

"Sorry where are my manners? Christopher Murphy."

Continuing to hear his velvety smooth voice caused her to think thinking maybe it was all right to trust and take him up on his offer. Sure, he was a complete stranger, but he was quite good-looking, and she was presently single.

"So what's your name?" Christopher asked.

"Brynn Culvers."

"So what do you say, interested in taking me up on my offer?"

She was more than eager to do so, but she was quite tired. At the same time, however, she didn't want to lose the chance to date him, make Christopher hers before some other girl at Mason High did. *Well maybe he'll let me give him my number*, she decided.

"Hey you know I really want to, but I'm kind of beyond tired at the moment. Maybe if you let me give you my cell phone number-"

What Brynn didn't expect was was Christopher's personality taking a turn for the worse.

"No, you come with me now," he ordered, staring deep into her eyes.

Returning his gaze, Brynn became aware of a strong feeling of no longer being in control of her body. She tried to turn away from him, but failed. She tried to speak but couldn't. All she could do was see and hear.

Oh crap, what the heck did he just do to me?

"I see you've got her under control," Brynn heard a voice say from somewhere close behind her. It sounded the same as Christopher's.

It was only a matter of seconds before she discovered who the owner of the voice was. He moved past her and stood right beside Christopher; whoever this was looked exactly like him.

"I sure have, little brother," Christopher said.

"Only by four minutes," he replied. "So you want to have her right here and now, or drag her back home?"

Oh crap I'm about to be raped by them.

"Sorry but no, Nathan has something far worse in store for you," Christopher said as though he read Brynn's mind.

What Christopher meant by this was shown to her when the two brothers revealed themselves as vampires. Dangerous, long fangs grew from their mouths.

Seeing this Brynn was filled with absolute horror especially after what Christopher had said. He and his brother planned to do something unspeakably evil to her. Terror coursed through her. She was about to become a meal for a pair of blood thirsty vampires. Given the condition she was in, there was little she could do about it.

The horror from realizing this grew one hundred percent with Christopher's, "come on Nathan, she's ours for the taking." The two started closing in on her.

"So what should we do with her, turn her or dump her?" Nathan asked.

"I say dump her afterwards. She's gorgeous and all, but I want to see what else this town has to offer. Have a chance to check out the other girls before we choose eternal girlfriends."

The only thing Brynn thought as Christopher and Nathan drove their powerful fangs into her shoulders was that maybe it wasn't such a good idea for her to have spent such a long time at the library.

***

In a record time they arrived with Brynn's corpse back to the house he and Nathan had purchased just prior to moving to Mason. Stepping into the living room, they he were met by their lovely personal assistant, Ginny Lawyers. She'd been responsible for taking care of the purchase. Like them, she was a vampire. Turned by Christopher, and according to her, she had no problem being one. Unlike most vampires, Christopher and his brother were able to walk around in the sun. Their father had been seduced by their full vampire mother.

"So I supposed the very first time hunting in Mason went smoothly," Ginny said.

"Sure did," Christopher replied, dumping Brynn's body on the floor.

"What's her name?"

"Brynn Culvers, Nathan and I spotted her leaving the Mason Public Library."

"So how was she?"

"Delicious."

"Well I sure hope you two left some for me."

"Nathan and I are vampires, not selfish pigs."

Not saying another word Ginny squatted down to help herself to the blood remaining in Brynn.

"Wow you weren't kidding Christopher, she is delicious."

"I told you so, Ginny."

"But it's not enough for me. I'm out of here to grab something for myself," she said, rising back to her feet.

"Nathan and I will head out with you to scope out the town for suitable mates. But first you think you could do us a tremendous favor and bury Brynn in the backyard?"

***

"Okay so tell me what's on your mind Amy?" Robin asked as they sat facing each other on the patio outside of a coffee shop.

"What has it always been for the past two weeks? I can't stop being bothered by what Shelby almost did to me. She was my best friend, Robin. How could she have been so selfish to try and murder me to take over my role as leader to you, Peter, and Andrew?"

"I have two words for you Amy, she's psycho. Your life's better off without her in it."

"You really think so, Robin?"

"I sure do."

"But I tried so hard to be a best friend to her. I guess that was pretty stupid of me huh?"

"No, of course not. Look I'll tell you what, if it'll make you feel any better, I'll be your best friend. I'm not as strong a telepath as Shelby was, but at least I'm not a psycho. I don't have any interest in stealing your role as leader. I'm quite content to just be a part of a group of friends gifted with special powers the same as I have."

Now why didn't she think of that, Amy wondered. Sure, they'd hung out on several occasions at Mason High, unlike her and Shelby, who was homeschooled. Was it time for Robin and her to start growing closer as friends? Especially now with Shelby sentenced to spend the rest of her life locked in a psychiatric hospital. All thanks to Robin frying her brain to prevent her from carrying out her plan to become leader.

"Hey you know what Robin, you're right. You and I have been friends almost as long as Shelby and me. With her locked up securely where she can't harm anyone, we're the only girls in our group of four. We should start growing closer as friends."

"Yeah I could sure go for that."

"So changing the subject, are you looking forward to the school dance tomorrow night?"

"I would if I actually had a date for it."

"I'm in the same situation. I really want to go, but without a date, it's going to be pretty stupid showing up there. Hopefully by the time of the dance I'm able to find someone to go with me."

"Yeah the same goes for me."

***

So far, Christopher and Nathan saw nothing they wanted. Ginny either. That was until they neared a coffee shop with an outdoor patio. Christopher saw just who he did. Sitting there was a raven-haired girl talking to a girl with similar looking sandy brown hair.

"Yeah I see who you're staring at big brother," Nathan said, catching sight of who had grabbed Christopher's attention. "I sure could go for a taste of Raven Hair."

"Uh-uh, sorry little brother, I've already picked her for myself. But you're more than welcome to lay claim to her friend."

"I don't have a problem with that. She's just as gorgeous as Raven Hair."

"I don't see anyone here who looks good enough to bite into," Ginny said, starting to head off. "I'll leave you two alone with those two lovely young ladies and search elsewhere. Catch you at home."

***

"Let's go claim them, Christopher," Nathan said as soon as Ginny was out of earshot.

"I can't wait to make Raven Hair mine forever," Christopher replied.

"So are you going to turn her right now tonight Christopher?"

"There's something different and unique in Raven Hair I never saw in the girls I had my sights set on in the past. I think I'll get to know her a little before I turn her."

***

"Hey look who's checking us out," Robin said, catching sight of Christopher and Nathan staring right at them.

"Yeah, I see them, Robin. They're sure something to look at."

And they were, at least the one dressed in blue jeans and a black work shirt was. As far as she was concerned, whoever he was would be perfect for the dance.

"Robin, while we're on the subject of hot guys and the dance, why is it you haven't ever expressed any interest in Peter and Andrew? I'm sure they'd love to escort us to the dance."

"Oh come on Amy. Peter's made it quite clear to us on more than one occasion he only has eyes for one of the tallest girls attending Mason High, Alison Duncan."

"Peter always talks about how he's so desperate for Alison, Robin. But you don't see him actively trying to make her his, do you?"

"No, I don't have any interest in Peter and Andrew. More than anything I consider them brothers. Okay now it's your turn. How do you feel about our two male friends?"

"The same as you, I think of Peter and Andrew as the brothers I never had. Returning to the subject of Alison, do you think she has the same feelings Peter has for her?"

"Honestly I don't have a clue but in my mind, they'd be perfect for each other, Robin."

"You won't hear any argument from me about that, Amy. She and Peter would be perfect together as a couple as far as I'm concerned."

And then the incredible, hot looking guys, guilty of checking them out from afar, arrived.

Studying the one dressed in blue jeans and black work shirt, Amy was caught by surprise. She felt a strong feeling of desire for him. This was a first for her. Never once in her life had she felt such a thing. She never had a chance for a relationship. All her time was spent on studying and homework or school related related activities, such as swim team and volunteering a couple hours in the high school library. Maybe it was time for her to finally start dating.

"Hey there girls," the one she was interested in said.

"What's up guys?" Robin asked.

"This is my brother Nathan, and I'm Christopher. We're new in town and we couldn't help but notice you're by yourselves."

"Yeah Robin and I are presently single and unattached at the moment," Amy replied, flashing a brief, inviting smile.

This night could not get any better, Christopher thought. Not only had claiming their first victim in Mason gone off without a hitch but the girl he desperately wanted to be his forever was single and readily available for the taking.

"So you don't mind if Nathan and I join you two?"

"Nobody's stopping you. Amy, you don't have any problem with it do you?"

"Uh-uh, nope I don't."

And she sure didn't. Feeling her chances would grow if she just had an opportunity to reveal she was interested in him, try and convince him to attend the dance with her.

"So tell us about you two Amy and Robin?" Christopher asked as he and Nathan joined them.

"As you know by now, I'm Amy and this is my best friend Robin Manners."

"So what's your last name Amy?"

"Sorry Amy Laughlin."

"Amy Laughlin, now that's sure a beautiful name."

He thinks my name is beautiful, Amy thought. It made her believe she might have a chance with him.

"Okay how about the two of you? Are you involved with anyone?"

"No, Nathan and I are as single and unattached as much as you and Robin."

Okay Amy your chance with Christopher has now just doubled, she thought.

"Christopher let me ask you something," Amy said.

"Sure, what's up Amy?"

"I uh realize we don't even know each other. But I was just wondering if maybe you'd want to get together sometime. Like at the school dance tomorrow night, and for your information, it's ballroom themed."

Amy's saying this signaled to Christopher he had her right where he wanted her. She was interested in him. It made his plan to have her as his forever that much easier.

"Are you asking me out, Amy?"

"Would it bother you if I was, Christopher?"

"Amy as much as I'm flattered by you asking me on a date for the dance, we just met."

"But you wouldn't be making a mistake if you said yes to her, Christopher," Robin said. Her intention was to fix the two of them up before the dance.

"You know what Amy, yeah I'll be your date for the dance. On one condition, you and Robin accept an invitation to spend some time at Nathan's and my house afterwards."

"I don't have a problem with it. Robin?"

"Nope I don't have a problem with that Amy. It's about time I started dating as well."

As Christopher sat there facing Amy, the only thing he felt, was pure happiness He had every single right to feel this way. The girl he so desired wanted him just as much as he did her.

"So Amy, why don't you and Robin tell Nathan and me a little about yourselves?"

"Sure what do you want to know?"

"Maybe tell me your interests. Or if you have any brothers or sisters?"

"That sure would be something if we had siblings, given our circumstances. Wouldn't you agree Amy?"

"Okay now I'm interested in finding what you exactly meant by that, Robin," Christopher said.

"Christopher, I was really hoping Robin and I wouldn't have to reveal our little secret. But since I really want us to start getting to know each other, I might as well tell you. Now I really don't want to scare either of you, but Robin and I have been gifted with, how do should I say it, superpowers."

Okay things are so much better, Christopher thought. Not only was he about to make Amy his forever. But she just revealed she had a special gift.

"Now that's sure something I wasn't expecting you to say."

"Okay you're scared of what Robin and I are."

"Are you kidding me? If anything, I should be impressed someone with such an ability is attracted to me. So tell me the powers you and Robin have."

"Robin has telekinesis, and I have the power to control animals of every type, you name it I can tame it in no time. Our other two friends, Peter has the power to bring the dead back to life and Andrew's the shape shifter. So tell me what you think about them?"

"Like I said I'm impressed, Amy. It's not all the time I get to meet someone with such interesting powers as you and Robin have."

"Okay now it's only fair you and Nathan reveal a thing or two about yourselves."

"Sure, I don't have a problem sharing. Nathan's and my hometown is in Blood River, Minnesota. Both our parents are dead. Our adult cousin Ginny Lawyers is our caretaker until we turn eighteen."

Christopher revealing that he and Nathan were orphans filled Amy with immediate sadness.

"Oh Christopher I'm so sorry. You must have been so heartbroken without parents. And that goes for you as well Nathan."

"Nathan and I survive."

Before she could say another word, Amy was caught off guard by her cell phone's ring tone.

"Hold on, I have to answer this. Yeah hey Mom, uh-huh Robin and I are still sitting here at the coffee shop. Yes I'm well aware tonight's a school night. Sure I'll be right home."

"I guess our first meeting together is about to be cut short," Christopher said once Amy's call came to an end.

"Yeah despite me having a superpower I'm still a teenage girl underneath it all."

"Well I guess the next time I'll be seeing you will be tomorrow," Christopher said as Amy and Robin stood in unison.

"You guessed right. Catch you two later."

"Okay so do you have any interest in Nathan?" Amy asked from behind the wheel of her red Ford Focus while driving Robin home.

"As a matter of fact, I could see myself dating Nathan. One thing's for sure I'm really looking forward to not only the dance tomorrow night, but hanging out with them afterwards."

"So are you looking forward to tomorrow night also?" Robin asked as Amy pulled up to the front of her house and came to a stop.

"I can't wait for it, Robin."

"See you tomorrow new best friend," Robin said as she got out and started rushing toward her house.

***

"So how did hanging out with Robin go?" Kim Laughlin asked her daughter from the sofa just as soon as Amy entered.

"Great news, I found someone to go with to the dance tomorrow night." Amy replied, joining her.

"What's his name?"

"Christopher Murphy. He and his brother Nathan, who's agreed to take Robin, just moved here from Minnesota."

"Well I sure hope you two have a great time," Kim said.

"Yeah I do as well," Amy said rising to her feet. "Now it's time for me to head off to bed, I'm exhausted."

"Okay good night sweetheart," Kim said watching Amy mount the stairs, leaving her alone with her thoughts.

If Amy, Robin, Peter, and Andrew ever discovered the reason for being the way they were, they wouldn't be so pleased. There was no doubt in Kim's mind they'd be downright pissed off.

The cause of her daughter and her friend's existence was a result of a being from a planet a million miles away from Earth called Tarnex-4. His name was Kandex Axelmore, and one afternoon when she, Diane Manners, Christy Michaelson, and Betty Miller happened to be shopping at Save-A-Lot grocery store, Kandex had passed by each woman, lightly touching them, thus creating Amy, Robin, Peter and Andrew in them.

***

"You should be proud you're carrying what you have in you I am a Tarnexian," Kandex informed them that same night, paying each one of them visits. Initially fearful of this-and furious as well, over their bodies being violated and filled with the offspring of a man they weren't involved with. Didn't love. They supposed the reason why they found it in their hearts to forgive him was the fact of "the offspring will be gifted with abilities normal Earth children could only wish they'd have." Meaning they'd be different. Special. It was for this reason that they made the hesitant decision to carry these children to term-the four of them developing a strong bond with each other during the course of their pregnancies. As much as their husbands were initially opposed to this idea, they valued their marriages more. They begrudgingly accepted Amy, Robin, Peter and Andrew as their own children.

Ceasing to think about this, Kim was just glad the first boy Amy expressed interest in was born right here on Earth not coming from some far-off planet forty light years away.

***

Entering her bedroom, Amy was overcome with a sudden desire to sit at her desk and write her personal thoughts into her treasured diary.

Within seconds, she was sliding into her chair, reaching for the diary and a pen, and opening it up to a clean page.

> *Dear Diary March 17th*
>
> *So I've just returned home from spending the past couple hours hanging out with Robin at our favorite coffee shop. With all that transpired there, I can't help but feel one hundred percent excited over not only having our friendship brought up a level to best friend status, but I also just met the most gorgeous guy ever, named Christopher Murphy who just moved here to Mason, and his equally hot brother Nathan. It's a good thing I was first to express interest in Christopher before any of the girls at Mason High are able to snatch him up for themselves from right under me tomorrow. Well I'm pretty much beyond tired so I'm going to bring the writing to an end for now. Oh yeah one more thing, I'm sure glad I now have a date.*

***

Lying in bed, Christopher was the only thing Amy could think about. Oh, how she so desired to make him hers. And the way things had went between them not even an hour ago, she was certain she would receive this wish.

***

It didn't take Ginny long to find just what she was in search of. Her intended prey, a pair of identical twin sisters, age sixteen or seventeen out and about on a moonlit stroll.

Sorry girls, you made a terrible mistake in walking out here tonight, Ginny thought to herself as she began heading straight for them.

"Is there something we can help you with?" the one positioned on the left asked as Ginny stood in their way.

"You can start off by telling me your names." Ginny said.

"And if we refuse?"

"Trust me you want to tell me your names," Ginny replied, willing her vampire fangs to grow.

"I'm Amber Beckstone and this is my sister Leslie," and her face grew strong with sudden nervousness, eyes widening with fear.

"Amber and Leslie, now those are quite attractive names. Now what I need you both to do, come with me I've just nominated you to be my dinner tonight."

"Oh come on, you don't have to do this," Leslie pleaded.

"Uh-huh, I sure do. Now come on, get a move on, I don't have all night," Ginny ordered.

As soon as Ginny escorted Amber and Leslie to the mansion, she grabbed Amber by the neck, breaking it. In moments, she had her fangs out and buried them into her shoulder. She started draining the blood out of her.

***

"So I don't see those two lovely young ladies with you," Ginny said to Nathan and Christopher, her hand firmly gripping Leslie by her pony tail. "Did something go wrong with the two of you making them yours forever?"

"No uh-uh. Nathan and I are just going to wait until tomorrow night and our date to change them into our eternal brides, right after we escort them to the school dance. So I assume with her in your grip the hunt for blood went well?"

"It sure did. Her name's Leslie Beckstone, and since I'm full on her identical twin sister Amber's blood, you can have her if you'd like."

"I think I'll take you up on your offer, Nathan how about you?"

"Sure I wouldn't mind having her warm, sweet blood running through my veins," Nathan said pushing out long, canine teeth.

Watching them with horror-filled eyes, it took seconds for the other two vampires to close in on Leslie and do what they did best, drain her bone dry of blood.

***

Amy woke up the next morning with an incredible eagerness to hurry the heck up, get to school, get to know Christopher better.

The drowsiness slipping away, she didn't waste a second rushing out of bed to start her day.

***

Kim sat at the table, sipping a cup of coffee and facing her husband, Lucas. She couldn't help but wonder if it was the right time to reveal Amy's true heritage to her. Despite promising herself she wouldn't, she found herself questioning this decision.

"I can see there's something troubling you, care telling me what that is?" Lucas asked.

"Lucas, I know I said I wouldn't ever tell Amy about her true heritage, but I put some thought into it and well, what's your opinion?"

"Kim, as much as I have no interest in keeping a secret from Amy, I think she shouldn't be told about it until she turns eighteen."

"Yeah you're right, it's best to wait on that."

"Wait on what?" Amy asked, making an unexpected arrival into the dining room and joining her parents at the table.

"Oh we were just discussing whether or not to get you a brand new car," Kim said.

"But the one I have now is working just fine I have no need for a brand new one. The future however is a different story."

"So how did hanging out with Robin go last night?" Lucas asked.

"Oh yeah, I forgot to mention Amy's going on her first date tonight," Kim said.

"What's his name?" Lucas asked.

"Christopher Murphy, I met him last night," Amy replied.

"Well it's about time you started dating," Lucas said.

***

"Thanks for picking me up," Robin said as soon as she climbed into the Ford Focus.

"Hey we're best friends now, it's the least I could do," Amy replied, pulling off.

As expected, Peter and Andrew were waiting for them as she pulled into the first available parking space.

"You'll never realize the incredible luck Amy and I had last night," Robin said climbing out.

"What's that?" Peter asked.

"We met a couple of the most handsome guys ever last night. We're about to go on our very first date to tonight's dance."

"So who are they?" Andrew asked.

"Christopher and Nathan Murphy and they just moved here from Minnesota. Amy and I can't wait for tonight to arrive," Robin said, flashing a smile.

"Speaking of dating Peter and Andrew, don't you two think it's long overdue that you did the same?" Amy asked.

"And we all know who Peter's desperate to get his hands on."

"So when are you going to make Alison yours?" Robin asked.

"Nope that's never going to happen. Alison's whole life centers co-running Mason High's basketball team and being best friends with Heather Fields. She has no time for a relationship or me."

"You never know unless you ask her Peter," Amy said. "As a matter of fact Robin and I were discussing how you and Alison would be so perfect together. So are you going to develop a backbone and ask her to be yours?"

"You know what, I should if I want to make her mine. It's just going to take me a while to get up the courage to ask her."

"It's a start. Come on let's get to homeroom."

Setting foot into Mason High, Robin, Peter, and Andrew with her, the only thing Amy could think about, finding Christopher.

"*I can read your mind, you're desperate to locate Christopher,*" Robin said.

"*Can you blame me Robin? I honestly believe things are going to work out between us.*"

"*No of course I can't. I just hope he makes you happy, you need that after what Shelby almost did to you.*"

Approaching a bathroom, Amy felt a sudden urge to head in there and use it.

"Robin, Peter, Andrew, continue to homeroom. I'll catch up to you."

Once finished, Amy headed down the hallway after her three close friends.

Turning a corner, the first thing Amy saw was Alison's older sister Elizabeth. She was about to make her entrance into Mason High's student newspaper, the Student Voice. She shared the editor-in-chief position with her close friend Nicole Bakersfield.

When Amy was little, the thing she always asked herself about Elizabeth was why she looked nothing at all like Alison. Different hair and eye color, faces, it was almost as if they weren't really biological sisters at all. The next thing Amy felt seeing Elizabeth was sadness. She recalled when they were children, how her best friend Jordan had been abducted—never to be seen again. But this was just for a couple seconds. She suddenly had a desire to find out if Peter had any chance with Alison.

***

"Yeah Mom, just as soon as school ends, I'll skip hanging out with Nicole here in the Student Voice and rush home for my yearly physical," Elizabeth spoke into her cell phone.

Setting foot into the Student Voice, Amy saw Elizabeth seated behind her desk; Amy placed her cell phone back into her purse. Studying Elizabeth staring right at her, Amy noticed their appearances practically matched each other's. Being that this was not what she came in there for, she quickly pushed the thought from her mind.

"Hey I realize we've never said a single word to each other, despite my being aware of your existence since elementary school. You probably don't even know who I am or my name."

"I know who you are, Amy. You have something you want to see printed in the Student Voice?"

"Elizabeth, I was just wondering if we could talk a few minutes about Alison," Amy said, sliding into the chair in front of the desk. "You see well, I know my close friend Peter has had a deep interest in your sister."

"The feeling goes both ways Amy. But if you and Peter are involved, I'll tell her to back off and that he's unavailable."

"So Alison does feel the same way Peter does for her. Elizabeth I'm not interested romantically in him, and neither is Robin. No the reason why I'm here was to find out if you could tell me if Peter has a chance with Alison. And it seems My question has been answered."

"Yeah she's expressed an interest in Peter."

"So why hasn't she let him know how she feels?"

"Let me put it to you this way Amy. You and Robin are the reason why my sister hasn't bothered telling him. Alison has this idea either you or Robin were already involved with Peter. I mean, you, Robin and Andrew are always standing around him."

"But like I said Robin and I aren't interested in him, so she has nothing to worry about from us."

"I'll tell you what Amy. I'll let Alison know she has a chance with Peter, that'll really make her day."

"Elizabeth, I'd say yes to that idea. But Peter sort of wants to go about taking his own sweet time in making Alison his, you understand."

"Yeah I sure do."

"Well I'd better get out of here if I don't want to be late for homeroom," Amy said rising to her feet. "It was nice finally getting to talk to you."

"Likewise Amy, and when my sister and Peter get together as a couple, I'm positive it'll happen again."

"Catch you later Elizabeth."

"Uh-huh I sure will Amy."

Moving slowly down a hallway, Amy saw a girl she'd said, "hi") to a few times in the past, April Lawters, alone in front of her locker. What bothered Amy was that there was no sign of her best friend Brynn Culvers. Almost immediately Amy was overcome with wanting to know just why exactly they weren't together like usual.

"Hey what's up April, I don't see Brynn anywhere around," she said, reaching her.

"Yeah she's probably just running late or something. Brynn's been guilty of doing that on occasion," April replied, only turning partially to face her.

As much as Amy wanted to believe April, there was something in her words which made her think there was something wrong. If there was, Amy thought, she didn't have time to find out what that was right now. She had to get to homeroom before she was marked tardy.

"I'll catch you later April."

Relief automatically filled Amy as she headed into homeroom and saw it hadn't started.

"*What took you so long?*" Amy heard Robin's voice fill her head as soon as she sat down at a desk.

"*You're never going to guess where I came from Robin.*"

"*Where's that?*"

"*The Student Voice, and I just found out from Elizabeth that Alison's single.*"

"*Peter's sure going to love knowing that Amy.*"

"*Uh-huh, especially since Elizabeth also told me she feels the same way he does for her.*"

Amy's ceased the telepathic conversation as Christopher, Nathan made their way into the classroom.

"*I swear to you, Robin, this morning is going so perfect.*"

"*I couldn't agree more.*"

"Good morning, class," Bethany Masters said as she entered the classroom. "Now as it happens, I'm in such a good mood that I think we'll do a fun assignment. Write poems of your choosing and read them out loud in front of the class. But first on my agenda is to introduce you to a couple of new students, Christopher and Nathan Murphy. Great I see you two have arrived. Why don't you come up to the front of the class and tell us all about yourselves?"

Keeping her eyes focused on Christopher and Nathan, Amy felt more than ever, Christopher and her were meant to be.

"Hi, uh, like she said, I'm Christopher Murphy and standing beside me is my brother Nathan. There's nothing special about us, except to say up until a day or so ago, we lived in Minnesota, and that's about it I'm afraid."

Hearing Christopher's smooth, harmonic voice filled Amy with deep pleasure. It was with this she felt more so that the two of them belonged together.

"Okay class, now that we've got that out of the way, you can all start on your poetry assignments," Miss Masters announced.

Not allowing a second to pass, Amy hurried to remove her specific notebook she used for this class out of her backpack along with a pen. Opening it up to a clean page, she began writing.

In my heart, I feel nothing but pure bliss.
My heart has been struck by
a strong desire of contentment,
pulsating passion.
In my future,
I see great things to come.

"*Now I know someone's desperately in love,*" Robin used her telepathy to speak in her mind.

"*More than you know Robin.*"

"Okay who's ready to read what they wrote," Miss Masters said a few minutes later.

"I am," Amy replied sticking up her arm.

"Great, come on up here Amy," Miss Masters said.

"*Go on up there lover girl,*" Robin spoke into her mind. "*Let Christopher hear just how you feel about him.*" (

Heading up to the front of the classroom and facing her fellow students, it was just seconds before Amy began reading.

"In my heart, I feel nothing but pure bliss. My heart has been struck by a strong desire, of contentment, pulsating passion. In my future, I see great things to come."

"Wonderful poem Amy," Miss Masters commented. "Now who's next?"

"I'll go Miss Masters," Amy heard Christopher say as she returned to her desk; this caused her to listen intently.

"Like a sparkling diamond, her appearance is captivating to set my eyes upon. Ever since I first saw her, there was not a doubt in my mind I had to make her mine forever.

"*Now I wonder just who he could be talking about,*" Robin asked again by way of her gift of telepathy. Amy now realized Christopher's heart belonged to her.

"So I'll catch you all at lunch," Amy informed Robin, Peter, and Andrew. The four had gathered a few feet away from Miss Master's homeroom after it came to an end.

Heading down the hallway and entering the library, Amy was caught by complete surprise. She saw Christopher seated at one of the long, rectangular tables calmly reading a hardcover book. Almost immediately, Amy felt a strong desire to approach him.

"Hey mind if I join you?" she asked, reaching him.

"No, I don't have a problem with that," Christopher said in that same smooth, harmonic voice she found so appealing.

"So that sure was a great poem," Amy replied as she slid down into the chair directly across from him.

"Yeah I might say the same about yours, Amy."

"You really think so?"

"I wouldn't have said it if I didn't, you have a real talent for writing as far as I'm concerned. So you all ready for the dance and to hang out tonight?"

"Would you be upset if I tell you it's all I've been thinking about nonstop since I first laid eyes on you last night?"

"To tell you the honest truth Amy, I'm quite impressed by having a beautiful girl with a unique gift being attracted to me."

"Do you feel the same about me Christopher?"

"I won't lie to you Amy, I do."

Glancing at the cover of the book Christopher had in his hands, Amy saw it was *Dracula*.

"So I take it you're interested in vampires?"

"It's just a book. Nathan suggested I read it, and that's what I'm doing."

"It's great, you'll love it."

"So far I do, and while we're on the subject of books, tell me what you like to read Amy?"

"Romances, paranormal, suspense, you name it, I love it."

"Hey it's nothing to be embarrassed about Amy. Some of the world's greatest books are romances. As a matter of fact I enjoy reading them myself."

"Well at least that's something we have in common."

"Hey come with me, there's a book I want you to check out."

"Since I now know you enjoy reading romances there's a book I really think you should take a look at," Christopher said as she stood behind him. Watching as he slid out a hardcover book inserted between two others of equal size and shape.

"What is it?"

"Black Moth."

"Never heard of it."

"It was written in 1921,and it's romance, set in 1751, the author Georgette Beyer was nineteen."

"All right I'll check it out," Amy said relieving Christopher of the novel. She was filled by a strong sensation of love for him.

Staring right into his eyes, Amy found herself overcome by a strong desire to grab hold of his face with the palms of her hands and passionately kiss him.

"Tell me what's on your mind Amy."

Should I tell him what I desperately want to do? She wondered.

"There's nothing for you to be afraid of Amy, you can tell me anything and I'll accept it."

"Okay you asked for it. I'm so desperate to kiss you, it's really pathetic. Is that wrong, I mean we just met last night?"

"No it's not," Christopher whispered. "I'm not going to be bothered letting you do so."

Not saying a word further, Amy gently placed the palms of her hands against either side of Christopher's face. Pushing her head forward, in just seconds, she had connected her lips to his. She realized Christopher and his heart now belonged to her.

"I can't wait for tonight," she whispered seductively into his left ear upon their kiss coming to an end.

"Neither can I Amy."

***

"So you all ready to hang out with Christopher and Nathan tonight?" Robin asked as Amy was driving through downtown Mason.

"Uh-huh, I sure am Robin. But in the meantime, I need to stop by Macy's costume shop. Try and pick up some masquerade ball costume."

"Yeah good idea and while we're there I might as well get one also."

"Good afternoon young ladies, is there something I can help you with?" a man in his early fifties from behind a glass counter asked them in a kind voice.

"Uh yeah, my friend Robin and I were looking for some masquerade costumes for a dance at our school tonight."

"Well you've come to the right place. Feel free to look around and see if you find anything you like."

As she and Robin started looking around, Amy's eyes suddenly focused on a mannequin modeling a certain navy blue dress and carnival mask. It was just perfect, she immediately realized.

"Yeah I could see you in that Amy."

"Uh-huh so can I."

"Excellent choice," the man behind the counter said.

***

Setting foot inside her bedroom after dropping Robin off, she went to her desk and started to pen her thoughts about what happened between Christopher and her earlier into her diary.

So it won't be long now before Robin and I are hanging out with Christopher and Nathan. There's no doubt in my mind Christopher's heart belongs to me, and mine to him.

***

"So you better be sure to have a great time tonight Amy," Kim said as Amy was about to head out the front door wearing the dress she bought earlier.

"Yeah, and the same goes for me," Lucas said as well.

"Thanks, I'm sure I will," Amy replied. Seconds later she was gone.

"I just know this is going to be one of the greatest nights ever," Amy said as she and Robin set foot into the gymnasium where the masquerade ball was taking place.

"Yeah I couldn't agree with you more."

Looking all around, hoping to spot Christopher, Amy was caught by sudden surprise with his, "may I have the first dance."

Almost immediately Amy was overcome with a strong desire for him.

"You may," she said, turning to face him. She eagerly offered up her hand for Christopher to lead her out onto the dance floor.

"So how are you feeling about us dancing?" Christopher asked as they stood hand in hand.

"This is going to go down as one of the best nights of my life," Amy replied with a smile.

"I'm glad you feel that way," Christopher said, starting to move his head towards Amy's neck. Not to sink his teeth into her neck, no that was for later; but to kiss her.

"You don't mind if I kiss you Amy?"

Amy felt excited to be asked. Of course, she wasn't going to say no.

"You may," she said, smiling pleasantly.

Amy felt great pleasure in Christopher kissing her hungrily on the left side of the neck. *Oh, how I want you so much Christopher,* she thought, the desire growing large inside her.

He didn't stop there. Kissing her the same way on her lips and causing the desire to blossom even farther.

"I want you so much Christopher," Amy moaned helplessly as he once again attacked her neck with his brand of kisses.

***

During the drive to Christopher and Nathan's house, following the dance, Amy felt nothing but excitement. The night was going perfect so far. She just hoped this continued when they arrived at the Murphys' house.

"Wow this sure is some fantastic house," Robin admitted as she and Amy climbed from the car a few minutes later. The four of them started heading towards a large gray three-story house at the edge of the block.

"Yeah, I won't argue with that."

"Hi you two must be Amy and Robin, I'm Ginny," a lovely twenty-something woman said as they entered.

"Amy, Robin, this is Ginny, Nathan and my caretaker."

She couldn't speak for Robin, but Amy wasn't expecting to see a lavish roast lamb dinner waiting for them.

"Wow Christopher, you didn't have to do all this."

"Great I overdid it. Look if it's too much, we can go out somewhere."

"No it's fine, and it's the thought which counts. Robin, I hope you're hungry."

"I sure am," Robin said as they joined Christopher and Nathan around the table.

"If you all will excuse me, I have some business to take care of," Ginny said, making a quick departure.

"But aren't you hungry?" Amy asked.

"Yeah, but I really have no interest in imposing on a special night for the four of you," Ginny said.

"What's that supposed to mean?" Robin asked.

"It means that Nathan and I invited you here for a specific reason."

"And that is?" Amy asked.

"Simple, Nathan and I wanted you to hang out with us tonight is so we could change you and Robin into our eternal brides."

Thinking about this caused Amy to consider the fact Christopher and Nathan might be insane. They actually thought they were vampires! But then looking at Christopher and seeing the seriousness on his face, she knew he was telling her the truth. More indication of his being one came as she tried and failed to read his mind-proving he had the vampire power to block her from invading his mind.

"Oh crap, you really are vampires," Amy said, shock brightening her face.

"That's right and the feast is to help celebrate you being made into our wives."

"Okay, forget it, Robin let's go," Amy said, feeling all desire for Christopher evaporate.

"Good idea. But just one thing first, it's time to show the boys what makes us so unique."

Christopher was ready for this. Beginning to rise before Amy and Robin could use their powers, he found that he was unable to move a single muscle.

Keeping his eyes focused on Amy and Robin, Christopher saw they were deadly serious and really pissed off.

He had no time to think about this further, as Robin used her telekinesis to break up a chair and drive one of the legs into his chest and the other into Nathan's.

Christopher couldn't believe after existing hundreds of years, he and his brother were destroyed by a pair of girls with superpowers. Well at least he and Nathan were killed by someone significant. He felt his skin transform into grainy dust and collect into a neat pile on the floor. The same happened to Nathan.

In less than a minute they were no more.

"I'm sorry it didn't work out between you and Christopher," Robin said. "But at least we still have our lives intact."

"You've got that right," Amy replied, high-fiving her new best friend. "Come on let's go hang out at the coffee shop."

"Uh-huh, that's just what I was going to suggest."

RV FOLK

DAVID BENNETT BLACK

*"Oh, that uh, that there's an RV. Yeah, yeah, I
borrowed it off a buddy of mine. He took my house,
I took the RV. It's a good looking vehicle, ain't it?"*
- Uncle Eddie - Christmas Vacation

An awkward silence among the married can be a sign of the last straw, and the drive between Barry and Tara jumped from no words to intense shouting matches. Deciding a trip, a getaway or anything, was needed to ignite their love once more, they'd packed their camping gear into their tent trailer, hitched it to their Chevy, and hit the road. The outcome of the weekend determining divorce or continued counseling, but both knew what they wanted before their seat belts were latched. Their connection was as dead as the meat in their coolers and as cold as the beers chilling on ice.

Ignoring one another's presence, Barry drove above the speed limit as Tara eyed the speedometer— a mere three kilometers higher than her self-imposed limit. Having a sore and dry throat from their last "conversation", she chose to sigh her anger as he simply shook his head, tensing on the accelerator and adding another four kilometers on the dial. A war of sighs shot back and forth like children misbehaving in the classroom until Barry flipped the switch to the radio. Searching through the white noise, he settled on the first station and turned the volume knob upwards, attempting to drown out his soon-to-be ex-wife from his side of the vehicle. Tara grabbed her coffee and sipped deep and loud, trying to calm her senses and dull the want to slap him.

Speeding along the empty backroad, the voice from the radio spoke curses and dread from the lips of a preacher, his composition tight and practiced and clear.

"For he who sins and he who stares eye to eye with Satan, the devil, the opposer, he shall stand hand in hand with his burning flesh while the rest of us grasp the loving hand of our Lord! Amen!"

They both hated the Catholic drivel but loved the thought of making the other uncomfortable and tight. Neither opted to change the channel, each thinking they were torturing the other.

"And he who denies the truth and the words and the will of His being, they shall be brought down to the depths of Hell with those others that belong! And, no Lord, no Lord! Do we not belong in that pit for we love and worship the mightiest words as His flesh and His flesh as our own. Is His flesh our own?! I know I can hear you from your homes dear children, is His flesh our own?!

Amen! Amen, amen, amen, amen!"

"Turn this shit off." Barry broke first as Tara hid her smile, prideful in her quiet win. She began to turn the knob, the voice shifting to another preacher. And another. Then the sweet sound of guitar and drum cut past the white noise of the dead channels as Tara turned the volume to its height. Silence between the former lovers returned as the ballad on the radio ironically spoke of passionate fucking and a deep embrace.

Another ten kilometers of driving, the first sign of the past hour reared its head and announced the Ma and Pop burger shop ahead, both hoping for a bright open sign to greet them once they arrived.

"You gonna stop there?" She said as she pointed at the sign. "Do you want me to?"

"Yes, I want you to".

"Well, I guess then" he responded, pretending to be put-out by the request but in actuality, was excited for a meal.

Four kilometers later, the restaurant appeared and the sign read 'open', the parking lot full as Tara huffed.

"Just get me my usual, I'm not eating around a bunch of people like this", she spat at him to no response, her husband slamming the door behind him as he grabbed his wallet from his ass pocket.

Fifteen minutes passed with Tara looking at the tree line along the road, her soon-to-be ex's presence bee-lining for the restaurant stealing her ability to take in the beauty of the surrounding woods. She watched the birds fly and heard the insects buzz, her eyes fighting to look away from the roadkill on the edge of the lot entrance. The smell of the dead skunk's corpse wafted through the parking area and did nothing but make her crave a toke. Anything to make this weekend go by smoother.

Barry exited the small shack of a restaurant, the crowd inside could be heard laughing and hollering to the outdoors as the open door allowed the sound to escape. He carried two brown bags, grease dripping from each as Tara licked her lips without noticing her animalistic hunger taking over. Slamming the door behind him, the same as when he left, he silently handed her a brown bag as she inhaled deeply. Grabbing at her food, a chicken burger revealed itself as she began to shake her head.

"Do you even know me? When have I ever ordered this?" she said, pissed off. "Just fucking eat it" he said, ending the two lined conversation with his tone.

The sound of chewing filled the air as the crisp wind entered through their open windows, fries being munched and burgers being swallowed. The ice cubes cracked against each other in their cups, the jingling of his keys matching the noise as he restarted the car, ready to drive whether Tara was or wasn't.

After another hour of sitting with the person on Earth they hated the most; they both began to talk at the same time, their mixing words hitting like swords clashing in the air, sending nothing but a loud clunk where conversation should have been. After a few seconds of debating who was allowed to speak first, Barry decided on his own that it was him.

"Why are we doing this?"

"Doing what?" Tara responded, knowing what he meant. "Trying"

"This was your idea, I'm just along for our final ride". "So, you really think this is it?"

"Barry, I don't see you being able to do a single thing this weekend to change my mind, you, we have had years of this".

"I know bu-," he tried to say before being cut off.

"When was the last time you tried to fuck me? Honestly. Can you even remember?" she said as she glanced out the window, the passing trees looking like a green blur.

"That's not fair," he said, with no reason behind the words.

"Well, you have two nights to change this, and I damn well know you don't want to just as much as me". She spoke as her gaze stayed glued to the window, her eyes falling to the gray blur coming from the metal barrier on the ground.

"Then again, I ask, why the fuck are we doing this?" Barry spat out.

"You tell me," she said to silence. "Just drive so we can get this weekend over with".

Wanting the divorce, his craving for normalcy of his life grew a new fear in his mind.

Did he really want to endure the Hell of his marriage for the sake of no change? What was worse? He stayed silent and tapped the accelerator more, their speed reaching 130 kilometers an hour. If they'd been watching the woods and not fighting, the family of four silken deer running through the trees next to them could have sent their minds on a path to ease, a possible return to love but their yearning to sign the divorce papers stole their final chance. They drove and drove until they arrived, the provincial park where they had first made love standing in front of them. The Pinery, small but wonderful, was a park that held an importance in both of their hearts, an importance that had grown to loathing hostility over the course of no more than seven married years. A last chance to reignite what was lost was all soaked in water and unburnable.

"Where's the permit number?" Barry inquired as he searched the front of the Chevy.

"Did you not write it down at home?" Tara asked, shaking her head.

"I thought you were going to".

"When? While I was packing every other goddamn thing in the trailer and you were doing fuck-all?" she hissed.

"They've gotta have our reservation anyways, I'll go talk to them", Barry said, defeated.

"Yeah, you will", Tara said as the door was once again slammed in her face.

Ten minutes passed and Barry re-emerged from the small permit lodge, a map in one hand and a piece of paper in the other ready to be placed on their dashboard.

"Not a lot of people here this weekend, they said there's only one other couple up where we are", he said as he entered the car, trying to avoid a fight off the bat.

"Good", Tara answered, not willing to add any more.

Driving at the ten-kilometer speed limit, they ventured into The Pinery, passing the small bridge hovering above a small creek and heading towards the sites. They passed the camp store, the ice cream sign calling both of their names, yet both stayed still and silent. To their left was the canoe rental. Memories of their first year together flooding their minds as they both remembered them renting their own. They both recalled the smiles and love, not understanding how their current feelings had developed but fully accepting them as they were. A fork in the road sent one way to the beaches and the other to their site, both wanting to go for a swim without the other present, eager to flirt with strangers and have new experiences. They took a left and headed for their site, the sound of church music filling the air as they drew nearer to the camping area. Soft, beautiful vocals fell from a woman's voice as sweet guitar rang out from the crackling speakers, the sound coming from a recreational vehicle overtaking a site ahead.

Hail Mary, full of grace, the Lord is with you.
Blessed are you among women And blest is the fruit of your womb

Neither knew the song but if they were followers of the cloth they would've recognized the tune at once. Shrill vocals that had been overtaking the airwaves since its 1974 release two years ago on all of the Catholic radio stations. Her voice was as haunting as the religion itself.

They drove closer and saw the RV, laughing at the kitschy decorations and generic camp signage splattered with religious garb and imagery. Neither of the failing couple had ever seen so many bumper stickers, each hollering another quote or depicting another apostle, all purchased to please their almighty lord in the clouds. The music grew as they passed, the owners sitting comfortably on their lawn chairs, surrounding a lit fire and waving. Frail and old, their skin was wrinkled and their hair was thinning, looking more like aging siblings than a couple. Their hands were grasped tight, a bible on each of their laps and a smile on each of their faces. Ignoring the two thumpers from the so-called greatest generation, Barry and Tara kept driving, their hands steady in their lap and pretending the obvious eye contact had not occurred. Trying not to laugh again, not wanting to do anything in unison, they sat still as their vehicle slowly moved, the elderly couple's song ending and the next beginning. Johnny Cash and the Carter Sisters softly singing "Were You There When They Crucified My Lord?". Neither of the younger couple knew the song and they were glad to escape it, growing angry upon realizing how close their site was to the bellowing Catholic tunes.

The part of camping that most couples hate and dread is the act of backing the trailer up and parking it, an act that can fuel the fire to a fight in the most loving of couples. For pairs on the edge of a cliff, pens in their hands to sign the divorce papers, the act of backing a trailer in could end in blood. Climbing from the vehicle to direct Barry's parking job, Tara began to deliver the hand signals to continue backing up. Tapping too aggressively on the accelerator, the trailer jutted back and came inches from a tree as Tara shouted at his dimwit move. Returning the gear to forward, he began again, thankful no other cars were coming as he blocked the entire road.

The next Catholic tune swung into the airwaves and reached their site as Johnny Cash came to an end; the unknown sound fell to their ears, the hymn "I Am The Bread of Life". Shaking their heads, they continued their attempts as Barry began to back up a second time. Tara pointed to the left, but Barry went right, scratching branches from a long and thick pine and sending the sound of nails on a chalkboard through the air.

"Goddamnit, Barry! Watch where you're fucking going!" Tara shouted, not realizing that her shout raised the attention of the elderly couple four sites down.

"Oh, fuck off", he said to himself as he pulled up again, ready for his third attempt.

Better than the first two but nowhere near perfect, they decided as a couple, in one of their final choices, to let the trailer sit in the middle of the site. Hopping from the car, Barry gave his parking job a once over and accepted how bad it was. Beginning to turn the crank to the legs and unhook the hitch, Barry noticed the voyeurs, the two old folks in no way attempting to hide their nosiness. Standing at the end of their site, they watched with open ears wanting the show to continue.

"Don't look now but those religious shits are watching", Barry whispered to Tara.

"Anyone would have watched that sad excuse of a park", she said as she ignored his request and stared directly at them.

"Can we just set this thing up? Preferably in silence?", he asked in more of a command. "You actually want me to help with your precious trailer this time?", she inquired facetiously. "Just grab the poles", he said as he walked away, mumbling a misogynistic slur under his breath.

He began to crank the top up, the orange canvas of their tent trailer spilling out as it rose. Clicking slowly to a speedy rate, the sound shouted a warning to stop as it reached the top, the beds ready to be pulled from the side. Each took one and grabbed at the wooden slats, pulling slowly so as to not whip it out of place. One success and one failure, Tara's side was perfect as Barry fell to the ground, the wood falling to his chest and knocking the wind from his lungs.

"You stupid fuck! she exclaimed as she ran to his side, not to help but to watch him fumble. "Are you going to help me?" he asked, knowing she was not going to.

He shoved the board from his body and rose to his feet, catching his breath before slapping the hard side of the trailer with the back of his hand, letting his anger out with a shout. "Let's just fucking pack up, this bullshit isn't worth it. We can see the lawyer tomorrow", he shouted, unaware that the elderly couple had now entered their site.

"We just fucking got here! I'm not driving six hours tonight. We can leave in the fucking morning", she spat out, ready to turn back time to before their marriage.

"I'm not sleeping in the same bed as you".

"No shit, you just gotta fix that first", she said as she pointed at the fallen bed on the ground and the gaping hole in the side of the trailer, waiting to be velcroed shut.

"You kids need a hand?", the elderly man said to them as they both jumped.

"No, we're good, almost set up", Barry responded for them both, wanting the elderly folks to leave. "I don't mean with that there", he spoke back.

The younger couple looked on at the older couple, not sure what to say.

"You two sound like you're havin' a rough go of it", the wife began to speak, her rotten breath passing to the other three. "We'd like to help".

"What do you mean?", Tara inquired, confused as Barry picked up the bed and began sliding it back into place.

"Me and my husband are holistic marriage counselors of sorts. With us and the big man upstairs we can help solve your biggest problem", the old lady said as the younger couple was done with her drivel.

"We're good, have a nice night though", Tara said, trying to push them away. "We think your souls need us, dear", the old man spoke. "We know it".

"Can you two just let us set up? Maybe we'll come by later," Barry Lied.

"Do you promise?", the old woman asked.

"Sure".

"Can you say it?", the old man added.

"What?" Barry asked, confused and angry and tired. "Can you say that you promise?" the old man finished. "Yeah, sure. I promise".

"Lovely", the old woman said with a big smile. "Chat soon lovelies", she whispered out as she grabbed her husband's hand and kissed him on the cheek before they strode away like newlyweds.

Their site was prepared in another fifteen minutes, just as the sun started to fall into the darkness, the moon beginning to light the sky. Neither wanting to fight, neither wanting to speak, they each sat on opposite ends of a large fire as they took turns feeding the flame with overpriced logs. No hot dogs on a stick, no marshmallows enjoyed and no campfire songs sung, they sat in silence until the last log was burned and they were ready to retire to their separate beds, forgetting about the elderly couple waiting to grace them with their presence.

II

Waking on opposite sides of the tent trailer, wet and cold dew covered the interior walls and dripped to their dry faces, the liquid alarm clock starting their day. Each craving their morning coffee and shit, but neither would be allowed to occur. Pots tapped one another outside of the tent, strangers on their site seemingly preparing a meal, using their picnic table and supplies. Barry unzipped the fabric window and saw who they had forgotten, the elderly couple cheerily making breakfast as the smells of freshly cooked bacon wafted into the trailer. "Finally! Good morning, sleepyhead!" the old man shouted, acting as if all was normal. Barry checked his watch, the time screaming 6 a.m. into his still waking ears. "Where's the wife?"

"Still sleeping", he answered, unsure if he was in a dream.

"Well, wake her up then! Breakfast is getting cold!" the old lady spoke.

"We know you must have forgotten to come by last night, you don't seem like rude people and we don't stick around rude people", the man said as he flipped an egg on the grill.

"So, we thought we'd make it easier for you this mornin' and make you some food before we get to work!" the woman added.

"Before we get to work?" Barry asked in a daze as he began to rise, slipping on yesterday's jeans and a clean undershirt before entering the brisk air. Tara pretended to sleep, unwilling to deal with the religious couple so early on such a day.

"Of course, you both need saving and you know it. We all know it, don't we, dear?" the man said as he placed his arm around his wife.

"We sure do, so does the one up there", she said as she pointed to the heavens and placed a dry kiss on her husband's cheek. She had a rosary around her neck, the beads worn down from daily prayers said since her first communion.

"I think we're doing okay", Barry spoke as he approached the picnic table, wanting to kick them the hell off their site. "We actually brought our own breakfast".

"We know", the old man said. "What do you think we cooked?".

"Do you think people of our age would bring enough food to feed a family?" the woman added. "Your coolers were out in the open and your stove ready to be lit. You do know of the raccoons here right? You really should lock these things up or else it could all be gone once you wake up!"

Barry noticed the irony of the statement as he stared at all of their packed food on the table, cooked and surely to go to waste. Enough of a feast for eight, the present four wanted none as the elderly two took their seats at the picnic table.

"How long are you two staying for?" Barry asked, trying to change the subject and figure out when they would be leaving, hopefully sooner than later.

As the elderly man began to speak in his frail voice, Tara opened the door to the trailer and exited into the cool, morning air, the dew sticking between her toes in a pleasant waking of her senses.

"As long as we need", the man responded with an air of mystery.

"Will you two be taking a seat or do you usually eat on your feet?" the lady asked as she tapped the empty plates on the table and signaled them to join.

The aroma of the bacon was enticing, although the company was deadly, their thoughts believing the two to be no more than harmless zealots. They each sat, leaving a large space between their thighs, removing any possibility of their skin touching. Scooping eggs and bacon on their plates, they began their meal as the elderly pair watched like the stomach-stapled overweight, wanting to eat but unable to.

"How long have you two been married?" the woman asked as she continued to stare, her plate still empty.

"Seven years", Barry responded as Tara jumped in quickly afterwards. "Do we have to talk about our marriage?".

"Why else would we be here?" the man inquired, his plate just as empty as his wife's. He picked up a bottle of the younger couple's orange juice and filled their glasses to the brim, signaling to drink and to drink deep. "Drink".

"What else would we want to discuss?" the woman added. "How about anything?" Tara spoke with a piss.

"How about this?" the elderly woman whispered before quoting the word of her Lord. "Therefore what God has joined together, let no one separate. Anyone who divorces his wife and marries another woman commits adultery against her. And if she divorces her husband and marries another man, she commits adultery".

"Do you two read the word of the Lord?" the man asked as the sedative in the meal began to work; Barry and Tara felt faint, sweating and cold.

"What's happening?" Tara inquired as she looked at her hand, her vision doubling by the second.

"What is this?" Barry asked as his weight grew, his head slowly falling to his greasy plate.

"We are here to ensure your entrance to heaven, my children. As the word says, 'so they are no longer two, but one flesh. Therefore what God has joined together, let no one separate'".

As they fell to a dream from the drug-laced meal, another quote rang in their ears, whispered by the woman as the old man rose to his feet, a shotgun clearly hidden under his morning robe.

"'The man who hates and divorces his wife, does violence to the one he should protect'", the elders spoke the word of Malachi together before the man finished alone. "'And violence will certainly be had to ensure entrance'".

They slowly began to wake to the sound of music, their bodies bumping up and down from the shoddy wheels on the elderly couple's RV. Tied down, their hands were behind their back and their mouths gagged, saliva dripping down their waking chins. Jailed in the back of the mobile camper, they could see the elderly couple who sat in their respective chairs, the man piloting as the woman watched them wake. The music played and sliced a hole in their minds, seeping through with biblical bile.

The woman rubbed her rosary as she whispered her prayers to herself, the man singing to the Christian tune blessing the airwaves. His voice was hollow and wrong, the tone misplaced on the scale and shaking with his age. Drifting in and out of consciousness, the divorcing couple felt their presence leave the park and travel to an unknown place as the RV jutted up and down with each rock under its tires. Barry attempted to speak, nothing but nonsensical sounds falling from his still drugged mind came out.

"Oh, joy. You're awake", the lady spoke softly as she rose from her seat, her hand gently letting go of the rosary wrapped around her neck. The beads fell to her chest and softly landed on her white, wool knit, the sweater clearly home crafted. Her frail demeanor limped to the back of the RV as more potholes met the tires and the axel shifted with each bump. Her soft perfume moved to the waking minds, the scent opening their eyes fully to her view.

"I don't think that I ever properly introduced myself, or ourselves for that matter. I'm Mary Ann and this is Terrence, but everyone just calls him Terry. I tend to call him Ter-Bear but you better keep that nickname from your lips, dear", Mary Ann spoke as she eyed Tara as if she was a proven adulteress.

"Nice to properly make your acquaintances", Terry spoke as his eyes stayed on the road, his hands ten and two on the wheel.

"What's your names, my dears?" she asked, their drugged lips unable to respond as their heads shifted from side to side, feeling the opposite of lucid.

"Don't be rude now, you know we don't tolerate such moods".

Barry attempted to speak his name, the 'B' perforating his lips as the 'A' attempted to follow, the 'R' slurring afterwards, all amounting to nothing but the sound one makes when too cold to speak.

"Burrr", he stuttered his best attempt at an answer.

"How much did you give them, dear?" Mary Ann asked Terry.

"I didn't know how much they were gonna eat. They'll be fine soon enough", Terry responded. "Can they still listen?" she asked.

"Their eyes are open?" "On and off".

"Wait for them to be open for good, their ears will be open as well by then", he spoke as he turned down a dirt road, a dense forest waiting to be penetrated about a kilometer away.

"Can you two hear me?", Mary Ann inquired, their mumbles answering enough of a 'yes' for her to agree to a rant before the arrival and salvation.

Like a watched clock ticking slower by the second, both of the drugged two began to come to their senses. Beginning with touch, the reminder of the stale air hitting their skin returned as their eyes peeled open, red and dry and wanting to close forever. They saw the crosses gracing every surface, some bloodied and some like a cartoon, each depicting their Savior's' final moments. Dirty dishes jingle jangled in the sink as the vehicle moved, the clanking vibrating in their waking minds. And the stench, their nostrils began to toil as the elderly couples' unwashed bodies sifted through the air, almost visible in its strength, joined alongside an obviously unemptied sewage tank. Once, a long time ago, they would have grasped for each other's hands, wanting the embrace of safety but the passion was long gone and there was no net waiting to catch either's fall.

"Right now, you two are on a path to the damned and we promise, with all of our hearts, this divorce will not taint your souls' entry to the afterlife, my sweet and beautiful children", the woman spoke softly as the two in bondage fought to speak.

"Amen, darling", Terry answered to no question, the words coming involuntarily, his muscle memory working his tongue and vocal cords.

"With our help and the power of confession, everyone will be overjoyed with the outcome", Mary Ann spoke louder as she grasped her hands together in prayer, looking to the ceiling of the filthy RV before closing her eyes. "Oh Lord, who art in heaven, hallowed be thy name, with your love and your glory, these two will accept your love and my Lord, oh my Lord, it will be as glorious as your rising sun, as beautiful as your bright moon, as perfect as your bleeding wrist and as ample as your promise in death".

"Where are you taking us?" Barry was finally able to speak, a large cough following the last syllable. Drooling, his bondage disallowed a wipe, forcing the saliva to slowly drip from his chin and to his lap.

"I told you I didn't give them too much", Terry gleefully stated as he took his eyes off the road to look at the kidnapped couple. "Might as well let 'em rest, tonight's the night".

"But I have so much to tell them", Mary Ann spoke as she shrugged at her husband. "And the rules can be told around the last supper", the man said as he went for the radio, turning it on as another Catholic tune was slowly fading out, the preacher from the day before returning to haunt their new predicament.

Barry and Tara both began to squabble, their slurred words rising in volume as the preacher shouted damnation to all. Blasting the radio to full volume, his deep voice washed away their cries.

"For who listens to what we produce and lay out, you are bless-ed and ho-ly, you are one of the children, those that turn away to the modern filth poisoning our youth and raping our morals. We know you all repent! We all know that you shine! And want to be seen! And he does see, he does watch and he does wait, with all the love lost in this world of Satan's wrath, he does it all with love and admiration for you, you my listeners, and only you. Raise your hand to the Lord and praise Amen, amen as this next song falls from the heavens to us, gifted to you by our long hand".

Another song, this time a chorus sung hymn, the words of "Crown Him With Many Crowns" snuffed out the shouts and questions from the back of the RV as Terry turned down a hidden driveway. Various Bible quotes layered the trees, pampered with signs demanding no trespassing on their property, bullet holes in the yellow metal to prove the threats. The crowd of churchgoers sang in the recording, the radio shifting in and out of service as white noise began to steal the gospel song. The deeper they went, the more the station tattered until it was gone from existence, nothing but a deafening buzz filling the car and drowning out the continued shouts of the unlucky.

A dark barn with decaying paint filled their view as the RV began to slow, a small house waiting to home the four for the evening coming closer as they arrived. Broken down and filthier than the RV, the muck on the exterior must have been caked on for years as though the older couple hadn't wanted or needed to clean what was narrowly seen. Terry shifted the keys from the ignition with his boney and frail hands as his shotgun leaned on his lap, ready to be grabbed and pointed at either of the two at any moment. Silence overtook the speakers as the captives' screams grew audible to the elderly couple, their slurring gone and their strength returned.

"Let us the fuck out of here!" Tara shouted, the inclusion of "us" surprising Barry.

"Soon enough, my dears. Dinner first and then the task, a little game to promise your entrance past Saint Peter's gates", Mary Ann spoke as she left the car, slamming the door behind her as Terry followed, leaving the couple alone in their ropes.

Trapped with the last person they could have wanted, silence overwhelmed the captives, neither wanting to work together even if it meant ignoring an escape plan. Minutes passed and the only sound was their seething breath and their moving bodies, each trying to escape on their own terms. Haunted by the imagery of God's executed son from every angle, they each felt a kinship with the Holy Man from Nazareth in their cages, one trapped by nail and the couple by rope. The heat came fast, and the air grew stale, stealing proper oxygen as the sun burned the exterior of the RV. Even if they wanted to talk, the will to speak was stolen from the smoldering burn, the scorched heat waves growing more visible by the minute. Their attempts to escape grew to nothing, their bodies sweating away the energy needed to break free from the rope. Feeling like they were about to plummet into a drugless sleep, the couple heard the beginning of footsteps moving along the rock path outside before the door swung open, the fresh air filling the cabin like a downpour and cooling their waning bodies. They each sucked the air deep, filling their lungs to the max and expelling with coughs spewing saliva to the floor.

Dressed in her Sunday best, Mary Ann returned, her white gown laced with flowers and her silk shoes hugging her wrinkled and aged feet.

"Are we ready, my dears?" the elderly lady spoke with a shake in her voice and a gleam in her eye.

"Fuck yourself", Barry spat out along his dry saliva.

"Don't be rude, boy. We are doing nothing but helping your souls", she spoke as her soft voice returned with the final words. "We love you as he does and tonight will prove it".

"What is tonight?" Tara asked as she breathed heavily and sweat ferociously. "Your saving grace", Mary Ann whispered. "Don't fret, this isn't our first rodeo".

The old woman slowly walked to the captive two, stretching her skinny and boney arms to the knots behind their backs. Pulling with all her power, she grunted and huffed as the rope came loose, freeing Barry and Tara from the recreational vehicle's grip. Both standing as if springs were stitched to their asses, they began to bolt, passing Mary Ann and running for the exit, unaware of the shotgun butt waiting to greet their attempt to flee. Barry jumped from the door and met the cold metal of the shotgun on his temple as he fell to the ground. Tara screamed, not for her husband but for herself, the only exit covered by the deranged.

"You coming, honey?" Terry shouted from outside of the RV as Tara quivered, wanting to rip the old lady's teeth from her mouth.

"As soon as this one does!" she shouted back as she shot puppy dog eyes at her victim. Tara felt odd, the love of a grandmother seething through the body of a devil standing at her feet. "You gonna go or does he have to come in here, darling? Please, just go of your own free will, the Lord gave it to us for a reason, you know", Mary Ann whispered as she stepped closer to Tara's shaking soul.

She began to move her feet as slowly as she could, shuffling a centimeter at a time and avoiding the inevitable. The barrel of Terry's shotgun popped into her view, slowly gliding into the RV, followed by the man wielding the death machine.

"My wife doesn't even walk that slow", he said as he pointed the weapon at Tara's chest, speeding her pace up immediately.

"Oh shush, you", Mary Ann smiled at his joke as they both exited, the warm day feeling like a winter chill compared to the inside of the vehicle.

With a bloodied nose, Barry followed the group in whimpering silence as the shotgun pushed the way like a dog herding his sheep. A pleasant smell greeted their entrance as the log burning stove kept their final meal warm, the scent of fresh meat cooking filling the small cabin-like home. The walls were wooden and covered in black mold, ignored for years and rotting the foundation. A shag carpet tickled their feet after Mary Ann demanded them to remove their shoes, the crusty worm-like tentacles of the rug sticking to their sweat with each step.

"We don't have no temple to slaughter the lamb in this day and age but our kitchen will suffice, it always has in the past and the almighty understands our duty, He did hand it to us, you know", Mary Ann spoke as they entered the kitchen. "Do you two like lamb?"

Neither of them answered, their gaze holding on the shotgun shifting from face to face, ready to go off at any moment.

"Well, I bet you do. Who doesn't? I bet you also have a couple questions. First, eat and fill your body with strength, then the answers, my dears", the old woman added before she grabbed four bowls and began spooning a lamb and bean stew out with a metal ladle engraved with another image of their savior.

"Eat", Terry spat out, the first sign of anger croaking from his belly since they had met. He stuck his wooden spoon deep into his bowl and filled his mouth, swallowing with a deep breath of relief and proving that the good was safe to digest.

Both sat, not remembering taking their seats as the fear of the bullet hid what was in front of their faces. A spoon in one hand and shotgun in the other, Terry tapped the barrel to the table and slurped another spoonful as he silently demanded them to eat for a second time. They trembled as they grabbed their utensils and began shoveling the surprisingly tasty meal into their mouths. Next was the bread and wine, the staple of the meal, needing to be digested to appease the Lord. Dipping his loaf into his drink, Terry killed two birds at once as he sucked on the wet bread before chewing the mush and swallowing. Tapping his shotgun to the younger couple's glasses, they quickly grabbed their wine and began to drink, hoping for the dry alcohol to dull their senses. They each swallowed the entire glass, hoping inebriation would calm their nerves and allow an escape, but they found no alcohol and followed the virgin wine with dry bread.

An entire meal devoured at gunpoint, they scraped the bowls with the spoons in an attempt to appease their captors, hoping the small act would allow them mercy, the dreams futile. And then it was time for the task, time for their souls to be saved and time for only one to be the victor.

"'Marriage should be honored by all, and the marriage bed kept pure, for God will judge the adulterer and all the sexually immoral'", Mary Ann quoted her book. "Have you heard those words before? Read them?".

Both were unable to answer as the shotgun held their attention, the barrel still moving from person to person.

"Are you aware the adulterer is sentenced to an eternity in hell? Do you want that for yourselves? Please don't allow the gun to frighten you, think of it as help from the Lord, his hand making sure you stay straight within our game", Mary Ann spoke as if this was all normal - because it was for her.

"Get on with it", Terry spoke as his hand began to shake, the heavy gun too much for his aging muscles.

"Oh, shush", Mary Ann said as she shoved Terry with love. "Tonight, one of you will enter heaven's gates while the other repents for their sins, begging for forgiveness in breaking a commandment. If neither of you oblige, God's hand will send you both to the afterlife this eve, my husband's bullets rocketing your souls to Saint Peter".

"What?" Tara asked as the puzzle was yet to reveal itself to her fearful mind. The games outcome chilled Barry as he realized what they wanted.

"Whoever survives, they can confess immediately and go on their way, knowing that both of your souls have been saved".

"Whoever survives?" Tara asked as Mary Ann placed a single blade on the table, long and thick and sharp and ready to steal one's life.

"Only one of you will leave this kitchen, the loser already digesting their final meal but neither of you should fear, my children. Both of you will be saved from Satan's grasp, this matter of divorce settled in the only way, granting you both access to sit by his right side in heaven".

"Death in one will ensure entrance for both, as long as the victor repents, and repent you will", Terry added as he settled the shotgun on the table, still grasping the trigger. "And please, if the winner does remarry, make sure it is with the soul you truly plan the rest of your life with. We won't be around forever to solve these problems for people like you two. You should honestly be thankful you met us now, before we whither and age any further. Lucky you are to have us. Lucky you are to have those that care".

"And if we do not?" Barry inquired with sweat on his brow.

"As we said, then you will both meet the bullet and die married, primed for God's side".

Barry and Tara each moved their gaze from the shotgun aiming at their throats to the knife on the table, the only key that would open their door to freedom, the door only big enough to fit one.

"Please, do hurry, this is the most dreadful part of saving. I truly don't enjoy the sight", Mary Ann said as she stepped behind her husband, placing her hands over her eyes and peeking through the cracks.

"Just because I want to divorce him, doesn't mean that I want to murder -", Tara began to say, her lapse in judgment leading to her premature death as the weapon was stabbed deep into her jugular by the man she once loved.

The knife grasped tight in Barry's hand, the blade pulled from her throat as blood began to pour to the table, Mary Ann growing sick at the view as Tara's confusion mounted. Gurgling, she tried to speak, tried to yell and curse her murderous husband, the man who wielded the knife without a moment's thought. Ready to repent and do what they required for him to leave unharmed, Barry ignored his dying wife as he hoped for the future, sighing in relief at his newly found single status.

The floor grew covered with Tara's blood as her life left her body, the sudden death shocking her final breaths, confused at the lack of pain and the sudden action. She fell to her knees, grasping her neck and falling into a final dream as she left the Earth. Lifeless, gone and limp, her body lay on the floor in front of the three, Barry's mind wondering what was next.

Shocked at his choice, his thoughts joined the moment as he realized what he had done, feeling as though the hand of a higher power pushed his own. Dizzying at his actions, he watched his wife's corpse vibrate as he questioned his choice, wondering if it was truly his to make or if a separate being pushed his hand.

"One more thing, my dear. Can we trust you to keep this evening between us? We have plenty of more work to do and plenty of more souls to save", Mary Ann spoke as she stepped over the body on the floor, grabbing a tablecloth and covering the dead.

Seething, his eyes moved from his dead wife to the shotgun in Terry's grasp, his mind jumping from idea to idea, each ending with the death of the elders. Barry lunged at the old man, Terry pulling the trigger as the gunshot fired, a double barrel worth of pellets evacuating from the chamber and demolishing Barry's charging legs. Falling to the ground with a sharp yelp, his blood joined his wife's as he became immobile, watching Mary Ann wrap her arms around Terry and kiss him on the side of his neck.

"Will we ever find one we can trust?" she asked into his ear as Barry shouted bloody hell. "Until then, the barn's vacancy will grow", Terry responded as he kissed his wife while the wounded man rested his head on the chest of his dead wife, passing out from the loss of blood. "I wonder how long this one will last"

III

Waking to the stench of shit and the rough rot of hay, Barry felt a salted burn in his legs as he looked at the ground, age-old manure caked everywhere and filling the room with the feces of the dead and gone. Finding himself in a stable, he heard groans coming from the other stalls, human but pained, each another captive of the elderly couple's path to heaven. Wordless groans came from around him as he tried to join in, his question coming empty as blood fell from his mouth, he noticed a fresh emptiness between his teeth. A removed tongue and ability to speak, his new life as one of the elderly's pets began, as Saint Peter waited for his entrance.

The barn door opened, and the morning sun shot into his new home, his new flatmates staring from their own prisons, each maimed in their own special way. The visible one was missing an arm, his leg chained to the wall as he licked his salt rock hanging from the wall with the nub of a tongue, acting as the animal to please his owners. A hunger filled the air as footsteps stopped and buckets hit the ground, the sound of livestock feed hitting the plastic and filling to the brim with their meals. A hose began, the water filling the remainder of the feeding dishes, creating a steamy stew for the imprisoned. The first meal of many. Terry approached Barry's stall and plopped a feeding bucket to the ground, kicking it to the new inhabitant as the vomit-like substance sloshed to the ground. Barry was reminded of his youth and the reading of *120 Days of Sodom* the slop in front of him mirroring the hell the rich's captives were forced to eat. The sound of slurping and swallowing filled the stable as the hidden others began their meals, the smell turning Barry's stomach as he refused the first offering of many.

"You'll get hungry enough to eat soon", Terry spoke as he grabbed the hose, spraying the man in a cold shower, removing the blood from his wife that had stained his skin. "Remember what we've done for you, your entrance into heaven is as set as Mary Ann's perfect pudding desserts. You will learn to thank us as these others have. And you'll learn to accept these words, you're welcome. Death will come soon, and the afterlife will be plentiful and nothing but bliss. Until then, you're lucky we don't shoot horses with broken legs"

Barry felt the cold water slowly dry on his flesh as he refused to accept his new life, his naked body dripping in his new home.

As Tara entered the gates of heaven, looking down at her Earthly husband, ready to live more so in death than she ever did in life. Saint Peter opened the gates for her upon her arrival as the Lord thanked the elderly couple for acting his will, sending them the location of the next couple needing to be saved.

Cold Moon

Tucker Struyk

"Believe me, for I know, you will find something far greater in the woods than in books. Stones and trees will teach you that which you cannot learn from the masters."

Saint Bernard of Clairvaux

I.

Rafe Lowell lay flat on his back. In the dark, his eyes traced the bumps and indentations of his stipple ceiling. From the window, a pale moonlight crept across the ruckled bed sheets and illuminated his naked flesh—exposed to the midwinter chill. Beside him lay his wife, Eva. Her body faced the door—with her back to him as she snored. He steadied his breathing to match the her rhythm. Without warning, the bed was launched upright. It stood upon the footboard at a ninety-degree angle. He clung to the bedspread for dear life. His grip slipped against the fabric. He turned to Eva, with disquiet on his face, but she was fast asleep. Her rapid eye movement flickered beneath a pair of closed eyelids. His eyes darted about the room. Everything else was in its proper place. He relaxed back into the mattress. Somehow, despite having their feet planted upon the footboard, they remained in bed.

He rolled onto his side, where his wandering gaze found the arched window. Beyond the scrogs of his yard, he saw a row of walnut trees dappled against a black canvas. He sat upright and lurched forward with a squinted stare. Eyes glimmered from the trees. There, perched upon the highest branches, was a wolf pack. About six or seven wolves, with glowing irises and bushy tails, howled at the cold moon in the night sky. Rafe fell back into the mattress and feigned sleep. The wolves bared their teeth. Their ears pricked at the creaking of bed springs. His eyes shot wide open, but he dared not move. Suddenly the window opened without a touch.

Gusts of brisk air licked his bare skin. A breeze whistled in his ear. Wolves gathered outside and together they approached. Snarls and growls advanced towards the foot of the bed. Rafe could not compose himself any longer. He grabbed Eva by the shoulders and shook her.

She did not stir. He leapt from the covers, but his feet slipped out from under him. He was splayed out on the floor in front of the pack. The wolves tore into Rafe, with hooked claws and the gnashing of teeth, until he was consumed by their hunger. His screams were drowned out by gnawing sounds. In the quietus, his resistance melted to elation. He welcomed the release.

II.

Rafe awoke moments before the culmination of his dreams. He lay flat on his stomach. His morning wood pressed firmly against the mattress. He rolled over to find nobody there. Just the outline of his wife. He pawed at Eva's indent in the bed to feel for the warmth of her body—it was faint, but still there. Somewhere, in the process, his erection subsided. He hopped in the shower for a cold rinse, shaved, brushed his teeth, and dressed in a button-up shirt and slacks. For a moment, he froze in front of the full-length mirror. He almost did not recognize himself. His figure lost all definition in its cotton constraints. His sunken eyes bore the same baggage as those around him—muscle tissue, weakened with age, draped over the hazel eyes of his youth. A vernal image of himself gave way to a new, mature one. One he had yet to reconcile with. The moment passed. By the time he made it downstairs, Eva was cleaning the dishes from a meal of eggs with bacon she had made for herself and their son, Colin. They sat across from one another at the kitchen table.

"Good morning," said Rafe.

Colin mumbled an ambivalent, "Morning." His eyes never left the messenger app on his phone.

In a halfhearted gesture, Eva batted her eyes to Rafe. "Good morning, dear," she said. Her loving gaze was lost in the luster of the morning light. She shifted focus back onto Colin. "Go get ready for school. You only have a few minutes, if you want me to drop you off on my way to the office."

Colin pushed in his chair and swung a bookbag over his shoulder.

Before he could pass him by, Rafe grabbed Colin by the upper arm. "I can drop you off," he said. "We're headed in the same direction, after all." He grinned.

Colin rolled his eyes. He gave Eva a sideways glance. She cleared her throat. Her eyes grew wide with pleading. "Don't take it personal," she told Rafe. "He just doesn't want to be seen with the school principal. You know how kids are." Rafe's smile flatlined to a straight-faced glower. Eva patted his back. "C'mon, you were eleven once. You understand."

Rafe nodded. He poured himself a cup of coffee and watched Eva and Collin back out of the driveway. His eyes scanned the trees that lined his backyard. Though he saw nothing, traces of his ephialtes still haunted the periphery of his mind.

III.

Sequestered to the back of the administration offices, sat an executive desk adorned with trinkets and framed family photos. There, the hands—of an analog clock mounted on the wall—rotated in perpetual motion. Every tick-tock tally marked one less second spent in purgatory. Next to the clock was a picture of the building back when it opened. With wire mesh windows and a chain-link fence edging the curtilage, the two-story school took on the outward appearance of a prison. Rafe sulked behind a cheap computer monitor. He hated Red Cloud Middle School. The class schedules always needed rearranging to cater to everyone's preference, the curriculum standards were never met to the superintendent's satisfaction, and year after year the students behaved like savages—he felt the torment would never end. When he had first accepted the position, he had sought out an opportunity to make a difference in children's lives—be the father figure that he never had. Now, those daydreams had faded to waking nightmares. Even his son chose to ignore Rafe's existence rather than embrace him as a role model.

A knock rattled at his door. "Come in," he said.

Prudence Grundy, the school's vice principal, entered. She sauntered through the door in a tunic blouse and a pair of flats. Her plastered-on smile had the effect of makeup on a clown. It amplified the pleasantry to an uncanny degree and, therefore, undermined its own legitimacy—made Rafe ponder at its intent. "Officer Huntley is here," she said.

"Great," said Rafe. "Make the announcement." He dismissed her with the flick of his hand. Eyes glued to an Excel spreadsheet that even he did not fully understand, "I'll meet you there."

He rubbed his temples with his fingertips. A headache swelled behind the eyes. The LED's overhead did little to help him. Prudence's voice boomed from the intercom, "All classes report to the lecture hall for an important school assembly." Her automatonlike tone made him uneasy. Everything about her seemed too polished, too performative.

Rafe followed the swarm of students on their march to the lecture hall. He glanced over the crowd. Not a single person stopped to say hello or even bothered to make eye contact. He sighed. His eyes glazed over in ambivalence. In a single file, students filled out the bleachers until there was no room left. Faculty members stood, against the wall, in the back of the auditorium. Among the assembly, Rafe spotted his son with a group of friends. They jostled one another in a playful tussle—elbows prodded at rib cages, pinches inflicted in return, swear words exchanged.

Then, as the boys settled in, Colin scanned the room. Yet, when his roaming gaze crossed paths with his father's corporeal form, his eyes passed right over Rafe—as if nothing was there at all. Rafe's parted lips came to a close. He licked the wounds foisted upon his ego. He cursed himself for expecting anything less from Colin.

Prudence took the stage to introduce the police officer as the guest speaker, then handed the microphone down the line like a baton in a relay race. Officer Huntley was met with smattered applause. He lifted a hand to show his gratitude and looked out at the crowd with a pained expression. "Thank you for that warm welcome," he said. "What I'm here to talk to you all about today is not a subject to be taken lightly. Some of you will find the content of my words to be disturbing. If anyone feels triggered, there's no shame in stepping out for a moment. Okay?"

Students leaned in. A promise of the macabre had their curiosities piqued. Colin's eyes traced Officer Huntley's movements across the stage. His friends all followed suit. Occasionally, they turned to one another with wide eyed reactions.

Rafe rolled his eyes. He watched the boys with disdain. His arms crossed in front of his chest. Officer Huntley's words washed over him in wave after wave of clichés.

"...My partner and I were 10-8 when, all of a sudden, we got a Signal 66 call—which means there was a suspected gang member," said Officer Huntley. "So, as backup, we arrive to talk to a young couple found carting an infant in a stroller along the side of the highway. Within minutes, it's clear they're not in the right state of mind and they're on drugs. Then, we checked up on the infant in the stroller." His bottom lip quivered. His hands clenched to fists. "There, we found the infant deceased due to the fentanyl he ingested. All because his parents wanted to get high."

Silence flooded the room.

"That's why I'm here today," said Officer Huntley, "to offer all of you kids an opportunity to better yourselves by signing a pledge to never do drugs." He signaled Prudence, off stage, to the materials he had prepared. "This is important, okay, because—it may not be today, and it may not be tomorrow—but the day is coming when you will be confronted with a dark temptation. A temptation that could cost you everything you love." Prudence crossed the stage to provide Officer Huntley with a sheet of paper and a marker. "Now, you can't predict when that will happen. So, some of you will have forgotten this pledge by then and you will give in to the ruination of your one and only life." He balked—too moved, by his own words, to continue. He took a deep breath and found the strength to carry on. "My hope is that, after today, others among you will remember this lesson and you'll say 'no' to temptation."

On Prudence's cue, the students applauded.

Students gathered, in a line, to write their names on an anti-drug petition, then shuffled along to the exit. On their way out the door, they passed Officer Huntley. Some students offered the cop a polite smile, while others looked right through him. Rafe studied the results as everyone left. He was pleased to find the officer had about as much cachet with the children as he did, that is until Colin made his way towards the exit. Officer Huntley was looking off in the distance—his mind already elsewhere, in the absence of social interaction—when Colin spoke to him. Rafe was too far off to hear them. Their heads bobbed to the tune of a good conversation. Colin's friends went on without him. Then, once their discussion came to its natural end, Colin gave Officer Huntley a high five and walked off.

Rafe made his way through the crowd. His teeth grinded together—in the subtle rotation of his jaw as he walked. He stormed down the building's main corridor, to the administration office, and shut his office door behind him. He held his hands steepled above the keyboard. He checked the time. Only a couple hours until nightfall. He pulled out his phone and shot Eva a quick text message. He told her to eat dinner without him, since he was swamped with paperwork and would be home late. Afterward, he checked his phone and smirked. Just as he had dreamed it would be; tonight, a full moon was expected.

IV.

During the twilight hour, saffron rays poured in from the double-hung window. Shorter, blue wavelengths scattered throughout the Earth's atmosphere—as longer, more vibrant ones reached the eyes of land dwellers. Hues of red and violet illuminated dust particles as they drifted to the bookshelf and made homes upon the bindings of volumes left unread. Rafe sat with his eyes closed. His head was cradled in the palm of his hand. He pushed down until all light in the room blurred to loops and whirls. He counted down the minutes left in the day. His eyes shot open. Gradually, his vision returned to him. Footsteps, from students dismissed for the day, ceased. The cubicles—of administration faculty members—were empty. He could sense the arrival of dusk.

Just then, Prudence poked her head in. "Hey, Rafe," she said. He put on a good face, but it was short-lived before he turned to the blue light of his computer screen. She continued, "I'm on my way out for the day." Her words hung in the air with no reply. From the doorway, she waited for him to acknowledge her. When he did not, she cleared her throat and said, "It's getting late."

Rafe nodded. "I've still got a few things to check off the to-do list," he said. "I'll see you tomorrow."

Prudence nodded. "All right," she said. "Don't work too hard." Despite her hesitation, she stepped beyond the door's threshold. Her loose-limbed footfalls carried on down the hall and out into the parking lot.

Rafe loitered there, at his desk, until all who remained was him and the janitorial staff. He collected his belongings and made a beeline for his car in the parking lot. With both hands on his knapsack and his head hung low, he managed to avoid any unwanted attention and kept his eyes focused on each step he took. The long night's moon pierced the ether—even in the day's final hour. He threw himself into the car and placed his key in the ignition. On the open road, cars weaved in and out of their lanes—thanks to the rush hour traffic. Sunlight dwindled to a blanket of black that enveloped the sky. Rafe bristled. He figured he had more time. Taillights glistened their red gleam in front of him. A yellow light beamed in from the streetlights that shone through the sunroof of his car. He clasped the steering wheel with all his might. As he parked the car under a stoplight, his hands fumbled with the gear shifter. He exhaled through labored moans. Claws burst from his fingertips. His fingernails cascaded to the floormat—as these curved talons took their place upon his hands. The light turned green. Cars honked behind him. He shifted to drive and pressed the gas pedal. He pulled into an empty parking lot at Clift Park. Aside from the stochastic assortment of ne'er-do-wells who lurked under the veil of night, he was alone. He put the car in park.

He writhed in the driver's seat. His jaw dislocated from its place to protrude outward—in the shape of a snout—as bones and nerves rearranged their internal form. He caught a brief glimpse of himself in the car's mirror. His thighs extended outward at an odd angle, his wrists were cow-hocked, all his fingers were molded together as paws, and hair follicles jutted out of every pore—no reminders of a tainted youth, nor marks of grizzled flesh. In the swagger of his step, he gained a newfound confidence. He shed the shame of his daytime persona and held two truths in the palm of his hand at once. He was an animal. He was a man. He was the Wolf Man.

V.

Wolf Man barreled out from the car door in a whirlwind of angst and virility. He lifted his muzzle to absorb the scents of the air. An aroma of decay flooded his nostrils. To his right, an opossum feasted on the rotted flesh of a rabbit flattened to roadkill. The opossum fled from its meal as soon as it caught sight of him. He smiled to himself. Fear enshrouded all the night's creatures with shame—for all absconded from the eye of an unwanted witness. In his new form, he was invincible. He ran faster than his legs could manage on their own. He positioned himself on all fours and pranced through the woods. He achieved a new top speed, but took on the appearance of a chimp from the Congolian rainforests—and a disfigured one at that. He spotted a group of teenagers on the basketball court. He retreated deeper into the forest. There, Wolf Man found comfort in the discarded pine needles and melted snow at his feet. His eyes surveyed the dark. He was alone. He howled at the moon above, cursed it for making him the monster he was.

A howl came from farther off in the woods.

Wolf Man pricked an ear. He galloped towards the sound. Misery afflicted every beat of his heart. He yearned for an equivalent. Someone with whom he could share himself, even the parts he was ashamed of. He searched in shadows. Deep within the thicket, he located the werewolf. A runt with yellow eyes and rounded ears. They stared at one another—in a standstill. Neither one knew how to make the first move or if it was even safe to. Wolf Man approached in slow and deliberate advances. He maintained a high posture—with his hackles raised. Squirrels stirred in their dreys, as Wolf Man let out a low growl. The runt kept his head down, his fur flattened, and his ears lowered.

As an act of communion to the primordial god within, Wolf Man mounted him. He set his hooks into the runt's tender flesh and refused to let him loose until they met their eventual end as one. They separated. Quiet whining was heard as they parted ways. Then, once the throes of lust and passion faded to the doldrums of normalcy, Wolf Man shed his carnal skin and shackled himself to the body of Rafe Lowell, who got back in his car and drove home.

VI.

Rafe ambled into the mudroom of his home with a look of guilt in his eyes. In the kitchen, he found leftover meatloaf in the fridge. He grabbed a plate and set it in the microwave. He sighed. His eyes made loopty-loops in their sockets as he watched the spinning plate go around and around. He never wanted to be the type of man who neglected his home life, not even for an evening. He went into the living room. Draped upon the sectional couch, Eva read a paperback novel. Across from her, hunched over a notebook laid out on the coffee table, Colin finished his homework for the day. Rafe stood in front of them, until he had their attention. It took them a moment to realize he had returned. "I wanted to apologize," said Rafe, "for not being at dinner."

Colin chortled. "Don't worry about it," he said. His snide laughter faded into a know-it-all smirk. "You're the one who's got to eat reheated meatloaf, anyway."

"No," said Rafe, "I'm serious." He exhaled through his nose. His arms held akimbo. "I want you both to know, as the man of the house, I'm here for you." His eyes flickered from Colin's to Eva's. "Always."

Neither one blinked. They stared at him, with a blank look on their faces.

Eva shrugged. Her eyes drifted from him, to the printed words of a sappy romance novel. "It's just one dinner," she said. "It's fine." She picked up where she left off. "We'll be fine."

Rafe nodded.

He stepped into the shower, where beads of water warmed him from the night's cold embrace and baptized him from past sins. Yet, even in that fiberglass-walled confessional, he relished in the secret knowledge of forbidden thrills—ones only he knew of, at least for now.

VII.

In the mirror's reflection, hidden underneath soap streaks and urine stains, Rafe forced a labored smile and recited prepared words that had lost all meaning to him. At the sink of a public bathroom, his anxiety bubbled to the surface in shaky hands and heaved breaths. He practiced his speech one last time before he spoke in front of the school board. He held on to the sink for dear life. His ability to relay the school's performance to the board was hindered by a crippling sense of self-loathing. A man walked over to the urinal behind him. After a drawn-out groan, Rafe left.

When he entered the meeting room, the board was ready for him. He adjusted his suit as he stood before them. His eyeline was held about an inch or two above the tallest head in the room, so as to avoid any faces infiltrating his concentration on the half-baked speech. "Ladies and gentlemen of the board," he said, "I'd like to start off by thanking you all for being here on such a snowy day." Board members tuned out just as soon as he began. They watched him with their heads rested upon their propped up elbows. "…Red Cloud Middle School's art department in the midst of..." Nobody took in a single word from him. They simply waited for his prattle to end.

Pragmatic words rolled off the tip of his tongue with ease. He, himself, stopped listening at a certain point. He had bespouted it so many times the speech was on autopilot. His thoughts drifted towards the matter of the night—of the Wolf Man and his pack. He envisioned the school board among their ranks. Trustees with toned muscles, chiseled jawlines, hairy chests, and tattered clothes. Some fit into the role naturally, while others required a little more imagination. It mattered little to Wolf Man. Whether it be alpha or omega, everyone had a role to play in their pack and a partner to play with.

"…any questions?" asked Rafe. None of the board members lifted a hand, or made any sign that they had heard him at all. He sat. His tensed shoulders relaxed to their former slouch. Board members eyed each other and imparted a few words in response to Rafe's assessment. Once he was done, they moved on the matter of budget and how best to serve the taxpayers who put them there.

VIII.

The sunset dipped below the horizon line. Moonlight rapped on the window's glass, but curtains were drawn in defense. Inside the Lowell home, Rafe sat at the dinner table with Colin and Eva. The family bowed their heads in prayer, then broke bread over mundane conversation. Eva prodded Colin until he went through each class period of his school day. Rafe and Eva nodded along to Colin's stories. Meanwhile, their thoughts were adrift. When Colin finished, Rafe opened his mouth to speak, but his voice was drowned out by Eva's. She parroted news headlines she had skimmed online, those designed to incite fear and spark topical discussion. He listened and waited for his turn to chime in.

"So, as you all know," said Rafe, "I had a meeting with the school board today"—

"Oh," said Colin, "I almost forgot." He reacted as though he had been awakened from a dream. "I need a parental signature for a field trip."

"What class is this for?" asked Eva.

Rafe checked the time on his phone. It was late. He stole a peek outside, through a crack in the closed curtain. He reflected on the night before: the snow between his toes, the goosebumps on his skin, the warmth of a leman under his weight. Hairs raised on the back of his neck. Even concealed beneath his popcorn ceiling, the full moon still bathed him in its glory. Wolf Man clawed at the underside of Rafe's skin. His testicles were swollen in eager delirium. He excused himself from the table. Colin and Eva shot him a questioning glare. "I'm going to go for a jog," he told them. "I'll be right back."

The two shrug him off, then proceed with their idle chitchat.

Rafe threw on a track suit and a pair of tennis shoes. He sprinted, from the mailbox to Clift Park. His legs carried him over slush and black ice. Then, without notice, he was plucked from his human form, like a berry from the vine. He panted, buried under the weight of a full fur coat. Finally, winter wolf syndrome consumed him whole—body and soul.

IX.

Wolf Man clung to the shagbark hickory trees of Clift Park. Tucked behind a dead leadplant bush, he discovered a creek and ran alongside it. In the distance, wolves cried out to the waning moon. His head cocked to one side. He heard the howls of several participants. He headed in their direction. His nose was kept low to the ground, as he picked up the wolves' trail. Wafts of musk filled his nostrils. Blood coursed through his loins. His eyes scoured in blackness, until he came upon a small clearing in the boscage. There they were. A pack of seven wolves in total. He came to a halt in front of them. His jaw dropped. They were the wolves of his dream. An unconscious memory, faded by the toll of the conscious world, had come to life. Among them was the runt he had met the night before.

Wolf Man took the first steps at a cautious rate. Then, the pack's alpha bared teeth and made his presence known. A series of snarls and yelps came to the alpha's aid. Wolf Man treated them in kind. He rushed the alpha forefeet first. His mouth opened and teeth flashed. The alpha was shaken, but maintained his stance. Wolf Man assailed the pack leader with a barrage of clawed attacks. He shoved the alpha's head below his own. The alpha nipped at Wolf Man's underbelly, so Wolf Man sank his teeth into the scruff of the alpha's neck. Wolf Man caught a mouthful of fur and the alpha tried to wriggle himself free. Wolf Man clenched harder, until he tasted blood. The alpha whimpered and backpedaled into his pack members. From that moment onward, they recognized Wolf Man as their own.

Together, the pack went on the prowl. They picked up a scent of deer scat and traced the herd from there. Hoofprints, left in the snow, led them to a young buck, alone, in the woods. The buck made a run for it, but they circled him and cornered him between a confluence of streams. Once the wide-eyed buck accepted his fate, the pack—even the former alpha—made room for Wolf Man to take the first bite. Wolf Man embraced his role and invited the runt to dine at his side.

X.

Prudence and her husband sipped red wine glasses on the back porch of their house, which backed up to the forest of Clift Park. She berated the man with trivial workplace gossip he had no concept of, but he listened just the same. "…it's always social injustice this or civil rights that with him," said Prudence, "and Mrs. Quirke, the poor thing, goes along with every word of it."

Mr. Grundy swallowed the last drop from his glass. His eyes looked off into the dark spaces between tree trunks. "Maybe they've got a point," he said. "It is a good topic for children to learn about at some point."

Prudence pursed her lips. "That may be," she said, "but surely not at such a young age." She shot him an evil eye. "Anyway, why are you taking their side? You don't realize how"—

Barbaric grunts and deep moans emanated from the forest. They were quiet at first, then they became louder and louder in a rhythmic cadence. Prudence sat upright in her chair. The tumult spurred her interest. The hushed voices and gruff tones struck a recognizable chord in her head. She gasped. Out in the wood, behind Clift Park, she heard men in the throes of sex. Once she had confirmation of her suspicions, she got up to walk over to the deck's railing and listen. Mr. Grundy crept up behind his wife and wrapped his arms around her. He chuckled. "Just ignore it," he told her. "Let's enjoy our night." He pressed his crotch against her backside. "It'll end soon."

She shoved him aside and proceeded to dial 9-1-1. "You're damn right it'll end soon," she said. "I'll be sure of that." She hung in there, through the dial tone, with another glass of wine. Someone picked up on the other end. "Hello, I have a noise complaint to make.."

Mr. Grundy shook his head. He went inside, but left what remained of their wine bottle for Prudence to polish off. She described the noises over the phone with venom in her voice. Yet, her heart fluttered with each new sound. She derived excitement from cataloguing their dark deeds. She took perverse pleasure from knowing she would be the end to their unnatural relations. She knew, she could return to their place in the woods, when no one was around, to scavenge for evidence of their copulation—devour the scraps of their love.

XI.

A police cruiser parked facing the forest of Clift Park. The headlights illuminated the snow covered ground and pine tree branches. Officer Huntley stepped out from the driver's seat and ventured into the woods. His eyes traced the outline of the flashlight's dim glow. He listened for the sounds described by dispatch, but heard only the crunch beneath his feet. He pressed on—unsure of what he would be stumbling upon. Suddenly, an animal soughed nearby. He clicked his flashlight off. He inched closer, in a foxtrot. Another, more defined, uproar came in the form of frantic huffs and perfervid grumbles that followed. From that Officer Huntley could only assume lechers and sybarites and, since stones and trees would sooner drive a man to sin than civility, the dwellers in darkness used night after night to satisfy their insatiable lusts. They were predators who lacked the need to hunt. Their prey came right to them, willingly. Each nightfall, they amassed new acolytes to frequent their wolves' den and new meat to indulge in—bone marrow and all. He rested one hand on his gun holster. A harsh whisper cut through the heartsease, and in an instant all was still in the air.

Officer Huntley flicked his flashlight on.

In the narrow beam of light, droves of naked men poured forth from the trees. They darted in all directions. Officer Huntley did not know which way to make his chase. Flashes of bare skin and genitalia passed before his eyes. He steadied his flashlight on two middle-aged men standing near a young man about half their age. They struggled to put their clothes on. The young man worked the denim waistline over his exposed penis and made a run for it. Officer Huntley froze. For only a moment, he studied the form of their figures and the veins of their muscles. He compared their manhood to his own. Meanwhile, the older men scurried in opposite directions. Officer Huntley made his choice of the two and sprinted after him.

XII.

Rafe scampered the best his paltry legs could carry him in his human form. Through ankle-deep snow, he trudged. His feet treaded over ice and pinecones. He worked his soles' skin raw. His track suit was left discarded at the site of the young buck's fall. He had grown reckless in the celebratory moments of his kill. Now, he was nude and open to attack. He glanced over his shoulder. Officer Huntley remained hot on his trail. Rafe felt the cop nipping at his heels. He was losing stamina and grew short-winded.

Rafe gave in to the rising waters that swelled in a floodtide at his back. He bemoaned the cursed moon that brought him here, to ardor's folly. He dug in his bloody heels. His whistle-stop footfalls came to a halt near the park's entrance. Officer Huntley tackled Rafe to the forest floor and pushed Rafe's head into the earth, as he clasped Rafe's forearms in handcuffs. Rafe went limp. A bulge, at the officer's groin, mashed into Rafe's back. Officer Huntley lowered his lips to Rafe's ear. He exhaled a hot breath and said, "You have the right to remain silent…" Rafe tuned out after the first right was read. His mind was propelled to what was sure to follow: a severance check, divorce, alimony—the list went on and on. Officer Huntley squinted. His eyes met Rafe's with a glimmer of familiarity. "Wait," he said, "I know you." Just the same, he carted Rafe toward the police cruiser. "You work at Red Cloud, right?" He pshawed. "They let a perv like you around kids? This world's gone to shit." With that, he closed the car door in Rafe's face.

A beet red complexion spread across Rafe's face and down his neck. His eyes—lost to a vacant stare—looked to the vacuum between molecules, to a nightmarish vision of what was to come. Yet, he realized, even in the backseat of Officer Huntley's car, he would not change his ways. He was bound to Wolf Man—to the pack—and they to him.

XIII.

Auroral sunlight peeked over the horizon line and bathed the brick walls, of Red Cloud Middle School, in shades of orange and red. At that hour, all who were there were faculty and extracurricular club members. Among them, Rafe was crouched in front of his desk. He gathered his belongings into a cardboard box. He hauled the box outside, though his arms struggled to wrap around the awkward dimensions. As he passed, he received judgmental glares from his former co-workers. They watched him go about his morning, as if he were a prisoner on the lam. They studied his every move, then relayed what they saw to the person nearest to them. He kept his head down and pretended not to notice. Internally, their condemnation enshrouded his brain in a shameful fog.

On his way out of the administration offices, he bumped into Prudence. The two locked eyes on one another. Her bug eyes did their best to appear unperturbed. She forced an uncomfortable greeting, as she attempted to blink away her apparent fear. Rafe reciprocated her welcome with humility. "By the way," he said, "congratulations on the promotion to principal." He gulped down the lump in his throat. "You're going to do great."

Prudence was taken aback, but flattered. She smiled. "Well," she said, "I certainly have big shoes to fill." Her smile faded. "Good luck with…whatever comes next."

Rafe winced. He soldiered on down the hallway and out the main entrance. Just then, he caught Colin walking in to school. "Colin," he called out. He saw Colin flinch, at the sound of his voice, but the boy did not turn around. "I'm sorry for everything I put you and your mom through." His words faltered from the tears lodged within him. He refused to let them be seen. "Buddy, please, I need to talk to you about this. It's only right that you hear me out here." Colin popped a couple of wireless earbuds in, so Rafe raised his voice. "I just need a moment of your time. Just a second." It was too late. Colin was already inside—safe from his father in a secured barricade. Rafe threw his hands over his head. His box clattered to the ground. Its contents spilled out onto the concrete.

He scrambled to recollect his trinkets, but a Subaru Crosstrek veered from the student drop off lane. He braced for impact. Yet, the car stopped within inches of him. Eva stepped out of the driver's seat. She lorded over him. Her brows furrowed. "Don't talk to our son like that," she said. "In fact, don't talk to him at all." The corners of her lips curled, in the hint of a smirk. "I've got a lawyer and we're coming for full custody, do you understand? Colin and I don't need a deadbeat like you around. We don't need…"

Rafe rose to his feet and proceeded onward, to his car. He left the box with her. There was nothing of value in there anyway. Once he shut the car door behind him, he turned on the radio, and sang along to the oldies station. He drummed his fingers on the steering wheel. His toes tapped on the floormat. Then, he changed the station again and again. He was in search of an earworm to replace Eva's cruel words, but none would suffice. Her insults rang in his mind the whole day through.

XIV.

Rafe settled in a studio apartment downtown, where he wasted what little remained in his bank account. He spent his days woolgathering in fast food parking lots and his nights at the bottom of a Jack Daniels bottle. Each glug was a pitiful attempt to shut out the retributions of his crimes to no avail.

Days blurred to night, in the vague recollections of Rafe's fragile short term memory. Beneath the long nights moon, his blood vessels writhed under the skin. Wolf Man lurked just beneath the surface of Rafe's being. With clenched fists and veins bulging from his neck, he fought the Wolf Man with all his will. He forbade Wolf Man's existence. He refused to embrace his inner self—not after what Wolf Man did to his career, to his family. He built up a mental blockade from Wolf Man. For a while, that seemed to work. He seemed calm, perhaps even normal. Then, a jolt of pain shot through his body and brought him to his knees. He wheezed. The Wolf Man could not be stopped, not with temporary solutions. He had to think in terms of absolutes. In a final bid for freedom, he penned a suicide note—a letter of both compassion and contempt for Colin and Eva—before loading the revolver at his side. His body tensed. He was at war with the demon within.

He placed the gun's barrel between his teeth, tasted the carbon steel on his tongue, and bit the silver bullet.

XV.

Wolf Man awakened on the laminate wood flooring. He rolled to his side and hacked up the silver bullet, as well as a small puddle of blood. He sprang to his feet. His entire body vibrated with seething rage. He repudiated society's rejection of him. He denied any wrongdoing. The hunt was as natural as life itself and he acted as its embodiment. Now, he had to demonstrate the folly of their ways. He clambered down the staircase, out the exit, and onto the crowded streets. He followed a woody scent with notes of citrus—Eva's favorite perfume brand—to the Lowell home. Once he made it to their front porch; he leered inside from the window. Nobody moved in his line of sight, but he smelled the salty aroma of sweat. He burst through the front door.

Lights were off in the entryway. Wolf Man followed his nose to the basement. There, they hid in the cellar. Wolf Man discovered them huddled in the room's back corner. Colin averted his eyes from the horror and Eva was already on the phone with local police. She told them to come quick. Wolf Man whimpered. They viewed him as the monster he always felt he was. For over a decade, they had taken every second he could spare them. When, in reality, they only ever wanted a part of him—a fraction of his essence. Inevitably, they called his bluff and, when his cards were on the table, he was saddled with a two-seven off-suit hand. Fine. If they wanted a monster, he would show them who he was. He pounced on Eva, tore her limb from limb, and dug into her like a fine delicacy. Colin screamed. His face was caked in crimson—a baptism of blood.

"Hold it right there," said Officer Huntley. He drew his gun and steadied his aim at Wolf Man. He hesitated, as he anticipated Wolf Man's next move. Before he could think to pull the trigger, Wolf Man swiped at Officer Huntley and slit the cop's throat with a clawed hand. In the wake of Officer Huntley's death, Colin fell silent, and Wolf Man fled into the night.

Near Clift Park, snowflakes floated in the air and flecked the vacuous sky in white speckles. There, deer wandered the open fields and, from the trees, wolves stalked them, in noble pursuit.

HER HAND IN MARRIAGE

ABIGAIL TAYLOR

I. To Have and To Hold

Ben Crawford's journey began as the snow started its thaw and ice slushed off into the rivers. Patches of soft green peeked around the lazy drifts of white powder and the post oaks were as richly dark as the shaggy bison that survived these parts. In his travels, Ben watched train windows pry open enough to cater the muzzle of a rifle. The whooping men's arms raised in victory at each fallen beast, their shouts silent in the engine's slipstream. Buzzards and lonesome prairie wolves hopped around the mud, slick with fat, taking meat and bone that the men wasted.

When he arrived at the territory, the snow had all but dissipated, leaving only the crisp, curling reminder of itself in the air. He stopped in the town, half a day's journey from his final destination, to provide his blue roan a rest and himself a bed. Perhaps a bit of the liquid courage as well. The journey had been long and the letter in his pocket was one of familial urgency.

He'd arrived as soon as he could, but this part of the New World still lacked a train system. The town itself was hardly more than a pop up of necessities hugged together and divided by a strip of perpetually wet road and planks of wood for women to walk on.

After tucking his horse into the only livery, pitiful and damp after a harsh winter and stubborn thaw, Ben stepped into the saloon. There, the proprietor, a Kiowa man, offered warm beer and a rope of tobacco. Ben rested his bowler hat on his knee and smoothed his tough hand through a crop of thick, brown curls. He took the beer and declined the tobacco.

"You seem troubled," said the man.

"Oh, only the road," answered Ben. Bartenders were such gossips, and Ben didn't want to give this one any mention of his family's financial troubles. His cousin Olivia, now Lady Dalgliesh, had exchanged her wealth for the prestige of a titled aristocrat who took her railroad inheritance and squandered it. The act alone put a strain on all the First Daughters who had stepped up to take the necessary sacrifice ensuring the Crawford Legacy since Virginia was first colonized. Olivia was not a First Daughter; Ben had heard his own parents complain often enough, and therefore didn't understand how hitching her post to minor royalty upset the intricate workings of the family's considerable wealth.

The how and when such generational wealth started to slip was not apparent, but the proof sat outside the saloon. Where there should've been a train station, sponsored by the Crawfords' sprawling estate, lay only prairie.

"What brings you out here?" asked the bartender, easing onto his elbows for a gentle conversation.

"The railroad," said Ben. His tone more snipped than he intended, but he'd rather not have idle chat. He'd spent too many weeks in his own company and needed to ease into the bending nature of a crowd, even if that crowd only consisted of a too friendly bartender and a handful of dusty ranch hands holding a card game on the other side of the room.

"Oh that. You're better off talking to those Dalgliesh people up the way. They hold the land for it….promises promises." The man pointed his wide, flat mouth in the direction Ben would take in the morning. "Spending it all on parties, see? I know because I'm also the mailman and they have their friends come in once a month to put on a big to-do. Last one was Christmas. Wedding or engagement announcement. Some such. Hired outside help. I had to go up to the house myself to deliver the responses. Some as far as Canada."

He dug under the counter and extracted an ammunition box, which he sat on the empty counter space between them. "Free drinks all night if you could take this for me in the morning. It'll save me a trip."

Ben's tired expression tugged a little. He couldn't help but like this man. "You trust me with their mail?"

"Well, stranger," the bartender's slim fingers dipped into a pouch and removed a large pinch of Virginia flake, which he stuffed into his pipe. "To be honest, if the mail don't make it…it don't make it. They've got these birds, see? Peacocks I think they're called, and they scream a mighty fuss. Bother the shit out of me and I'd just as rather not put up with the nonsense."

Ben agreed to the trade and the following morning rode out, later than intended, with two dozen letters neatly parceled together with thick twine. His tongue and throat were gummy with hops.

The promise of rain frosted the air and followed Ben to the manor house on the far west side of the territory where the plains began to dip and take shape into something more jagged than he'd seen in any other part of the world. There were large bands of red orange rock, escarpments he supposed, cutting the horizon. If he kept riding, he'd reach the desert by the following afternoon. Here, however, the grasses, post oaks, and mesquites pushed back the parched earth, tucked everything beneath a damp and unruly arm.

A shrieking bird greeted Ben at the fog-hugged iron gates. The size of a wild turkey but possessing the deep, shining plume of precious jewels, it hounded him up the carriage path, long tail dragging behind it like an abandoned flag. It bellowed several curses, as though mocking him, *whostherewhostherewhosthere!* with such force that a stable boy rushed out with a pistol pointed above his shaggy head to shoo the creature away with several warning shots. The peacock wailed and hurried into the safety of an ornate rose garden at the center of the cul-de-sac in front of the manor.

The stable boy slid the gun into his belt loop and took the blue roan, whose ears were pressed flat against its skull. He pointed to the arched, marble steps. "I was told you'd be here this day or the next, sir. They're waiting. I'll see your horse gets a good clean and hoof trim."

The stone manor loomed in the gray, dank air, weeping black at the cornerstones, cutting the sky with thick, twisting spires. Each window, long and yawning, carried a lit candle, burning bright and welcoming in spite of the imposing face of the structure. Ben tugged on the velvet cord hanging in a tiny alcove by the ornate cherry wood doors. He wondered if Sir Dalgliesh was so stuck in the Old World that he insisted on a home that reminded him of ancient deities, warring clansmen, and patents of nobility.

A butler received Ben wordlessly taking hat and coat, wet at the shoulders, and tucked them away in some unseen compartment of the oaken walls. He silently led Ben to the front parlor. Several times Ben lost himself in the sprawling tapestries and gilded frames that decorated the commissioned paintings of the landscapes and the Crawford-Dalgliesh families.

The butler opened the parlor door and the heavy waft of honeysuckle greeted him before the bright green paper plastered fashionably over the walls. A fire danced in a black marble hearth. Three women were seated with embroidery on the pastel pink chaise longues. An elderly man watched from a heavy leather armchair that was at odds with the rest of the room's decor. He twirled a bright amber whiskey in a crystal cut glass but stopped when the eldest of the women cried, "Ah, dear cousin, Bingley!"

"Ben's fine."

The butler bowed and removed himself from the parlor, clicking the door firmly shut behind him. A creeping sensation of falling into a bear trap caught Ben at the spine. Lady Olivia kissed the air around Ben's newly shaven jaw. With her cultivated accent, cured of the low-slung Americanism that she'd been raised in, she cooed, "I hoped your trip remained uneventful and none of those dreadful ruffians took the stagecoach. We've heard such remarkable stories!"

"I didn't arrive by coach. Or by train…as it happens," he added pointedly. Lady Olivia had the decency to blush and cast her eyes down in shame. There were fine laugh lines, which hadn't been there the last time he'd seen her, and drifts of scented powder and kohl that lined her lashes, gathered in the corners. Blue silk and pale lace draped her body, soft and well cared for by imported sweets.

"Good of you to come, Bingley," Sir Roger Dalgliesh spoke around a sagging, tobacco-stained mustache.

"Ben."

Sir Dalgliesh's small eyes quivered in delight at the sapphire tie pin catching the light. "I've heard you've done quite well with your, what was it, *bonanza farming* this season? A quaint title, don't you think? Rather something out of a penny dreadful the chambermaids like to read."

Ben didn't respond other than study the varying wrinkles gathered about the man's face and the lattice work of popped veins that covered his nose and cheeks. The soft palm of his hand did little to impress Ben.

Sir Dalgliesh chuckled uncomfortably. "Stoicism. I've heard you have it in spades…Might I introduce you to my daughter? Lady Johana, please make yourself known."

The girl, like her mother, had the distinct Crawford curls that framed the angular face inherited from her father, though his had started to sag out of the noble elegance. Her shoulders were exposed, as was the current fashion, allowing the graceful dip of her collarbone to accentuate the drapery of pearls around her stately neck. Her mouth, a pale blush only, parted so naturally it was as if her lips were too frightened to kiss themselves. She couldn't have been more than sixteen.

Ben bowed over her offered hand. She gestured to the third woman beside her and spoke, wine soft, "This is my sister, Lady Williamina."

Lady Williamina, slightly older and near identical wore her dark hair in an interwoven plait, tucked under a mourning veil. She extended her gloved, right hand to be kissed because her left was little more than a sleeve pinned with a pearl inlaid brooch. She wore the missing limb with pride, her chin tilted upward as though Ben might question its source, but he was a Crawford and didn't need to ask about the nature of the injury.

Instead, he turned to Lady Olivia. "She is your First Daughter?"

Lady Olivia touched Sir Dalgliesh with fond, simpering strokes. "Of course. Where would we be without our traditions?"

Ben's eyes narrowed curiously. He had not attended their wedding, being of an age that would be inappropriate for his mother to be seen in public with him. Sir Dalgliesh had the easy marriage since Olivia was the second daughter, and Ben was curious of how the leaching Lord first reacted to the necessary rituals Lady Williamina performed for her …*husband?*

Ah, the bartender had mentioned a wedding party around Christmas, and now there she was, a few scant months later, in mourning. No need to question the husband's whereabouts. The bartender did not mention a Crawford funeral, and that could only mean he broke the sacred vows; which meant that Lady Williamina was not only tarnished, but her First Daughter duties were negated.

Ben stroked his chin, observing the silent woman. He thought about Lady Olivia's letter of urgency and her refusal to put specifics to the page. So this was more than a money issue. It was an issue of the Crawford curse.

Sir Dalgliesh offered Ben a glass of whiskey, and his enormous mustache fluttered against his hot breath. "To business, I should think."

Their daughters swept out of the room, which now felt stifling in spite of the cool spring weather. That didn't stop Sir Dalgliesh from requesting a member of staff to toss another log onto the fire. His liquor untouched, Ben sat on the chaise lounge farthest from the hearth.

"Bingley," Sir Dalgliesh began.

"Ben is fine."

"Quite right," he sipped from his own glass and Ben calculated, by the shape of Sir Dalgliesh, how much money he guzzled away. "Bingley. As you can see, our eldest is quite undesirable and would be unable to wed, even if she were still intact, given her state of mourning."

"Truth be told, she's gone quite mad with it. Won't speak. Hardly eats," offered Lady Olivia, returning to her own seat and positioning herself as though posing for a new portrait. "The lout ran off with the dowry and spent it on a second family. Would you believe that he had another wife and children in the neighboring county? And he a so-called respectable county judge!"

"His fate was appropriate, I suppose," said Ben, taking a polite sip of the whiskey he'd been offered. It burned his cracked lips but ran smooth across his tongue.

Sir Dalgliesh released a bold laugh. "Quite right! Died of dysentery and his wife taken over by those Johnny Rebs your newspapers always speak of. I suspect the children were abducted and made savage or sent off to some orphanage. This land of yours, so uncouth. But," he let out a languid sigh and settled like a satisfied cat in his armchair, "there's oil. You yourself have seen quite a turn in profits, in spite of your branch of the family coming from a third daughter. There's no shame in new money these days!"

"Or for working it," Ben answered, thinking again of Sir Dalgliesh's simple, unused hands. "And you decided to invest in potential oil instead of the railroad? I had it on good authority that Olivia's dowry included a contract with the Pacific – "

"Oil first and then the train!" Tutted Sir Dalgliesh, speaking to Ben like he was an errant schoolboy. "What good is building a town if there's no proper jobs to be had? As I'm sure you understand, the duties of marriage have transferred over to Johana, and we agree that a union with you would be most fortuitous for both of our families. Johana's dowry includes shares of the oil and train, respectively, as well as the Dalgliesh family line. Your heirs would be viscounts, and they would have the profits of your…what is it, cotton?"

"Wheat."

"Naturally. You could afford to hire the necessary staff." He swirled the last of his whiskey before swallowing it and setting the glass aside. Ben chose not to mention that his fifty ranch hands and ten house maids hadn't kept him from breaking a sweat. He didn't expect someone as delicate as Sir Dalgliesh to understand the joys of physical labor and how it enhanced the mind as well as the body.

Lady Olvia cut into the silence. "All that, simply for you to take Johana's hand in marriage and keep that remarkable luck of the Crawford's strong."

Ben nodded, taking the proposal in thoughtful consideration, twirling the Crawford promise ring around his wedding finger. He was hardly out of university and Johana was a child. On the other hand, the marriage bond could be done the Crawford way and Ben could send Lady Johana off to the east coast, to business or boarding school, to receive a bit of the world and all it had to offer until she was old enough to understand her carnal duties. Ben wouldn't mind the waiting. In fact, he'd prefer it and would see to it that it was part of the vows should he take her hand.

"Her temperament is like her grandmother's, I'm told," said Sir Dalgliesh, as if this might be the sprinkle of sugar to entice Ben further. It did not.

However, he was bound in accordance with family law to be married soon and had yet to find a First or Second daughter from another beneficial family who might agree to the old ways. In truth, he rather hoped that his success in agriculture would provide a loophole, and he might remain a bachelor to his dying day. The discussion with his father, following Lady Olivia's urgent letter, dashed those frail hopes. Lady Johana remained the only viable option, or the entire family might crumble to desolation and ruin. All because of Lady

Olivia and her weak link of a husband. So-called 'patents of nobility' be damned.

"I'll take the evening to make my decision and discuss it with you and Lady Olivia tomorrow."

Dinner was a meal of pale consomme made from veal stock, imported whitebait, and quail eggs served with the roasted joint of a pig. They washed their fingers in rose water between courses, dabbed their lips with silk napkins, and sucked champagne jellies for dessert. All the while, Lady Johana turned out her best display of a soft, demure quality. A wife best seen and not heard, as she was instructed at finishing school. She used her right hand to serve and feed herself, the left resting loose in her lap, showing her capabilities and strength in that one side.

Brandy and cigars came next. Later, the men joined Lady Olivia in the second parlor. Furnished with club chairs made of African blackwood, trophies of Sir Dalgliesh's recent kills in the colonies mounted on the walls. Gorilla. Elephant. Kudu.

"I'll have myself a lion next," he chuckled, "and you know, my brother claimed in his last letter that he has the hand of a Zulu! Still wrapped around the spear! Marvelous."

Lady Olivia plucked at the cascade of amethysts that fell across her bosom. The brandy gave her cheeks a pretty flush. "It hasn't been since our tour of his island that we've seen sweet Fredrick." She turned to Ben, her eyes twinkling as though she was letting him in on some private joke. "They're just like twins. One can hardly tell them apart. We must make sure he comes to this wedding!"

"It hasn't been agreed upon yet," said Sir Dalgliesh, eyeing Ben with an accusatory glance through his monocle. Ben watched the fire lick dark shadows across the hunting trophies and subconsciously tightened the Crawford ring on his finger, his body eager to make a decision before his mind set to it. Lady Olivia noticed the subtle gesture and her smile turned vulpine.

The following evening, invitations were sent on heavy, perfumed cardstock. Ben watched the exchange from butler to bartender from the window of his suite and a vague sickness clamped down harder on his stomach than the Crawford ring did on his skin. Days were spent in the chaperoned company of his bride-to-be. Lady Johana was eager to show him her embroidery, her pet pony, the koi pond she insisted

Sir Dalgliesh build for her in the greenhouse on her fourteenth birthday.

"It's an honor," she told Ben one spring afternoon, while she made a daisy chain, and her parents sat some distance away at the table beneath a sprawling mesquite, set up by a servant, for high tea, "to be trusted with the blessing gifted on the family."

Blessing. Ben leaned forward and helped her right hand thread a green stem between its fellows. He'd only ever heard it called a curse by his parents. The price to pay for prosperity in the New World hounded each generation, but the steady flow of income was worth the rituals.

Sir Dalgliesh had assumed Ben was 'new money' but it was true only of his venture into bonanza farming. In reality, it was simply an investment with two percent of his inheritance. Ben's branch of Crawfords had made their name owning a shipping company that carried spices, such as pepper and cardamom, to Massachusetts when the land was still owned by King George III. Ben's great-great grandmother had given her entire arm for that windfall. Securing the family name. Securing the curse…the blessing.

In the days leading up to the summer wedding, he spent restless evenings drifting along the long, dark corridors, twisting the Crawford ring ever more tightly. He took to studying the family portraits the Dalgliesh royals and their distinct features, interwoven among dukes and duchesses, members of the high courts. Lady Olivia had been right in saying Sir Dalgliesh and Sir Fredrick had an uncanny sameness. On more than one occasion during these night walks, Ben caught Lady Williamina staring up at a large oil painting of Fredrick Dalgliesh, flattered in military honors, one booted foot mounted against the head of a Zulu king. She muttered under her breath and ignored Ben as he passed her.

Ben marked the movements of the servants during the day, airing out the Eastern wing of guest rooms, polishing the floorboards and handrails of the great marble staircases. When asked why he didn't employ anyone from the half-constructed town, Sir Dalgliesh gave a little bounce on the balls of his feet. "Savages and low country folk. They don't know how to do a good proper clean. No, it is a very English art, you'll find."

At night, the manor fell into the damp moonwashed fog. All remained quiet, as though sitting shiva long before the dead made an appearance, except for the peacock. It skulked along the sprawling property, hidden among the hedgerows, or balancing on a parapet of the ivy-covered chapel.

Whostherewhostherewhosthere!

One night, there came an answer. "Me. I'm here."

Ben's breath hitched in his throat, and he eased away from the library window, folded into the dark corners between the vast leather bindings of family history, waffling collections of poetry, and the simple fiction Lady Olivia was so fond of flicking through but never actually read.

"Me. I'm here."

The voice was unrecognizable to him, but the incongruous shape was not. Lady Williamina, dressed in a nightgown so gauzy Ben saw the indecent curve of her thighs through the skirt, pierced through by the gas lamps flickering in the hall. She used that light to guide her way into the library and strode with purpose for a discarded book by one of the long windows. Her thin, prematurely gray curls fell down her back, cloaking the nubby remains of her arm. Ben stayed where he was, having read in a medical journal that it was dangerous to wake a sleepwalking woman because she would be prone to violence.

And, as her father said, she was unstable in her grief.

She nudged open the window, rocking back and forth on her bare feet, and began turning the pages of her book. The full moon dipped behind a cloudbank. but she sucked in the air as though its pale, reflective light fed her. Her frantic fingers stopped on a page two-thirds of the way into the tome. She began to mutter slow, low, and then faster until the chant slurred into a soothing spell. Or a warning. "Anheirlessssonanheirlesssonanheirlessson."

Disturbed, Ben crept quietly from the library, and in the following evenings, remained in his room. Still, he imagined, he heard the dancing call of the peacock and Lady Williamina answer.

Who's there?

An heirless son.

II. With This Ring, I Thee Wed

On the day of the wedding, the manor was festooned in lavender, bright orange dahlias, and camellias that throbbed pink. The family gathered, First Daughters off to one side, separate from their husbands, in the customary mourning dresses and blood red veils. Lady Johana's gown was a tiered wedding cake of prayer lace, raindrop pearls, her white veil held fast by rows of amethyst, no doubt shipped from their uncle's mines.

Sir Dalgliesh joined Lady Olivia at the front pew. Ben did not see Lady Williamina, but it was not a surprise. In mourning, she could attend no celebration, and as a discarded Crawford, her presence would be considered a bad omen.

Lady Johana took Ben's hand, her gloved thumb gently brushing over the Crawford ring that bit into his now blackened finger. The presiding priest, a Crawford by way of marriage to another cousin, thrice removed, prompted them through their vows. There was no ask for either bride or groom to promise sickness or health. Only the repeated promise that the marriage would be in richer and in wealth so long as they both shall live. Amen. "You may now join each other as one."

Ben raised Lady Johana's veil revealing her face, painted in precise and careful designs put there by her mother, sister, and the maidens.

"Bone of my bones, flesh of my flesh," quoted the priest, nodding to Lady Johana, who had hesitated as she raised Ben's left hand to her lips. "She shall be called Woman because she was taken from Man."

Her tongue was warm around his skin, and the exhale from her nostrils fogged the Crawford ring as she bit down on the necrotic tissue and swallowed his finger whole. The gold band clacked through her shining teeth, and she presented it to the priest, who blessed it and fixed it under her tongue. The elders grumbled, then gently clapped their hands with approval. Once the ceremony was over, it would be removed by Ben in a kiss and he would slip it onto her right finger where it would remain the rest of her days on earth or until she had a son. Whichever came first.

Ben was removed from the pulpit, a red silk cloth placed over the dribbling wound and led to a throne in the middle of the peach groves. There, he and the Crawford men, and those married into the family, watched the red veiled First Daughters bring forward Lady Johana and place her on a red velvet cushion. They tilted her face east, to accept the rising sun, and lifted her left arm. Crawford maidens dressed in white communion gowns brought forward their ribbons. Each had a different pastel color. They kissed Lady Johana's feet before looping their ribbon, one by one, over her arm. The First Daughters began to sing as they danced around Lady Johana, a grinning May Pole. *Blessed*, they said, *see how you are blessed?*

The morning slipped into late afternoon and with the final ribbons braided tight, the wedding party migrated to Lady Johana's beloved greenhouse. Bowls of rose water were placed along the white cloth tables, and champagne bubbled from a fountain fixed above the koi pond in a divine arch. The grumbling elders were sated with hors d'oeuvres on a silver serving tray, rimmed in the flower chains Lady Johana spent so many months making, was presented for Ben to hold.

The First Daughters escorted his bride, blushing with adrenaline, onto a tufted cushion facing Sir and Lady Dalgliesh. The maidens circled around her holding the fraying ends of their ribbons, waiting for the cut. The ribbon that fell first from the braid signaled the next to be wed. Lady Johana's eyes were glassy, her fixed smile radiant. Ben swallowed and steadied his hands before he tipped the serving tray. A flood of worry drenched his insides. What if he failed as a provider? What if he was not the proper sort of husband? What if she never became fond of him and the light in her eyes faded once the ceremony was over? What if they were the sort of people who only liked the idea of marriage, rather than the thing itself?

He quieted his mind, focused on the scene before him and what would happen next. The what ifs could wait. The only promise he had was this moment. Now. His new bride.

Lady Olivia kissed her daughter's painted cheeks and held firm to the slim, lace encrusted shoulders. The priest presented Sir Dalgliesh with a bone saw resting on a silk pillow. Precious stones glinted at the handle and were swallowed by Sir Dalgliesh's soft hands as he began sawing. It was a testament of devotion that Lady Johana's weeping remained silent. Tears and sweat smeared the swirling designs along her pretty face.

Sir Dalgliesh's movements were rough and quick, almost too fast for the maidens to see which ribbon fell first, or for the First Daughters to rush forward and collect the blood into a plain, clay bowl. Lady Johana's teeth began to chatter and clack against the ring that was meant to be tucked under her tongue. The First Daughters removed her veil, soaked it in the bowl, and fixed it back to her lovely tiara, nestled in the mountain of curls. Lady Olivia hiccuped and pressed her stained hands to her breast. "I'm so proud!"

Sir Dalgliesh brought the arm to Ben and placed it in the center of the flower chains. Ben's own father took a gold-plated carving knife, stripped the still pulsing flesh from the elbow joint to wrist, and placed it into Ben's open mouth. He held it there as he walked to the other end of the greenhouse, flora tickling his face as the elders spat upon the proffered arm, and out the back door. Husbands of The First Daughters waited by the fire they'd built and began to crackle the smooth, white epidermis. Ben swallowed the warm, raw flesh. It wriggled heavily down into his stomach. He turned, ready to show his mouth to the priest who would then bless a goblet of the blood that bride, groom, and Lady Olivia must drink to complete the union.

But as he turned, he saw a dark figure sweeping across the acreage. Unseen, the peacock wailed, *WHOSTHEREWHOSTHERE-WHOSTHERE!*

Ben and the other husbands rushed towards the greenhouse, but Lady Williamina had already breached the front. The wedding party froze in a strange tableau, so suddenly, that The First Daughters' red veils still fluttered.

Lady Johana turned her shining, wet face from Ben to her sister. Her teeth were bright against the smears of paint and blood. She spoke weakly, disoriented in her devotion, "Now all my favorite people are in one room!"

"Not too late! Not too late!" Lady Williamina cried out. Her movements were viper sharp and right arm strong, certain of itself, as she bowled past the weeping First Daughters and seized the gilded carving knife from Ben's father's slackened hand.

"It is the grief!" Lady Olivia grasped, begging the audience of her family to forgive the upset as Sir Dalgliesh tried to restrain his daughter from ruining the last half of the ceremony.

Sir Dalgliesh's walrus mustache billowed from his lips. "Apologize! Williamina this is unbecoming! What is the meaning of this?"

"To eat the heart of an heirless son is to break the curse forever!"

Lady Williamina slashed the carving knife and her father's neck split open.

"Oh, my Fredrick," Lady Olivia whispered. The only man who was not in attendance. A man so identical to his brother that a lonely housewife might take to his bed and hide the truth in the shape of their likeness. Her words alone were confirmation enough in the shaking silence caused by Sir Dalgliesh's sudden murder. He fell back on his knees, folded like a serving napkin, with his gloved fingers wrapped around a neck that pulsed with a sigh of air that was still warm.

And then The First Daughters shrieked.

Some fainted, while others demanded their husbands remove Lady Williamina from the greenhouse. Which they did, but she kicked and bit and continued to scream, "Eat the heart to break the curse! HIS HEART!"

Lady Johana looked waxen beneath the gore that shimmered across her diamond cut features. She fixed her sad eyes onto Ben's as her maiden cousins burst from their positions around her and rushed to the body of Sir Dalgliesh. Teeth bared, ribbing at the sinew, the loose muscles of his neck, drenched in the splatter of blood and intestine as they tore into his torso, to get at the heart. To devour. To break. Guts and rib bones splattered across tight corsets. The pillowy lungs were chewed and discarded. The lady mongrels fought over the choice cut: the heart. Let them be the ones to rid themselves of the curse. Let them keep their arms.

Ben watched Lady Johana, imagining he could hear the slow churn of her beating pulse over the crunch of bone and snap of raw tissue. The First Daughters and their husbands attempted to beat away the maidens but were met with snarls and frenzy. "More hearts! More hearts!"

The elders were turned onto the tables. The slick, loose skin of their bodies mixed into puff pastries and orange puddings. Their ribs cracked as easily as crab claws. They were licked clean to the tender parts.

With a smile, Lady Johana pushed her tongue through the center of his gold band. Ben saw pieces of himself wedged between her teeth. He stepped forward, slipping on the fresh rivers of guts that covered the flagstone. Cradling Lady Johana's chin in his hands, he extracted the ring with a gentle sucking of his lips and dipped her finger inside of him. She tasted of salt and talcum powder. And she was pale. So pale and lovely.

"I'm cold," she smiled sweetly.

"I'm right here with you," he told her.

III. Until Death Do Us Part

LOVE IN THE REEM

VINCENT ENDWELL

It was honestly funny how guys thought Christine's matter-of-factness about big life stuff was so threatening. As if she couldn't be seriously interested in a guy and *also* good at relationships, instead of falling over herself like they did around her. Guys felt the same way about Christine's obsession with true crime – at first kind of cute and shocking, but then they started to wonder if she was planning to kill them which wasn't even remotely why she liked true crime. Christine just had a tendency for weird shit to happen around her, and she felt she should be able to spot it. That was all.

Now, Dylan hadn't been like that. He had already liked true crime before they'd started talking about it together, and he had *also* been a fan of the Wine and Crime Club. They had talked about that podcast the first night they'd met at Zach's, talked about it for hours in fact. So maybe that was it, Christine thought. Maybe Dylan was a little savvier than the rest. Maybe that was why she was falling for him.

Despite being a relationship pragmatist, here she was with Dylan, waiting for bread under the fairy lights, and her heart was beating like a trapped frog bouncing. It would have been a warm Tennessee night even if it weren't February, and Christine was only wearing a light jacket, yet she was still sweating underneath her plastic gloves and white mesh veil. Across from her, Dylan appeared to be faring no better in his suit jacket, and he kept tugging at the collar with his polyethylene hands. His face was invisible beneath the swaying black veil made of the same material they made gym class jerseys out of, but she imagined his cheeks were probably red as the Valentine's hearts scattered across the tablecloth. He was the kind of pale Scandinavian blood that turns a livid hue when he blushes, part of why she thought he was adorable. She resolved to make him blush at least once every day as long as they were together. It was a stupid little promise, but it made her feel warm inside.

So maybe romance wasn't all bullshit.

"What a nice night," Dylan remarked. His throat was clearly a little tight, and Christine thought it cute that he got so nervous around her. He just wanted everything to go right all the time, little ex-honors student perfectionist. "I was so worried it was going to rain, and we weren't going to be able to sit outside."

"Of course you did, you nerd," Christine said, because when *she* got nervous, she started to tease him mercilessly. "You also probably wrote, *talk about the weather* on your notecards for when you can't think of anything to say."

"Okay, ow," said Dylan, injured, and she remembered he couldn't see her face to know she was joking, and so she put her hand across the table for his. He laced his plastic fingers through hers, the gripping ridges on the fingers rough and warm against the back of her hand. She loved how small her fingers looked in his-and hoped that this counted as an apology. "That was a low blow."

"I'm sorry," she laughed. At the table over, a woman wore a very thin white veil with fever-red lipstick smudged against the inside of it, leaving a bloody smear. Christine imagined her own awkwardness bleeding through just like that, invisible to her but obvious to everyone else, and tried to be fucking normal for once. "I'm an asshole, seriously. Tell me about your day."

The sky was muddy brown but bone dry. Beneath the patio, the water of the Splitridge Swamp lapped at the supports, and the crooning of the red-frogs sang all around like a Venetian serenade. Someone had scattered the accoutrements of Valentine's Day over the patio and restaurant like pox. When she'd entered, she had passed through a veil of hanging paper hearts and a pair of sliding glass door plastered with stickers of cartoon red frogs with Cupid wings. Some people might find them in poor taste, Christine guessed, but honestly, they were kind of cute even if the frogs were adorable little vectors of contagion. You couldn't be doom and gloom all the time, after all.

At their table, beside the bucket of stinking bleach sanitizer, a bloom of red roses and wax flowers sprayed out from a center piece, their petals and leaves threatened by the candleflame nestled within them. Christine was reminded vaguely of an Advent wreath; there was just something about it that felt religious, like it was promising that something would arrive.

Dylan laughed his big, awkward laugh, and began telling her how Zach, Kev, and him were going out again to look for the mill house. Christine sat up with sudden interest, like a dog perking up its ears at a can opener.

One of Christine and Dylan's joint true crime obsessions was, of course, the–murder of Jeremy Ries. This was one of the very first things they had talked about – the evidence pointing towards Colonel Langley, who could have set the fire that killed Hieronymus Johnson, the question of whether the mysterious "E. Haskill" had been a victim or an accomplice – and since meeting each other, they had only grown more fascinated with the story. Obsession fed obsession, after all, and Dylan and his crew were already explorers of a stripe. With Christine to bounce things off of, they'd been going out more and more lately, which Christine *loved*.

Dylan's story today had her on the edge of her seat. Him, Zach, Kev had all driven out to the mill house ruins, that site of Johnson's demise right out on the edge of the marsh. Langley might have killed Ries out there, too, it was a point of speculation in the whole sordid affair, though Christine was partial to the somewhat controversial 'Spirition theory. Before they'd reached the ruins, though, that idiot Zach got the truck into a patch of mud so deep it nearly took the thing off its axles. When Dylan went down the road to get help, though, he happened across a man named *Sline*.

"Do you know him?" Dylan asked, which Christine told him was a weird question, except that she *did* have a habit of encountering strange people, and she *did* have a habit of adding them to the running list in her mind of people to check up on if a strange murder ever occurred. She'd rehearsed, multiple times, the kind of information she would tell the cops if something truly fucked up ever happened in town. For instance, that harlequin performer who hung out by the Temple but wasn't an employee, she'd *checked*, or that lady with bug-eyes at the Wawa counter who had told her *in detail* how to cook red frogs, or that guy all in black rags who had followed her home one night, standing just outside the circle of the streetlight. She had actually almost called the cops on him, but he vanished as soon as she picked up the phone.

This Sline, though, she hadn't met. As Dylan relayed, it looked like he lived in this small shack, all rough wood with no windows, and he was sitting out down by the marsh, waxing an ancient rowboat. He was wearing outdated clothes, a style that a workman might wear in the 70's – a patterned red shirt and worn leather boots. When Dylan approached him for help, the man Sline looked up with these *eyes*, pale in an already pale face. They were gray and cataracted, but the man seemed to have no trouble seeing. When Dylan finished explaining, this Sline said nothing at all but simply got up and walked away, along the edge of the water.

Baffled and annoyed, Dylan went back to the others, but as they stood around arguing, they heard the growl of an engine back down the road. Sline had come back with an old, rusted truck with a winch, and after some effort got their truck pulled out of the sinkhole.

"Oh cool." Christine had to admit to herself she was a little annoyed that the guy ended up being helpful. "I thought he was going to come out with a gun."

"Well, but then he warned us that we shouldn't be in the marsh," Dylan said, leaning forward. And technically his forearms shouldn't have been touching the table, but it had been sanitized anyway, so what was the risk, and Christine wanted to hear the story. "He just kept saying that it was going to be a bad one. And that those 'Bible-thumpers' in town weren't going to be happy. Which…" He raised his shoulders to his ears, then lowered them back down like weakened hydraulics.

Christine told him that the story was fucked up and she loved it. Dylan said that he thought she would. He seemed way more at ease now that the awkwardness of veils and polyethylene and Valentine's Day formality was fading. He was so funny like that – such a sincere guy, just wants to do things the old-fashioned, proper way - but he should know the way to a girl's heart is by telling a bizarro creep story. She insisted that next time he went out to try to find the mill house, he *had* to take her along.

The server arrived with water and to take their order. A second passed where Christine couldn't tell their gender, and the plastic server's veil, cut with tiny holes and printed with pink hearts, sucked up against their mouth like a baby suffocating on a plastic bag. The voice was high, so Christine thought, *girl*? but she wasn't quite sure. There was something not quite right about the server's face in its outline against the plastic, something not a face's shape. And there was something about the set of their brow and eyes, as well, half-visible through the translucent print. It almost seemed like they were glaring at her. Like this waiter hated her with a fire low and deep.

They were saying this year's reem was worse than usual, though Christine thought people were overreacting. A week ago, someone had yelled at her in the store for taking her gloves off for a minute because her hands were sweaty, which seemed insanely extreme. It was just all so stressful anyway – people should cut each other more slack. Caroline in particular was the worst about it, hiding in her house all the time and barely talking to anyone. They'd had a blow-up a few weeks ago, too, and now Christine was waiting for an apology that probably wouldn't come.

You could buy veils at Family Dollar now, but this one she had ordered special so that her mother would stop yelling at her for wearing the disposable ones instead of the ones she'd kept in a box for decades. Her mother believed they made them better the last time the reem came; Christine was honestly not convinced but didn't want to argue.

"So," Dylan said, with the kind of low pronunciation that meant the start of a new conversation. His shoulders were tight, and he seemed to be knotting his hands underneath the table, plastic whispering against plastic. "Chrissy. Can we talk about… us?"

Christine's pulse quickened like someone realizing that the dance has started around them and they need to step in time. Usually, she was the one asking these questions – it was rare that the guy took point. "Yeah, of course," she said. Her chest felt tight, as if her heart had grown more lobes like a blooming flower. "So I feel like it's *pretty* clear we're dating at this point."

Dylan chuckled with relief, scratching the back of his neck again with a little more vigor. "I mean, I think so. I like you a lot, and I could really see a future for us. I'd like to take it a step at a time, but I'd like to keep, ah, keep talking about it with you, and such." He gulped like one of the frogs by the water. It seemed like he had approximately half of a rehearsed statement and had reached the end of it.

"Me, too," she said sincerely, chin on hand, skin touching glove. *Should she*—Well, whatever. "Do you think we should work through some of those early relationship questions? I know I've been thinking about – we should talk about what we want and where we see things going. Like, are marriage and kids even things you want, long-term?"

Dylan took a sip of water, carefully timed, lifting his veil just a little at the bottom to slip his glass beneath. The glass slid out of the veil, and he wiped his lips on the back of the polyethylene glove, beneath the black mesh. Now, you were really not supposed to do that, but again, *everything* was sanitized. Admittedly, there were some dead frogs lying on the sidewalk to their right, and the restaurant was pretty close to the water, but, like, what can you do? Not live your life?

His answer was up-front: he did want marriage, and he wasn't sure about having kids – not for a few years, certainly. That was hopeful, because that's about where Christine was. She dove into it, how she definitely saw herself married and had a few ideas for a wedding, but she had never been that into kids and would have to really think about it. She had a lot she wanted to do with her life and her career, and Dylan seemed positive about that. He nodded, said that building the tutoring business was important. He said it in a way that felt honest, not the kind of affect guys put on when they want to support your dreams but are going to turn around later and wonder why you're not in the kitchen.

He surprised her next with a question of his own – what were her dealbreakers? She had to think on that for a minute. There were a few more red frogs on the pavement by the water, warbling like a choir at gunpoint, some of them scuffling with each other like bulldogs having a fight. A lot more of them were dead than alive, she realized, little red bodies littering the mud like autumn leaves. Many of the shops on the boardwalk were boarded up or else the cracks stuffed with fabric, and the windows of the apartments above were cellophaned in layer upon layer of foggy plastic.

Movement behind the window of one apartment caught her eye, and she paused mid-sentence to make out the shape. There was someone standing behind the glass, blurred and ghostly, gazing down at the street and the diners and the water. They moved, and she saw that they were wearing a veil which she had mistaken for a curtain, they were standing so still.

"A dealbreaker. I mean, probably someone who doesn't take the reem seriously," Christine continued, more slowly. Her gaze kept being drawn back to the person, standing motionless behind the glass.

She started to wonder: if she had missed one person, could she have missed more?

Oh– she had. There were more people in those windows, in off-white veils like hanging drapes, all gazing down to the gentle lapping of the swamp. Her skin started to crawl with the realization that they must have been standing there the whole time, or else moved very slowly into place. Maybe they were waiting for a parade? Fireworks? An advent of something?

"Though not as insane as some people are about it, obviously," Christine said, warily. "I mean, if you're taking super unnecessary risks, that's not good, but like, I don't know, you have to go out for mental health reasons sometimes."

As she spoke, she dipped her hands into the bucket of bleach and sanitized the palms and backs of her gloves. Like a contagious yawn, Dylan did the same, rubbing bleach over his gloves and trying not to nick the edge of his suit jacket. He nodded along, and gave a thick little cough, like he had a frog in his throat – ha, ha – and was trying to hide it.

Christine considered. "I guess that applies to anything. Like, housecleaning. I think like… reasonable levels, you know?"

A sudden clatter of footsteps broke through the noise, and Christine spun to look. A black-clad figure emerged from behind the white buildings of the boardwalk and raced down the cobbled road. For a moment, she almost thought she recognized them and grabbed Dylan's hand before she was sure.

But it wasn't the man in all the black rags who had followed her that one time. This person *was* dressed all in black, though. Their footsteps pounded like sudden drumbeats, and Christine's heart pounded faster, no longer just from an incipient crush.

The person careened up the brick street of the commons, racing urgently like an emergency surgeon's knife. It wasn't so strange these days to see someone covered from head-to-toe, but there was something costume-like about this person's clothes – the shorn rags, the tight bindings on their legs, the slippers that so neatly danced around the dying bodies of the frogs on the sidewalk.

Then the runner slowed, staring at the restaurant and its outdoor diners through that dark feathery veil. For a moment, they were only about twenty feet away, looking right at Christine and Dylan.

Christine's skin crawled, and her throat suddenly seized with sandy dryness. She crunched Dylan's fingers beneath hers, looking for reassurance that she wasn't crazy, that this person really was just *staring* at them.

Then the stranger croaked loudly, with a voice muffled and hoarse and strung through with incredulity.

"Idiot lovers of plague!"

Heads turned across the patio, swaying in their black and white veils. Christine flinched, sudden shock crawling up her spine as the runner continued, voice tolling and falling against the rippling water.

"Disease-spreaders! Sickness-bearers! The frogs love you! The frogs worship you! You are fuckers of frogs! You are married to bacteria! Your children will be pestilence and vermin!"

Silence hovered like an archway about to fall.

Then the interloper started racing once more as if time was limited, time was running out, dodging around the frogs like a hopping heron and vanishing into the dark. People started to chatter, gossiping and discussing first with confusion, then anger, then laughter. Christine released her grip on Dylan's fingers only long after the figure had left sight. The white-veiled watchers, unnoticed by the other diners, stood still in the windows.

"What the fuck?" Dylan said.

Christine laughed uncomfortably, trying to shrug off the dread coming over her like a chill. "That was so fucking rude. Also, incredible timing," she said. "That's exactly the dealbreaker I mean. If you start, like, *berating* random people, it's totally over."

Dylan laughed roundly. "Great, I'll remember not to do that."

"Wow, really glad we had this talk."

Christine sipped water to clear the blockage from her throat. She still felt tight inside, and it hadn't really lessened since the start of the date. She must have been more nervous than she thought for all this pressure to be inside her ribs and jaw. She started to feel the onset of a headache, as though her stress and nerves and general sense of romance had all crawled up inside her skull like mice inside the drywall. The sip of water did nothing, just made more obvious how dry and *hot* her throat was. The faint taste of bleach didn't do much for her either.

"Actually," she said, rasping a little, "that was exactly the kind of weirdo I attract, for whatever reason. So maybe that should be your dealbreaker if you date me. Whatever curse I have is going to rub off on you, and you're going to start getting all sorts of creeps around you as well. Like *Sline*."

Dylan squeezed her hand. "Honestly? That sounds awesome. I'd love to encounter crazy weirdoes with you any day."

Christine laughed but also kind of meant it. Her heart fluttered again, seaweed in a warm, shallow current.

"By the way," said Dylan, reaching beside him to a bag he had kept hidden beneath the table. He pulled it up and set it on the table (which he probably shouldn't have done – contact-mediated disease and all that, but whatever), and it was red and glittery and Christine was already excited, despite herself. His voice warbled a little again. He was *so* nervous, and he gulped again, a broad and silly sound. "I was going to wait until later, but now actually seems like a really good time. I got you some presents."

The waiter came back, and there was a little flurry as they left their plates before them, but honestly Christine barely noticed. Dylan pulled out a wrapped package first and handed it to her. She struggled to open it through the gloves, and so she pulled one off and set it to the side. When she pried open the paper, she gasped with joy.

It was a bullet journal, with a soft cover and an elastic strap around the side, and it was printed with something she recognized immediately – the original typewritten text of Jeremy Ries' last work, *A Pyramid Fit for a King*, which was entered into evidence in Colonel Langley's trial and conviction for Ries' murder. It was the same color as the yellowed paper, the strange and haunting words wrapped all around, and it was exactly the kind of esoteric and macabre and *fun* that she loved.

"You know me *so well*," she said, laughing, flipping through the soft and round-edged pages. Her heart was full to bursting. "Dylan! I swear to god you asshole! You know me so well!"

He laughed, looking at her in a way that (she imagined) was full of endearing happiness. "I thought you might like it. It seemed like your style. Organized, pretty, murder-related."

"You asshole, it's so good!"

"There's one other thing," he said and pulled out an envelope. Christine took it. In the corner of her eye, she realized that the waiter had never actually left – they had been standing just a little ways away, with what almost looked like a cruel smile on their face beneath the heart-printed plastic like a weirdo. Ignoring them, Christine slit open the envelope and pulled out normal printer paper – and then realized what was printed on it.

Two tickets to a live taping of the Wine and Crime Club – happening here, in town, down at the Lenore in just a week. They were recording an episode on the mill house fire and the death of Jeremy Ries.

There was a sudden high-pitched noise, and she realized it was her, squealing with excitement. Distance and touch be damned – she got up and embraced him, squeezing him to her with all her strength. His face felt misshapen beneath the veil, but she must be wrong, it was so weird that they had to wear all this fabric all the time.

"How did you know?" she exclaimed. "Was it because I talk about this all the time!? Oh my god, Dylan, this is the *best*, you have no idea how excited I am!"

The singing of the frogs crescendoed like an orchestra, piercingly loud. Ripples lapped in the water like a tongue. Someone coughed wetly at a table nearby. Something clicked in her head, and the thought crossed her mind that the reason the waiter's face looked so misshapen was because of bandages, wrapped around their chin and head, covering some kind of injury or protrusion. Had the waiter even said a single word? Had she heard them speak?

"I thought you'd like it," Dylan said, and she could hear his cute smirk, even though his voice was a little thick. "I figured we could go together next week – it should be a great show –"She wanted him in her life, sharing every weird moment, visiting the sites of murders and arsons, laughing at the macabre. God, it was so stupid that they couldn't just kiss; they were already eating food, outside, by the edge of the water. She lifted his veil and hers and pressed her lips to his.

Her heart expanded again. A lump seemed to grow in her throat and just behind her eyes. His tongue tasted odd, swollen and feverish, and the heat of crush and the chill of disgust fought in her like scuffling frogs. She couldn't seem to catch her breath. As she pulled back, she noticed a lump in his cheek, like a jawbreaker pressed against his teeth. Dylan was completely flustered, absolutely Valentine-red, and he laughed again.

Then when he spoke, that lump protruded like another tongue beside his, poking out of his mouth. It was an eye. Bulbous and frantic, the yellow iris flicked in the fleshy socket like it was looking for someone in a pushing, shifting crowd.

"I'm glad you like it," he said, sloppily. Another eye roved beneath his cheek, yellow and peering, a curious bystander. Confusion, fear, dull happiness blurred in her. She reached up and touched her own throat with her unclean gloves, and found a lump bulging beneath the skin like a ripening fruit.

The coughing around them grew worse. People doubled over their meals, lungs heaving damply, roundly. Dylan started to cough again as well, and this time it was productive. Eyes, each hanging by a long viscous red string, fell from his mouth like egg sacs, or a bloom of flowers. More and more sagged from his mouth, filling his mouth, becoming his mouth. Christine's head throbbed like it wanted to split, little viscous balls cracking their way from her skull as if through a shell. They pressed and oozed beneath her dress, between her ribs. Her head throbbed with the eyes behind her eyes, and her vision warped, then turned red, then black.

For a moment there was nothing.

Then sight reemerged, fractured, flicking in many uncontrollable directions all at once. She watched, she stared, she gazed, and she saw him right before her, and all that hope and liking flowed out like a font. Eyes dripped down her face like tears of joy, each telling her with bright and glittering detail: *romance isn't dead.*

It was just like having a crush. The pressure built and built until she couldn't take it, and yet she felt so wonderful. Amid all the torturous confusion, the amorous bafflement, the anxious, agonizing beauty, she wouldn't trade it away for anything.

"I don't just like it. I love it," she said, and her words fell muffled and thick through her mouthful of staring, roving eyes. "I honestly can't wait. You've made me really, really happy."

PERFECT GENTLEMEN

KEVIN M. FOLLIARD

Jolene wrapped the final tress of her hair around the hot curling iron. She twisted, held, and released. An auburn spiral bobbed alongside her ear, and she shook her head with pride.

She struck a pose and admired herself in the full-length mirror. Her black dress slimmed her curves; she swirled the skirt, spinning to show off her other side. All her life, she'd thought herself homely, fat, pug-nosed. But finally, she knew better. She was gorgeous. Johnny had told her so.

Johnny had been the first person to tell her she was pretty. The first person she'd believed at least. Daddy always said she was pretty. But that's what Daddies did. Treated their daughters like princesses. Kept them safe in their castles.

Jolene was almost thirty years old, and Daddy still insisted on meeting men before she could date them. She'd met Johnny just a few weeks ago, but already she knew he was the real deal—her perfect match. She wanted to keep him secret from Daddy's prying eyes for a little while longer.

Jolene explored the oak jewelry chest in her walk-in closet. She selected a set of pearl earrings along with a diamond studded purse. She fingered a long pearl necklace. Around her neck, she always wore the wooden whistle Daddy had given her as a child. The whistle was carved from cypress in the shape of a gator skull, and it was attached to a silver chain. It definitely didn't go with the outfit. She removed it, tucked it into her purse, and then fixed the pearls around her neck.

She took one last look at her low-cut summer ensemble and blew her reflection a kiss before leaving her room. She descended the steps and knocked on the glass doors of Daddy's study. He looked up from his reading, smiled beneath his white mustache, and beckoned her in.

"Just wanted to say g'nite, Daddy!"

He eyed her top to bottom. "Where on Earth is a daughter of mine goin', showin' that much skin?"

"Daddy!" she huffed. "This is how all the girls dress in the heat!"

"You look like you're goin' on a date." He raised a bushy eyebrow and took a sip of his sazerac.

"I'm not." She crossed the room and kissed Daddy's cheek. "It's a fundraiser at the school. A benefit for the women's shelter."

"You're not in school anymore, Jolene."

"Well I still have friends!" she said. "At the university. It's important to give, you know."

"I know," he said. "I'll be waitin' up for you."

Jolene glared. "Don't, Daddy. I'm a grown woman."

He sighed. "Where's your whistle?"

She rolled her eyes. "In my purse, Daddy."

"I want you to wear that all the time."

"Doesn't go with the outfit, Daddy. I've got it, though. You worry too much."

"Not only am I an old-fashioned old man," he took her hand, "but I will always be your Daddy. And I will always worry. You look gorgeous, Princess. Be careful."

"I will!" She blew her father a kiss before she exited the study. "*Don't* wait up!"

Jolene stepped into the muggy, ninety-seven degree night. She fanned herself as she made her way to her yellow convertible. "Lord Almighty!" she declared. "I'll be sweatin' like a pig before he even sees me!" She put the roof up and blasted the air conditioner.

She hit the remote on her visor, and the front gate creaked opened. Jolene's car rumbled over the marsh bridge. She pictured Johnny's perfect smile. *It doesn't matter if I'm sweatin' like a pig,* she thought. *That fool boy would still make me feel like a movie star.* She squealed aloud.

They had met at a Bourbon Street bar. Not quite a hole in the wall, but not the kind of place Daddy would have approved of either. Jolene had exhausted her options in high society. This was uncharted territory—a place where Jolene thought just maybe a nice, normal fella might be waiting.

A big oaf, with a sloping brow and red veins on his nose had started hitting on her. She was flattered at first. She rarely received attention from gentlemen. But then the oaf started getting frisky, right there at the bar. Jolene repeatedly told him to stop, but the man was drunk. She was just about ready to scream for help, when Johnny came along. He tapped the oaf's shoulder, reprimanded him, and socked him right on his big red nose. The drunk scrambled for the door, tail between his legs.

Johnny had been such a gentleman, making sure she was okay, calming her down. Jolene's heart had been racing so fast that it took her a full minute to even notice Johnny's picture-perfect smile, neatly combed dark hair, and soft brown eyes with flecks of gold around the edges. Needless to say, her heart rate quickened right back up again, but in a good way.

They'd seen each other just four times since then, but every time Johnny had been a perfect gentleman. Johnny loved music. He was in a jazz band, but only for fun. His real job was working at a shipping yard on the Mississippi. "A fella's gotta have humble origins and make something of himself," Johnny had said. "I've got my passions, but my head is fixed firmly to neck and shoulders." He had sounded just like Daddy in a way: self-made and self-reliant.

Johnny didn't even drink. He had only been out that night for his cousin Tyler's bachelor party. "Only a glass of champagne at weddings," Johnny had said. "I like to stay on my toes. That's how I'm able to protect beautiful ladies." Jolene ate up every word that came out of Johnny's mouth like it was honey.

Her phone vibrated inside her purse. Normally, nothing could take Jolene's eyes off the road, but the thought it could be Johnny trumped safety. She reached over and fished it out: *So happy 2 C U! Im 15 mins urly!* She swooned as she read the text, then swerved to stay out of the opposite lane.

After twenty minutes of dark country roads, Jolene arrived at Johnny's uncle's cabin. It was built on a deck overlooking the bayou. She stepped out of her air-conditioned car into the humid oven of the Louisiana night. Before she was even halfway to the door, it swung open revealing Johnny's tall strong silhouette.

He put his hand above his eyes. "Is that an angel I see comin' up my walkway?"

Jolene giggled. "It might be a greasy pig, I'm afraid!"

"Don't you talk like that about my girl!" Johnny raced down and grabbed her.

Jolene squealed with delight. "I'm all sweaty, Johnny!"

"No one's sweatier'n me, darlin'!" He kissed her long and hard. After he released her, she got a good look at him in the moonlight. His dark hair matted against his head; beads of sweat ran down his perfect forehead and chiseled jaw.

"Hot dang! Your uncle doesn't have air conditioning?" she asked.

Johnny shook his head. "Can't get it to work. Would you rather go out to a restaurant? I've got a bottle of wine on ice. I was gonna fan you out on the deck."

"Mmm." She kissed his cheek. "That sounds perfect. Let's stay here."

Johnny fingered her pearls. "Well, aren't you extra beautiful tonight? I'm afraid I'm under dressed." Johnny was wearing a black polo and khaki shorts with tennis shoes.

"You're not underdressed." She gestured to her own ensemble. "You're just *this* special."

"You know how to make a gentleman blush." Johnny guided her by the arm. "Right this way." He escorted her up the walkway to the front door and held it open. "Ladies first."

Jolene brushed his arm and giggled as she entered. Inside, the cabin was small and dark. Two men stood across the room. She paused, startled. She had thought it would be just the two of them. The smaller man had a narrow face, buck teeth, and a blond widow's peak. She recognized him. "Oh," she said, trying to be polite. "Your cousin Tyler's here. Well that's . . ." her eyes shifted to the other man, ". . . nice."

The hulking man wiped the sweat off his sloped brow with a massive fist. Snot dribbled under his red nose. It was the oaf from the Bourbon Street bar.

The door slammed and locked.

Jolene spun around. "Johnny, what's this all about?"

Johnny smiled. "Relax, cupcake, nobody's gonna hurt you." Gone was all the charm and sweetness of Johnny's normal voice, replaced by cold indifference.

"Hurt me? Johnny, I'm scared."

Johnny smiled. "Scared and stupid both." Jolene rushed the door, but Johnny grabbed her by the arms. "I said relax!" he shouted. "It's in your best interest to cooperate, *angel*."

Jolene screamed as the two men grabbed her from behind. She struggled and twisted uselessly.

Johnny fished into his pockets and produced a white rag and a small bottle. He untwisted the cap. "Stop strugglin', girl." He held the rag to the top of the bottle and poured.

"Help me!" Jolene screeched.

"Nobody'll hear." Johnny approached.

"Johnny, please!"

"*That* Johnny's a fairytale, Princess." He held the rag against her face. "Now take a deep, calming breath."

Johnny sneered. His gold eyes glinted. Jolene's vision faded to white.

***

Johnny supervised while Earl and Tyler carried Jolene's unconscious body to the van. Earl had her under the arms, and Tyler trailed behind, holding her feet. Earl let her upper half thud on the floor of the van.

"You stupid hick!" Johnny called. "I told you, we don't hurt her! Treat her good and get her back in one piece. A good kidnapping and ransom should be a painless operation!"

Tyler chuckled. "Painless my butt! You're the one that broke her heart. She'll never forget that. Not in a million years!"

Johnny spit. "That's nothin'. That's kid stuff. If I didn't break her heart, some gold-digger would've. Rich girls with rich daddies and faces like that don't have a prayer. I did her a favor. The family won't even miss the money we're askin' for, and she lives out the rest of her life as a stinking rich, stinking ugly old maid. Win-win."

"Sure," Tyler said. "Whatever you say, Johnny."

Johnny lit a cigarette. "Tie up her arms and legs; be gentle."

"How come we gotta do all the work?" Earl grumbled.

"Cuz you two are idiots." Johnny took a drag, held it in, and puffed out. "Besides, I kissed that girl no less than ten times. On the lips. I did all the dirty work."

Tyler snickered like a hyena as he uncoiled a length of rope. "You really are a pig, Johnny. You're the reason why none of us nice guys can't never get a date."

"That and you're ugly." Johnny flicked ash on the dirt. "Let's get a move on, gentlemen."

Tyler took the first shift behind the wheel, and Johnny rode shotgun. Earl remained in back with the unconscious girl.

"Hand me the purse," Johnny said. Earl passed up a small black bag studded with diamonds. Johnny whistled. "Dang purse is worth more than the two of you put together." He opened it and fished inside: gum, tissues, makeup, a silver chain with a wooden charm. At last, he found the girl's phone. He scrolled through the contacts until he found *Daddy*.

"Daddy," he laughed. "Pushin' thirty and saves her father's name in her phone as *Daddy*."

He composed a text message: *Sir: your daughter has been kidnapped. We have reasonable demands which we'll forward soon. The girl is safe. Be smart. Keep the police out of it.* He sent the message and chucked the phone out the window.

"Why'd you do that, Johnny?" Tyler asked.

"They can trace these things. We'll send the demands separate. Untraceable calls. I've got a system up north."

"Where we goin', boss? Dallas?" Earl called from the back.

"We're not crossin' state lines until this is over. That's a rookie mistake, gets the FBI involved right quick. I got a safe house north of Shreveport. Great place to lay low."

"What happens if the old man doesn't give in?" Tyler asked.

"He will."

"Yeah, but what if he doesn't. I'm just askin'."

"He will," Johnny repeated. "His daughter's his life, means more to him than money. I gotta say, his girl was easy pickins. Head over heels. That's what happens when you shelter your kids. They turn into Gullible Gerties."

"What do you know about kids?" Tyler said.

"I know about women, and I know about kids, and I know about brainless hicks who should shut up and drive," Johnny said.

"Don't expect us to shut up when it's time to divvy up that ransom money." Tyler laughed uneasily.

"You'll be handsomely compensated," Johnny said. "Handsome enough for a couple of Bayou Billies, at least."

***

Jolene awoke to gravel crunching under tires. She tried to open her eyes, but the lids pulled back down again like lead weights. A car door opened, and balmy air swooped over her body. Strong hands squeezed her limbs and carried her.

"Easy now!" came Johnny's voice. "Just get the old swine indoors."

Jolene struggled to open her eyes. Her vision unblurred and a sea of stars sparkled above her. She turned her head and saw a grassy meadow in the moonlight. A black creek snaked off into the distance. "Johnny . . ." she said. "Leggo."

"She's wakin' up," came another voice.

"Then get her in," Johnny said.

Jolene closed her eyes again. She heard a door open and iron hinges creak. The men laid her on straw, and the metal gate clanged shut.

Johnny said, "Earl, stay with the girl."

Jolene struggled to sit. She rubbed her eyes and opened them. She was in an old barn with a big wooden door and high ceiling. The hulking man, Johnny's friend Earl, stood by the door with his arms crossed. She moved forward and banged her forehead on hard metal.

"Ow!" She rubbed her head. Iron bars surrounded her; some kind of animal cage. Jolene grabbed the bars and shook. "You let me out of here!" She screamed, "Help! Let me out of here! Help!"

Earl shook his head. "Nobody around here, miss. Not for miles. Save your voice."

Jolene slumped. How could she have been so stupid? How could she have thought any man could be as perfect as Johnny? She should have listened to her daddy.

The thought of Daddy made Jolene grab for the chain around her neck, but she only found the pearl necklace. She looked up at Earl. "My purse," she said. "I need my purse. Where is it?"

"You'd best be quiet 'til Johnny gets back." Earl picked his big red nose.

Jolene tried to mask her revulsion. "Sir. Mr. Earl, please. May I please have my purse?"

"It's in the van," he said.

"Could you fetch it for me? I'd appreciate it."

"Johnny threw your phone out the window," Earl said. "You're outta luck."

Jolene nodded. "Makes sense; you're smart men. Really, I know that. But as it turns out it's not my phone I care about right this minute. Please, would you fetch my purse?"

"What for?"

Jolene choked out a low sob. "I have medication, sir."

Earl glared. "Medication?"

"Anti-anxiety pills. Please. If I could calm down, I think . . . I think that would make all of this go smoothly. It's money y'all are after, right?"

Earl stared.

"My daddy'll pay. No worries. But it'll be best for me if I can try to relax."

Earl scratched his head. "I don't know about this."

"Mr. Earl, I can tell you're a kind man. I can tell about people; it's a gift. This is all about money. Johnny put you up to this. This isn't what you'd normally do if you had another choice. I can see it in your eyes. I saw it there that night when I first met you at the bar. You know there's no harm in giving me my pills. I got no phone. There's no harm."

"No funny business?" Earl said.

"None whatsoever."

Earl nodded. He pushed through the barn door. Jolene watched him rummage in the back of a white van. He returned moments later with her diamond studded purse. He opened it and fished through. "Which bottle?"

"Better just give me the whole purse, so I can read the labels myself," she said.

Earl hesitated, and then passed the purse through the bars.

Jolene found the silver chain. She lifted it out, revealing the wooden reptile skull. She placed the snout of the whistle between her lips and blew.

***

Outside, Johnny heard a long, high-pitched squeal, like a train halting on rusty tracks. The sound ended with a strange guttural growl.

"The heck was that?" Tyler asked.

"Not sure." Johnny quickened his pace to the barn and pushed the door wide open. The girl sat in the straw behind bars, smiling like the cat that swallowed the canary. She twisted a small object in her hand, attached to a silver chain. The diamond studded purse lay beside her in the straw. "You stupid, Earl? Why'd you give her that?"

"She said she wanted pills," Earl said.

"She's a liar!" Johnny reached through the bars and snatched the purse. "We don't know what else she might have hidden."

"It's too late," the girl said.

"Ain't nobody around here for ten miles to hear your bird call, stupid," Johnny snapped. "Hand over that thing; it's annoying."

"I won't blow it again," Jolene said. "Won't need to. What's done is done." She exhaled in satisfaction.

Johnny looked her up and down. "Whatever makes you happy, Princess." He took out a phone. "Listen up. I'm callin' your daddy. This phone is untraceable, and we're gonna make this whole transaction easy as pie. When I put the phone to your ear, tell Daddy everything's peaches and that he should pay up ASAP. Got it?"

Jolene shrugged. "Sure. I ain't worried now."

Johnny eyed her suspiciously. He dialed the number.

The phone rang four times before the old man answered. "Hello?"

"Hello, Colonel Unger. Your daughter is safe, and she'll remain that way so long as you cooperate."

After a long pause, the girl's father said, "I understand."

"Good. Now, I trust you took me seriously and did not involve the authorities. I guarantee that would make this entire situation stickier for both parties, and nobody wants that."

Another long pause. "I understand."

"You say you understand, but does that mean you have not involved the authorities in any way?"

"I have not involved the authorities in any way," Colonel Unger said.

"I have your word on that?"

"You do."

"You're a smart man, and I respect that. My demands are reasonable, and I have no desire to drag out any unpleasantness. Six million dollars for the safe return of your daughter."

"Six million," he repeated.

"That's chump change for you, Colonel, and you know that. I'm not a greedy man. Just a man who wants to live comfortably for a long while."

"Six million dollars is doable," the old man said. "It'll take time to gather the funds. I'd rather not arouse suspicion."

"We wouldn't want that," Johnny said. "Following this phone call, you will receive a text message with routing numbers and wiring instructions to an offshore account. When the money clears, we will arrange for your daughter's safe return. Sound good?"

There was a long pause. "I want to talk to Jolene."

"Colonel, I thought you'd never ask," Johnny said. "Say hello to your daddy, angel." Johnny held his hand over the receiver and whispered. "Make it nice and sweet." He held the phone to her.

"Daddy?" Jolene said. "Hello, Daddy . . . . I'm so sorry, Daddy. I should have listened to you . . . . Oh no, I'm okay . . . . Well, you needn't worry about that, Daddy . . . That's right. I blew the whistle . . . . Mmm hmm . . . . Of course he'll hear it." She let out a girlish giggle. "Give it time. He'll make it."

Johnny yanked the phone away and glared at Jolene. He put the phone back up to his ear. "That's enough. You can hear that your daughter's in high spirits."

"Yes sir," the Colonel said. "Please take good care of her, and I promise you'll get what's coming to you."

"Much obliged," Johnny said. "Good evening, Colonel." He ended the call, then scrolled through his messages and found the prepared wiring instructions.

"You sure he didn't call the cops?" Tyler asked.

"Hard to say." Johnny sent his text. "We'll take his word for now."

"You sure that phone's untraceable?" Tyler rubbed his palms nervously.

"Stop worrying." He glanced at Jolene. "And you! What the heck were you talking about? Let me see that whistle."

Jolene held it against her chest. "It's mine! A gift from Daddy."

"Give it here, or I'll have Tyler shoot you in the leg."

"You wouldn't!" she protested.

"Boss, I don't wanna shoot her in the leg," Tyler said.

"You'll do it if I tell you to."

Tyler turned to Jolene and shrugged. "Yeah, I probably would. Just show him the whistle, Princess."

She inched towards the bars and held out the wooden whistle. Johnny grabbed it and pulled it through, but the girl clutched her end of the silver chain tight. "Don't take it away from me."

He turned it over in his hands. It was carved out of cypress in the shape of a lizard skull. He tossed it back through the bars. "It's just wood, thought it might be electronic. A pager or something."

She shook her head. "Much better than that. My daddy gave it to me. Got it from a very special family friend."

"And who's that?"

The girl's smile widened. "Gator Snout."

Johnny stared at the girl. "What kinda stupid name is Gator Snout?"

"It's a good name for a swamp monster," she said.

"Your daddy got that whistle from a swamp monster?"

Jolene nodded. "And I blew it, and now he's comin'. He's gonna rescue me, and the whole lot of you are gonna die."

Johnny exchanged glances with Earl and Tyler, then the three of them busted out laughing. Jolene laughed along with them. "It's true," she said. "I know it sounds funny, but it's absolutely one hundred percent true."

Johnny clutched his sides, trying to calm himself. He reached through the bars and mussed up Jolene's red curls. "Oh girl, you're gonna be *fun!*"

She giggled and flopped back in the hay. "I'm *serious*, Johnny. Gator Snout can hear that call from anywhere in the world. He'll come stridin' on up from the bayou in the dead of night." Her smile faded. "And he will rip the three of you apart."

Earl stopped laughing. "That's not funny, Johnny."

Johnny ignored him. "You're gettin' a little ahead of yourself, Princess. There's a swamp monster, named Gator Snout, and he's gonna help you *why* exactly?"

"Because he owes my Daddy the favor," Jolene said. "You see years ago before I was born, when my Daddy's company was brand new, they acquired a piece of land east of New Orleans, deep in the marsh. He got it for real cheap; but he knew if he pumped it dry, filled it with concrete, and built a couple factories, he'd be sittin' pretty."

"Uh huh." Johnny lit a cigarette.

"But as soon as they started development, machinery kept gettin' smashed. Soon, workers were disappearin'. Just gettin' sucked right down into the murk. Only their bones ever came back up."

"Well, I'll be darned." Johnny flicked ash.

"A Voodoo priest told Daddy that somethin' lived there. Something primal—ancient as the Earth. Older than America. Older than the Native Americans."

"Gator Snout, huh?" Tyler snickered.

Jolene nodded. "Uh-huh. Gator Snout is immortal. He's got long, powerful legs and arms, with big sharp claws, a bony whip-like tail, pointy spines along his back, and sharp jaws with thousands of teeth. He's as pitch black as outer space with big red eyes, fifteen feet tall and almost forty feet in length."

"Oooh!" Johnny puffed a cloud of smoke. "Easy now, girly. You're scarin' Earl."

Earl looked away. "No, she ain't."

"Well my Daddy didn't want any more trouble. He agreed that he'd never develop on that land, and he'd never sell that land to anyone who might. Turns out Gator Snout was grateful. He gave Daddy this whistle." She held up the little wooden skull. "Said any time my Daddy or one of his kin was in danger, all they had to do was blow."

"That a fact?" Johnny chuckled.

"You bet it is. And now the three of you are gonna regret all this. Boy are you ever."

Johnny tossed his cigarette on the dirt floor and snuffed it out with his boot. "Sounds interesting, sugar pie. You don't think this is just a tall tale your Daddy told you at bedtime to make you feel good and safe?"

Jolene huffed. "It's true. You'll see. Gator Snout's comin'. I've never blown that whistle before because I've never wished it upon anyone until now."

"You've never blown it before, so how do you know he'll come?" Tyler asked, a dumb smirk plastered over his face. "What if he don't hear it?"

"That's right, we're pretty far away," Johnny said. "I'm sure Gator Snout means well, Princess, but he's a busy fella. Can't be everywhere at once, you know."

"He'll come," she said, stone-faced.

"Listen closely, girl." Johnny leaned forward. "The only thing that's going to save you is six million dollars of your Daddy's money. That's it."

"No amount of money's worth this." She spat in the hay.

"Spoiled little rich girls who never grow up and never stop believin' in their rich Daddy's stories don't understand what money's worth." Johnny spit through the bars, between Jolene's eyes.

She wiped her forehead. "No. I mean nothin's worth what's gonna happen to you. *Nothin'.*"

* * *

The following day, the old barn baked like an oven in the summer heat. Jolene spent the day splayed out on the straw like an animal, beads of sweat running down her neck and chest. Earl had set up an industrial fan by the door, but all it did was blow hot air around. Johnny had disappeared for the day with the van. Earl and Tyler took shifts; neither one spoke or made eye contact.

Jolene fanned herself with her purse. Her black dress itched, but she had nothing else to wear. *They'll be sorry,* she thought. *Gator Snout's still makin' his way up here. Slow but sure. And when he gets here . . .*

In the middle of the afternoon, Earl brought her a tall glass of ice water, which she guzzled in seconds. She kept her eyes on him as he dozed against the wood walls. She crunched ice cubes in her mouth one by one. *That's what it'll be like when Gator Snout crunches their bones,* she thought. *Crunch. Crunch. Crunch.*

When Jolene finished her ice, she hid the glass in the straw. She cradled the wooden whistle in her hands. *He'll be here soon,* she assured herself. *Probably nightfall. It took him a day, that's all. Maybe he only travels in the dark.*

The sky outside the half-open barn door was turning pink when Johnny's white van pulled up. He got out and had words with Tyler, but Jolene couldn't hear. After a few minutes, Johnny relieved Earl and approached the bars. He tossed a brown paper bag at Jolene's feet.

"Eat."

Jolene opened the bag. The stench of onions and beef wafted out. "It's a hundred degrees in here, and you brought me a burger?"

Johnny shrugged. "Wait a while. It'll get cold."

"You're a pig." She picked out a piece of hamburger bun and ate it.

"I saw your friend Gator Snout while I was out." Johnny smiled. "Said he wanted a cut of the ransom money. I said fine."

Jolene picked at a piece of hamburger. "You wouldn't be smilin' if you really saw him."

Johnny laughed.

"You won't be laughin' soon."

"You're funny, Princess. I'm sorry about how all this went down. Really, I am."

Tyler entered the barn. "Hey, Johnny. You'd better see this." He handed Johnny his smartphone.

Johnny's smile faded. "Billionaire industrialist Colonel Arnold Unger's Daughter Missing," he read aloud. "Son of a snake!" He threw Tyler's phone across the barn.

"Hey! Easy there!" Tyler chased after his phone.

"You know what this means?" He punched the wall next to Jolene's cage. "It means your fool Daddy's gone behind our backs and gotten the police involved! And some dope broke the story! Well that's it." He pulled out his phone. "The price goes up."

"Hey Johnny," Tyler said. "We need to think this through."

"Shut your hick hole and let smart people do the thinking!" Johnny held the phone to his ear. "Hello, Colonel. I can't help but notice that not only is my account empty, but the whole dang internet is ablaze about your little lost Princess!"

Johnny shook his head; his face burned red. Jolene could make out her father's faint pleas.

"It sounds like you've got a whole world of sorry excuses, Colonel. You know what this means, of course. Price goes up. Double for every day you keep us waitin'. Startin' today. Twelve million. If I don't have my money by midnight tonight: twenty-four million."

"Johnny, Jeez!" Tyler whispered.

"No excuses. I tried to be reasonable, make this whole thing painless, and you went and ruined that . . . . That's more like it."

Jolene clutched her whistle. *Poor Daddy,* she thought. *Worried sick. He's gotta know. He's gotta know these are dead men. Once I blew the whistle, that was it for them.*

"You just give me a moment on that, Colonel." Johnny held the phone up to his chest and whispered to Jolene. "You make nice and comfy now, hear?"

Jolene nodded.

Johnny held the phone through the bars, and Jolene cozied up to it. "Daddy?"

"Jolene," Daddy sobbed. "Jolene, I will do anything for you. I'll pay anything, don't you worry. This'll all be over soon, sweetheart."

"Don't you dare pay, Daddy," she said. "I blew the whistle. Just sit tight."

"Jolene . . ." he sobbed. "Jolene, you know . . . that might not work, you know. And I'm just going to do everything I can—"

"Course it'll work, Daddy. Gator Snout can hear his whistle clear across the country, and—"

"Oh Jolene, you know that whistle it's . . . it's never been blown. It's . . . I just want you to stay safe." He regained his composure. "Be brave."

"All right, Daddy." Her heart pounded. *Why wouldn't the whistle work? Why wouldn't Gator Snout come?* All her life he'd never spoken more sincerely about anything. "Daddy, I—"

"That's enough," Johnny took the phone back. "Colonel, you've put some mighty funny ideas in your daughter's head." Johnny paused, then laughed. "Why that's the understatement of the year, Colonel. But what I'm about to say is not an understatement: If I have to put this phone up to your daughter's ear one more time, she will be in a considerably sorrier state. Get. Me. The money." He hung up.

Johnny put the phone back in his pocket. He balled up his fists, took a swing at the air, and screamed.

Tyler broke a long silence, "Johnny, you sure that phone's untraceable?"

"Shut your mouth!"

Jolene held an iron bar with one hand and lifted her whistle to her mouth with the other. She blew softly. The scratchy, high-pitched noise cut the silence.

Johnny lurched at her. She backed away and dropped the whistle. He shook the walls of her cage. "You stupid, spoiled brat! If you blow that whistle one more time, so help me God, I'll shove it down your throat!"

"I don't have to blow it again," Jolene assured herself. "He's comin'. Gator Snout's already on his way. First time I blew it, he heard."

"Your Daddy told you make-believe stories about nice monsters who help pathetic lost little girls when they blow whistles. But that's all it is, sweetheart: a story. And that's why you're so gullible and stupid. And that's why you're in this whole mess in the first place. Because you'll believe *anything*."

Hot tears burned the corners of Jolene's eyes. "It's true though."

"There ain't no Gator Snout, pork pie. And unless money from your Daddy, who's richer than *God*, appears in my account, you will bake like an Easter ham in this hot cage before anyone, no matter what kind of snout they have, ever comes to find you."

"Johnny . . ." Jolene sobbed. She inched forward. "I'm sorry. I'm scared, and . . ."

"And what?" He spat. "You want me to hold you? Make everything better?"

"I just want to tell you somethin'," Jolene barely whispered. She worked her hand through the straw.

Johnny leaned close and gripped the bars. "Speak up, angel!"

Jolene's hand fixed around the glass. She smashed it over Johnny's head. She slashed his fingers with the jagged edges.

Johnny screamed and clutched his bloody hands. "You stupid pig!" Blood dribbled down his arms. "I would kill you right now if you weren't worth so much!" He shouted at Tyler. "Who gave her a glass? Which one of you stupid morons!"

Earl appeared in the barn doorway; his jaw dropped.

"Worthless hick!" Johnny clutched his hands. "I should put a bullet right through your head, Earl! You're lucky I won't!"

Johnny held his bloody hands and rushed to the door. He turned around. "No food and no water for this pig. You hear that, Tyler?" He shoved his way past Earl, who followed.

Tyler pulled a handgun out of his pocket and aimed it at the bars. "You heard the man, miss. No food."

Jolene tossed the brown paper bag through the bars.

"That glass too. That's not gonna work twice." He motioned with the gun.

Jolene tossed the half-broken glass through the bars. It rolled through the dirt over splats of Johnny's blood.

Tyler nodded. "And that stupid whistle. Come on, enough of that."

Jolene clutched Gator Snout's whistle. "No," she said.

"Don't play games with me."

"No, please. I won't blow it again. It makes me feel safe."

Tyler cocked the gun. "I don't care."

Jolene sniffled. She took the silver chain off her neck and stared down at the little wooden skull. Her father's words echoed in her mind. *That might not work you know . . . it's never been blown.* "Oh Daddy, you wouldn't lie to me," she whispered to herself.

Tyler's shadow darkened her hand. "Hand it over, Princess. Now."

She tossed the whistle through the bars, buried her head in the straw, and cried.

***

Johnny's bandaged hands shook as he lit a cigarette outside. The situation was getting out of control. The more things dragged out, the more likely they were to get caught. It was stupid of him to up the ransom so much. That only gave the Colonel an excuse to take longer. And now he had to show he meant business.

If there's no money by midnight, he thought. *I'll have to take a finger . . . maybe an ear. That'll motivate him.*

Jolene sobbed inside the barn. Johnny took a drag of his cigarette and observed her through the open door. She had both hands on the bars. Her face was red like a screaming infant. Earl dozed against the wall. Tyler fanned his unbuttoned shirt collar with a magazine.

"Gator Snout's comin'," Jolene cried. "He's comin'!" She banged her head against the metal.

"Pipe down in there. I can't hear myself think!" Johnny shouted.

"He has to come!" Jolene sobbed. "He has to!"

"I said, shut up!" Johnny turned his back, but he could still hear Jolene muttering under her breath. Banging her head.

"Gator Snout's comin'."

Bang.

"Snout's comin'."

Bang.

"Snout's comin'."

Bang.

Johnny strode into the nearby clearing. The girl had lost it, and he couldn't stand the sound of her anymore. The whole thing had been a bad idea, right from the start. But there was no turning back.

A scratchy, high-pitched cry echoed into the night. "God dangit!" Johnny flicked his cigarette butt into the grass and stormed back to the barn. He flung the door open and shouted. "I told you to stop it with that dang whistle!"

Jolene raised her head, wide-eyed, cheeks wet with tears. Earl covered his mouth and yawned.

"Uh, Johnny . . ." Tyler held the silver chain with the little wooden skull. "Nobody blew no whistle."

The cry sounded again, fainter this time. Definitely coming from outside.

"He's here," Jolene said under her breath. "Lord have mercy, he's here."

Johnny grabbed Tyler by the collar. "You and Earl playin' a joke on me? Because I guarantee you, that'd be a big mistake!"

"Nobody's playin' a joke," Earl said.

The scratchy call resounded again, like worn out brakes screeching. Everyone remained still.

"You two check that out," Johnny said.

Tyler and Earl exchanged nervous glances.

"You deaf, boys? I said check it out!"

"Hey Johnny—" Tyler started.

"It's probably an old big rig that got lost in the back roads," Johnny said.

"But what if it's not?" Tyler whispered.

"You've got a gun, brainless. Just get out there!" Johnny pointed to the door.

Tyler placed his hand in his pocket. He and Earl headed outside.

"It's him you know," Jolene said. "I knew it. I knew he'd come."

"It's nothin'." Johnny said. "It's the wind. It's a truck. It's not anything or anyone come to save you." Johnny checked his phone and logged into his secure account. "Furthermore, it's after midnight, and I don't see no money from your Daddy."

Jolene shrugged. "Who cares. You'll never live to spend it anyway."

Johnny approached the bars. "Who cares?"

She nodded.

He snatched her wrist and yanked her forward. Jolene's skull thunked against the iron bar and she collapsed. Johnny wrapped his arm around her elbow and pinned her. With his other hand he produced his pocketknife. "Here's why you should care, angel! Because for every day Daddy's late, I cut a little piece of roast pig off and send it to him."

Jolene screamed and struggled, but Johnny held her arm in place. His hand shook as he held the blade to her fingers. "So what'll it be? A thumb? The pointy finger? Maybe this cute little pinky? Ain't that the one that goes 'wee wee' all the way home?"

"Johnny! Stop!" Jolene pleaded.

Johnny tightened his grip around Jolene's arm. She screamed.

A second scream overlapped. A man's scream. Jolene and Johnny both fell still. Silent. The man screamed again, echoing into the night. Jolene wrenched her arm back through the bars and backed into the corner, away from Johnny.

Johnny headed for the door, but Earl barreled through and grabbed him by the shirt. "Johnny! It got him! Lord Almighty, Johnny!" Earl's eyes were wild with fear, his face white as paper. "It got him, and I couldn't see him! I ran, Johnny! It got him!" he raved.

"Shut up! Get off me!" Johnny pushed Earl away.

Earl broke into tears.

"What the devil's gotten into you!" Johnny snapped.

"It got him, Johnny." Earl took a stilted breath. "It got him."

"Tyler?"

He nodded.

"What got him?"

"I didn't see."

"Well maybe somethin' spooked you."

"Oh, but it got him."

"Well let's get him back."

"You don't understand." Earl shook his head. "There ain't nothin'
to get back. Tyler . . . he's just a smear in the grass now, Johnny."

Johnny glanced back at Jolene. Her eyes said *I told you so.* Johnny
pushed Earl out of the way and stormed outside through the barn door.
He searched the field but couldn't find a trace of Tyler or anything else.

Then he caught it. Slight movement down by the creek. Something
tall, long, and lanky waded in the water, then ducked down low. Pitch
black. Barely visible against the midnight blue horizon. "Oh, my
Lord," he whispered.

Johnny took another step farther from the barn. It couldn't be real.
Not a chance.

The shadowy creature raised its head, tilted its narrow snout into
the air, and swallowed something. Its eyes burned red. It stepped out
of the creek on two long legs. It was as big as a dinosaur. A famished
dinosaur. Practically a skeleton. It lifted its arms into the air and flexed
sharp tapered claws. A row of black spines lined its back and tail. Its
jaws pried open wide, and the screeching whistle resounded through
the night.

The creature charged.

Johnny stuffed a bloody bandaged hand into his pocket and
fumbled for the van keys. He raced to the driver's side, scrambled
inside, and locked the doors. As soon as he started the car, Earl
pounded on the passenger side.

"Don't leave me, Johnny! I'm beggin' you!"

Johnny checked the rear-view mirror. No sign of the creature. "Get
in fast!" He unlocked the doors.

Earl opened the door and started to climb in. There was a loud
scrape, a swift black shadow, and Earl was gone.

"Sweet Jesus!" Johnny shifted the van into drive and sped off with
the passenger door hanging open. "Sweet Jesus, I'm sorry! I'm sorry
for everything I've ever done!" He accelerated the van. Thirty. Forty.
Fifty miles per hour on the dark country road. He checked the mirror.
The farmhouse and barn shrank in the distance. He slowed to take a
turn, and the vehicle jolted. Something pulled the van from behind.
Tires screeched and kicked up dust.

Black claws tore through the roof.

"Sweet Jesus!" Johnny screamed. "Sweet Jesus, I'm sorry!"

The monster's scratchy roar thundered above. Johnny slammed the breaks. A massive black shape tumbled over, splintering the windshield in a spider-web pattern. He put the van in reverse and accelerated backward. Through the cracks in the glass, he saw the creature flip onto its long legs, snap pitch-black jaws, and lunge forward. Its red eyes glowed. Its tail whipped behind it.

Johnny floored the gas. The van rumbled off road, then slammed to a halt. The air bag exploded against his face. He'd backed into something.

The windshield shattered. Dark claws groped between the driver and passenger seats. Johnny wormed his way to the floor.

The claws retreated. Johnny struggled with his injured hands for the seat release. The driver's seat reclined, and he crawled into the back of the van. Jaws snapped through the windshield behind him. The back-left side of the van had collided with a tree. Johnny tried the right door, but it was stuck. He kicked until it finally released and fell off its hinges.

Johnny raced for the light of the open barn. The creature screeched behind him. Johnny's heart pounded. He reached the barn, slammed the door, and barricaded it with a wooden plank. His bandages had come undone, and the cuts on his hands oozed fresh blood. The creature's screams drew closer.

Johnny backed away from the door. "Oh, sweet Jesus," he repeated. "Sweet Jesus save me."

"Ain't nothin' gonna save you now," Jolene said from her cage. "Not even money."

He turned and fell to his knees. "Jolene, I'm beggin' you please. Call that thing off, I'll do anything."

"That a fact?"

The creature banged against the barn door.

"Absolutely anything. Anything you want. I'll turn myself in, confess to everything, kiss your feet and call it candy. What. Ever. You. Want!"

Wood splintered behind him. The creature growled.

She crawled forward in the straw. "Anything I want, huh?"

"You name it."

The barn door exploded open. Johnny turned and faced the creature. It stalked forward, ducking down to enter the barn. Its red eyes fixed on Johnny; claws twitched with readiness. Hot shadowy spittle dripped from its snout and sizzled on the ground.

The creature reared back. Johnny winced.

"Hold up, Gator Snout!" Jolene cried.

The creature halted, tilted its head.

"The only thing I ever wanted, Johnny, was for someone to tell me I was beautiful . . . and believe him."

Johnny crawled up to the bars. "You *are* beautiful! The most beautiful sight I've ever seen in my life, I swear!"

She smiled.

"Jolene, believe me. I was a pig. I was a scoundrel. I was a greedy, filthy, lyin' sleaze! And if you have mercy for me, nothin' in this whole world will be more beautiful than that."

"That's sweet, Johnny," she smiled and caressed his hair. "And maybe two days ago I would've believed you. Gator Snout!"

"Jolene wait—" Darkness snapped over him.

***

Gator Snout pried Johnny apart in an instant and gobbled him up. Then he ripped open the iron bars of Jolene's cage. She climbed out and smiled. "I knew you'd come."

Gator Snout lowered his shadowy head. Around a spine on the back of his neck, the silver chain and whistle dangled. Gator snout delicately unhooked it with his talons and held it out for her.

"You want me to keep this?" she asked. "You've done so much already. I'm not sure I could ask for more favors."

He held the whistle closer to her.

"Well . . . if you insist." She secured it back around her neck. Jolene placed a kiss on her fingers and deposited it on the tip of his snout. "Gator Snout," she said, "you're a true gentleman. Perhaps the only one of your kind."

ABOUT THE AUTHORS

R.C. MULHARE

R.C. Mulhare once successfully defended her day-job workplace from zombies, through some judicious use of clearance-rack garden tools and survived a fight with Yog-Sothoth cultists in a hallway of a hotel in Providence; she's also picked up extra work editing the product blog of Umbrella Corporation.

In actuality, R.C. Mulhare was born in Lowell, Massachusetts and grew up in a nearby town, in a hundred year old house up the street from an old cemetery. Her interest in the dark and mysterious started when she was quite young, when her mother read the faery tales of the Brothers Grimm and quoted the poetry of Edgar Allan Poe to her, while her Irish storyteller father infused her with a fondness for strange characters and quirky situations. Between writing projects, she moonlights in grocery retail. She's also fond of hiking in the woods of the White Mountains of New Hampshire and browsing the antiques shops one finds all over New England. A two-time Amazon best-selling author, contributor to the Hugo Award Winning Archive of Our Own, and member of the New England Horror Writers, she has one hundred twenty stories in print through dozens of independent publishers including Atlantean Publishing, Macabre Maine, DBND Publishing, Hellbound Books, Nocturnal Sirens Publishing, FunDead Publications, Deadman's Tome, NEHW Press, Lovecraftiana Magazine, Tales of Wonder and Dread, and Weirdbook Magazine, with more stories in the works. She shares her home with her family, a vintage music-loving baby parakeet, about fifteen hundred books and an unknown number of eldritch things that rattle in the walls when she's writing late in the night. She's happy to have visitors through her page at: https://linktr.ee/rcmulhare

G K Lomax

(Co-Editor)

G K Lomax is a nom-de-internet. Behind it lies a rather strange individual from the fair English county of Essex. He has appeared on several broadcast quiz programmes, is constantly baffled by modern technology, and was once cursed by Sean Connery for the erratic nature of his golf. He writes weird fiction because he hates having to come up with happy endings, and sometimes thinks the end of the world can't come soon enough.

BP Christy

BP Christy is the author of *Lucidia: Book of Fates*, the horror anthology: *A Halloween Tradition*, and more than a dozen published short stories and poems. He is a member of the Writer's League of Texas and the Horror Writers Association, where he is a writing mentor, and holds a master's degree in creative writing and English. As a DAEP high school English teacher, he devoted most of his time to working with young people who could use a second chance.

Tim Jeffreys

Tim Jeffreys short fiction has appeared in Supernatural Tales, The Alchemy Press Book of Horrors 2 & 3, Nightscript 4, Stories We Tell After Midnight 2 & 3, Cosmic Horror Monthly #1, Shadowplays from P.S. Publishing, The Ghastling, and many other places. His ghost story novella, Holburn, was released by Manta Press in 2022. The sequel, Back from the Black, came out in 2023. Other work includes the comic horror novella, Here Comes Mr Herribone!, and sci-fi novella, Voids, co-written with Martin Greaves, and the novel The False Ones due for release in February 2025 from Crossroads Press.

www.timjeffreysblogspot.com

Mark Mackey

Mark Mackey, a long time resident of Chicago, Illinois, with no plans to relocate elsewhere, either city or state, has written tales included in various anthologies and has co-writtem the Soulless, a harrowing horror novel which commences on an ocean liner and concludes on a mysterious island. **https://www.amazon.com/stores/Mark-Mackey/author/B0054EB7PY**

David Bennett Black

David Bennett Black is a rapscallion. Born in a small town in Southern Canada to parents that died in the 1800s, he now lives in a much larger city with his partner and various bloodhounds. His work can be read and heard in many places, most recently through the Creepy podcast, where his story "My Child's Skin" was the number 1 fiction podcast in multiple countries for two straight weeks. With various shorts being published in a number of different anthologies in the next twelve months, he truly believes that people may actually start enjoying his company now.

Tucker Struyk

Tucker Struyk (he/they) is a queer writer and podcaster for Hookswitch Hotline. He has pieces published by Cosmic Horror Monthly, Murderous Ink Press, Eerie River Publishing, and several other publications. His piece "Our Father's Judgment" was published in the spring 2021 issue of 13 th Floor Magazine, where it was awarded an Editor's Choice Award, and his piece "Getaway" was given an honorable mention in the Fall/Winter 2022-23 issue of Allegory.

Abigail Taylor

Abigail F. Taylor is an award winning author. Her debut novella, THE NIGHT BEGINS, came out with Luna Press Publishing in 2023, and her next two novels MARYNEAL, 1962 and A HOME IN TISHOMINGO will arrive with Wild Ink Publishing in 2025 and 2026. When not writing or reading, She takes long walks, practices aikido, and watches trash tv while working on a never ending counted cross stitch. In a previous life, She was a horse girl and worked as an assistant director and script editor in the indie-film industry. To read more of her short stories or stay updated on her novels, visit her website: abigailftaylor.wordpress.com

VINCENT ENDWELL

Vincent Endwell is a writer, composer, and researcher originally hailing from unceded Onondaga territory (Central New York). Their work has been previously published in The Ghastling, Dark Horses Magazine, and Your Body is Not Your Body, an anthology from Tenebrous Press. Generally speaking, they think that seeing a ghost would probably be existentially comforting, but they are open to changing their mind on this.

KEVIN M. FOLLIARD

Kevin M. Folliard is a Chicagoland writer whose fiction has been collected by The Horror Tree, The Dread Machine, Demain Publishing, and more. His recent publications include his horror anthology *The Misery King's Country* and his sci-fi dinosaur adventure series *Tales from New Pangea* from Dark Owl Publishing. Kevin currently resides in the western suburbs of Chicago, IL, where he enjoys his day job in academia and membership in the La Grange Writers Group.

AARON CROCKER

Aaron was raised in the small town of El Dorado Springs, Missouri and later moved to Virginia where he currently resides. He holds a few degrees, the most applicable being a B.S. in English, Linguistics, and Communications from the University of Mary Washington.

In 2016, he wrote his first piece "Suburban Suicide" which took second place in a national divergent literature competition. From there he picked up a few more national and international awards in short and micro fiction competitions, sat on various short fiction judging panels, and has spoken at several writing events—the most notable being an invitation to address the Library of Congress in 2020 (virtually).

Over several years, Aaron published two moderately successful, limited-edition fundraising anthologies, and this is where he gained an appreciation for and enjoyment of publishing. From there, he dreamed up and founded Campfire Publishing, and although he quickly became aware of the editing skills required of such an endeavor, he is nothing if not dedicated and open to learning.